Dylan Dover:
Into The Vortex

Dylan Dover: Into the Vortex

Published by The Conrad Press Ltd. in the United Kingdom 2022

Tel: +44(0)1227 472 874

www.theconradpress.com

info@theconradpress.com

ISBN 978-1-914913-98-3

Typesetting and Cover Design by: Charlotte Mouncey, www.bookstyle.co.uk

The Conrad Press logo was designed by Maria Priestley.

Printed and bound in Great Britain by Clays Ltd, Elcograf S.p.A.

*For Andrew, Matthew, Jessie and Dylan –
thank you for your love, support, encouragement,
inspiration and patience. This would not
have been possible without you.*

DYLAN DOVER:
INTO THE VORTEX

LYNNE HOWARD

Book I of a series

PROLOGUE

Silence hung heavily over the four leaders, who gathered together in this secret place. They were the only ones who knew, and therefore the responsibility to decide what should be done fell to them alone. Their new world, only in its infancy and still so vulnerable, depended upon the goodwill of its citizens and peace was still not assured in the aftermath of war which had raged for so long.

The room was dark, hidden deep beneath the surface where they would not be discovered. A scroll hovered motionless before them and gave off a faint shimmer of light which was the only illumination in the otherwise blackened chamber. The four read and then read again the words which had been revealed to only them mere hours before.

Finally, the one named Alexia spoke her thoughts. 'We cannot hide this. The truth must be known. Our citizens must be informed so that we can collectively watch for signs.'

Her superior, Callista slowly nodded in assent. 'Perhaps you are right, Alexia. I was wise to have chosen you as my advisor.'

'No!' came the vehement response from another. He could not feel the warmth of the stone which pressed against his cold skin, but a familiar voice crooned to him softly inside his mind and he knew exactly what to say. 'With the greatest of respect to you, Callista and to you Alexia, I must strongly oppose any suggestion of alerting others to this prophecy. We should be the only ones who are aware of this possible threat to our world. We are powerful enough to be able to contain the peril to our people, if and when it comes to fruition. We have many resources we can utilize, which can alert us to signs of impending danger, without having to reveal this to anyone.'

'Baltazar, I agree with your assessment,' replied the other commander. 'Callista, you and I have both chosen our closest advisors well. Baltazar and Alexia are clearly great assets to the realm, but I believe as their advice is so opposed, that it shall have to be you and I alone who make this decision. Shall we discuss this elsewhere, my friend?'

Callista smiled wryly at being referred to as a friend by Atticus, who during the civil war had been her greatest enemy. They had been the leaders of the opposing armies. She moved closer to him and stood directly in his path in order to look deeply into his eyes. The limited amount of light radiating from the scroll was enough for her to determine that Atticus was genuine in his request, and she nodded her assent.

They grasped hands, Callista's dainty and pale, Atticus' strong and dark. Their physical appearances could not have been more different but their powers were almost equally formidable. In an instant, they were gone.

Baltazar and Alexia remained rooted where they stood. They did not move. They did not speak. Each knew the other's position, and each was convinced that the other was dreadfully wrong. And they waited.

It didn't take long. Callista and Atticus reemerged with a decision. It was Callista who spoke. 'We have determined that our society is too fragile at this time to receive this prophecy, if in fact it is as such. As leaders of the realm, we shall assume full responsibility to watch for any signs of its actualization. Baltazar, we are entrusting you to oversee the addition of any new members to our society, and to supervise the vortex of those who enter and depart. Alexia, you shall assist Baltazar in any way he requires. None of us shall speak of the prophecy to others. Any information that must be shared will be done here and here alone. It is imperative that this revelation not be leaked. That is our ruling.'

'The prophecy must be hidden away immediately. We cannot risk it being found by others,' commanded Atticus.

He approached the scroll which remained suspended in the air. The words were inscribed in flawless Latin, but Atticus easily translated the text into a language that they could all understand. And he read its contents out loud once to commit it to their memories, for it would not be seen again until or unless there were signs that it was coming true.

Hear now mighty rulers beware and take heed
The world you have created may not succeed.
Peace is so fragile, it's so easily torn
Your fate rests upon those who've not yet been born.
Together their powers are like no other
When passed through the hands of brother to brother.
Yet completeness eludes the powers of three
The last burning element, she too must be.

The power that heals, the power that destroys
Your fate to be sealed by one girl and three boys.
An unusual birth for they shall arrive
All on the same day and yet all shall survive.
Your world created shall be saved or no more
It shall be determined by siblings of four.
Look to the heavens and the stars that align
For the kings of three plus one more is the sign.

Atticus held his hands together as if in prayer, in front of the scripture. Then his hands split apart and wrapped themselves around the scroll until they came together on the other side. He closed his eyes and focused completely on the task at hand. Bits of rock and metal magically appeared and surrounded his hands. The pieces were shaking violently and rattled against each other, as if they were clamoring to move forward.

Atticus once more traced a circle round the scroll with his hands, bringing them back together where they had started. Then he took a step back. Once his hands were out of the way, the thousands of fragments forged together and created a vault around the parchment. With the prophecy safely encased in its magical tomb, Atticus once more waved his hands, and the vault disappeared.

'As leaders of this new immortal world, we are placing our complete and utter trust in you both, our deputies. We need your help to ensure that our vision of a peaceful society is fulfilled. One where all immortals, of any faction can exist in the open, without having to hide away any longer from humans. But like all new societies, ours is still very vulnerable. The scars of our civil war have not yet healed. This prophecy, if known, would cause our old disputes to arise once again, and we cannot risk that. We are confident in your loyalty. We shall not return here again, unless there is need to discuss the prophecy and we shall not mention it ever again, unless it becomes necessary to do so. Understood?' Callista demanded.

'Yes,' Baltazar and Alexia replied in perfect unison. 'Yes,' whispered the voice inside Baltazar's head. Then the four leaders of the immortal world returned to their society to govern the newly formed realm.

CHAPTER ONE

'Reus', the voice hissed menacingly into his ear. 'You must not fail. If you disappoint me, you know what the consequences shall be...' the words trailed off and then his superior abruptly turned on his heels and left Reus alone in the hallway.

Reus stood still for a moment to control the trembling that threatened to overtake him and give away his sense of fear to those who he would soon encounter. Any slip up could ruin Baltazar's plan and would result in Reus' immediate and very painful death. Reus had been under Baltazar's control for centuries and knew with complete certainty that he was expendable and easily replaced. His continued existence depended upon successful implementation of this plan, which had been in the works for many months. Reus steadied himself for another moment before he entered the birthing chamber.

On the table lay Maggie Warston, her distended stomach protruding higher than it seemed possible. Her nervous husband, Ben sat by her side squeezing her hand. The Master Deliverer had not yet arrived, which gave Reus a short time for introductions. He approached the couple and noted Maggie's anxious yet elated expression. She was eagerly anticipating the birth of multiples. In the world of the supernatural, doctors like those that exist in the human world are unnecessary;

however, those with exceptional powers were still needed to help heal immortals from traumatic injuries that could occur. Delivering one child or even twins would not likely cause any major injuries to the mother, but triplets or the even more unusual situation of four or more infants at the same time was a rare occurrence. Immortal children, even those yet to be born, had magical abilities which sometimes cloaked the presence of additional babies. For these unusual deliveries, the need for someone with strong powers to save the mother or any of the children should a problem arise was a precaution that the parents usually insisted upon, and for which Baltazar rejoiced. This made his plan to monitor unusual births that much simpler than if the parents had desired a home birth without intervention.

'So, the day has finally arrived. Congratulations to you both,' smiled Reus at the soon to be parents. 'I am Officer Eldonik, representative from the Ministry of Population and Census. I am here to record the births and report them on your behalf.'

'Yes, we were informed that a government official would be here,' replied Ben in a clipped tone. He was clearly irritated at a stranger being present for such a personal and intimate event.

'There is nothing to be concerned about. I am simply here to observe. You won't even notice that I'm in the room. But of course, you understand that for all exceptional births the Ministry sends a representative. It's just standard procedure.'

'Thank you, officer. My husband and I completely understand,' said Maggie and she gave her husband a smile to take the edge off her remark. Ben's shoulders slumped slightly as he relaxed under his wife's loving gaze.

Just then, the Master Deliverer known to his patients simply as Chai, glided into the room. He first made eye contact with Reus and gave him a knowing look. Reus felt confident that Chai would follow Baltazar's commands, exactly as he had been told. *I wonder what Chai has been promised by Baltazar. Or perhaps threatened…* thought Reus.

Chai approached Maggie with a friendly smile and placed his hand on her stomach. His grin promptly changed to a look of concern, which Maggie and Ben both noticed immediately.

'What's wrong? I can tell that something is wrong,' cried Maggie.

'We need to deliver these infants immediately,' stated Chai authoritatively. He quickly muttered the necessary spell as he waved his hands over Maggie's body from her head to her toes. A barrier appeared between Maggie's chest and the rest of her body, concealing her belly from both her and Ben. They could hear everything that was happening but could not see beyond the barrier.

Chai stood on Maggie's left side and Reus on the right. Reus gave Chai a nod to indicate that he should proceed. Chai hesitated a moment, and Reus could see regret flit briefly across Chai's face. *Clearly Baltazar is threatening him,* thought Reus. *No doubt about it. Chai is not a willing participant here,* but Reus was still certain that Chai would comply and would keep the secret.

Chai took a deep breath and then placed both of his hands on Maggie's stomach. He closed his eyes in concentration and began to chant quietly. The words for a safe delivery had a strong rhythm that were hypnotic and meant to ease the infants out of the womb with as little injury as possible to the mother. Reus watched as Maggie's belly split open to reveal the children nestled inside her. Chai knew what he had to do next. His chanting changed but his words were so quiet that only Reus could hear them. Chai reached into Maggie's belly and delivered the first child.

'The first child is a boy,' Chai said with fake enthusiasm. Chai ran his hands over the infant and within a minute, the baby let out his first cry. Chai held the child and passed his hands through the barrier to give him to his awaiting parents. While Maggie and Ben excitedly examined his fingers and toes, and cooed over his head of hair, Chai quickly delivered the remaining children. But he did not recite his incantations over these new immortals, and so they did not cry. Nor did Chai hand the babies over to his parents, but rather, he placed them in the arms of Reus.

Acting upon Baltazar's instructions, Reus immediately scanned the bodies of the infants looking for any unusual markings to report back to his master. He noticed on the second born child something strange on the inside of his right wrist – three small circle shaped markings that ran in a diagonal line. He then checked the same place on the third born child and found an identical line of dots. He did not notice any such markings on the others, but he also did not have adequate time to do a thorough inspection and of course, he certainly could not check the infant who was already in his mother's arms. Reus, with all but the one child securely nestled in his arms, snapped his fingers quietly and silently disappeared from the birthing chamber.

As soon as Reus was gone, Chai began his intonations again. He knew what he had to do. His ability to conceal the truth and persuade the parents of his lies was imperative. His voice sounded anxious and Maggie and Ben instantly noticed.

Chai's words became faster, his voice more frantic. Maggie and Ben simultaneously cried out to see their other children, but Chai ignored their pleas and persevered in reciting the magical spell that was known only to him as the Master Deliverer. Maggie cradled her first born son and kept her eyes locked on Ben's, as the two parents waited with fear in their eyes, to hear the cries of their other babies. After several minutes, the room went silent. Chai stopped his chanting.

'Please Chai, where are our other children?' pleaded Ben. The barrier dissolved in a whirl of colorful splinters that splattered rainbows around the room.

'I'm so very sorry,' whispered Chai. 'The other children are gone. I couldn't save them from their fate.' Chai held out to the parents what appeared to be the bodies of two perfectly formed, but completely still baby boys. Their eyes were closed. Their bodies were motionless. No breath stirred in their tiny chests.

'No!' gasped Maggie as grief overwhelmed her and she dissolved into tears. Ben too had tears streaming down his face as he stared at the two lifeless beings that Chai held before them.

'I know that this is devastating for you both,' stated Chai, 'But you must focus on your son who lives. Your other children will always be in your hearts, but you must move on without them. Cherish the son you have been blessed with, for I know that he is destined to do great things.'

Before Maggie or Ben could ask to hold their second and third born sons, their little bodies disappeared in a quiet whoosh which transported them to a world unknown even to immortals.

Chai quickly attended to Maggie's wounds from the delivery and healed her stomach so that within minutes, her body was as perfect as it had ever been with no signs of the traumatic delivery and no signs of being pregnant with three healthy sons and one healthy daughter. *They will mourn the two boys,* thought Chai. *Perhaps it is better that they never knew a daughter existed,* he decided.

Maggie and Ben left the Birthing Chamber with bittersweet tears for the son they were taking home and the sons that had disappeared. Chai remained in the room by himself for some time. Most of what he had said to the parents was true, if you didn't consider his lies of omission. The parents had just interpreted his words differently than he meant them. But Baltazar would be pleased. Chai and his family were safe... at least for now. He hoped that his debt to Baltazar was served and that by keeping this secret, he would no longer be under Baltazar's control. And yet Chai knew only too well that when Baltazar wanted something, he would do anything to achieve his goals. Chai did not know what Baltazar had in store for the warlock infants that were snatched from their parents this day or why the parents were only to know of three infants and not the fourth. Nor did he know why Baltazar wanted these children so badly, but he hoped that they too would be safe.

Chai cleaned the room quickly, wanting to leave this place as soon as he could. His usually capable hands trembled as he waved them over the stained surfaces, and he moved around the birthing chamber in great haste, his hurried efforts making him clumsy and distracted. Chai felt regret and terror weighing in equal measure upon his heart.

He put his hand into his pocket to reach for his handkerchief to wipe his forehead and as he did, his fingers brushed against a small, smooth stone. As his skin grazed the object, he felt a warm, pulsating sensation radiate through his hand, then travel up his arm before spreading through his torso. Chai's mind immediately felt at peace, all the trepidation falling away, leaving his thoughts clear and calm. A soft whisper in his ear reassured him that all was well and that he would not think of this incident again.

Chai resumed his duties and finished his tasks efficiently. Then he left the birthing chamber to return home to his family, the events of the day not causing him any further distress. His role had been fulfilled, at least for now. The stone glimmered softly close to Chai's body, where it would remain unless an intervening force pulled it away.

CHAPTER TWO

'Dylan, make sure you are home for dinner,' called out Olivia Dover to her only child as he was tying the laces of his running shoes.

'Mom, you say that every day when I walk the dogs after school. I know to be back in time to eat, you don't have to remind me,' replied twelve-year-old Dylan with just a hint of exasperation in his voice. He couldn't really get angry with his mother. He knew that she was over-protective, especially compared to his other friends' parents. But then again, he was an only child and he could recite by heart the long, convoluted story of how he was adopted into his family. It was no wonder that his parents, especially his mother, worried so much about him but sometimes he wished that his mom would lighten up, just a little bit!

Olivia walked over to her son and planted a kiss on his cheek. He was twelve, but a little small for his age. His tiny 5-foot-tall mother was still several inches taller than her son, and quite a bit heavier! Dylan was thin; too skinny always complained his mother and she constantly tried to put some weight on him with the delicious, high calorie foods she plied him with. But it didn't matter how many chocolate chip pancakes or homemade strawberry banana milkshakes he ate, Dylan was just destined to be lean. Olivia gave him a wide smile that radiated her love and adoration for him, and his irritation at her disappeared. How could he be even remotely upset with someone who only wanted him to be safe and happy?

'Bye, Mom,' he said with a smile that made his grey eyes twinkle. Dylan's mother couldn't help but notice, as she always did, the unusual yet beautifully strange eyes that her son had. They were grey but the color seemed to change depending on his moods from a pale grey, so light that his eyes appeared almost translucent to a deep, dark shade that looked almost purple, reminding her of storm clouds right before the skies erupted into gales of rain and shook with clashes of thunder. Right now, his eyes were a soft grey, showing that he was happy. Dylan's light brown hair was short in the back but at the front, his hair hung longer and constantly flopped into his eyes. Olivia reached out with a gentle hand and pushed the soft locks out of her son's face. She smiled at the cowlick that constantly parted the front of his bangs at an awkward angle, no matter how much gel or hair spray he used. She pulled his face close one more time and gave him one more kiss in the middle of his forehead, right where the cowlick divided his hair. 'Love you, Monkey,' she said knowing that at this point, Dylan was just tolerating her and that he really wanted to take off.

Their dogs, Oliver and Halle were also anxious to go, wagging their tails furiously as they sat patiently waiting at the front door to be released into the outdoors. With a quick check to make sure that he had his cell phone with him, Dylan opened the door, and gave a final wave to his mother. Just in time too for the dogs tugged him to be off on their walk, and Dylan stood no chance in resisting his two gorgeous, very large, very strong dogs. These dogs were huskies and outweighed Dylan by at least twenty pounds!

As they walked, Dylan thought over the events of the day. He was happy that he had finished all his work at school, so he had no homework to worry about that night. He made a mental note to remember to bring a tennis ball to school the next day to play with his best friend, Jack at recess. And then his mind drifted to Keisha, the prettiest girl in his class who actually spoke with him that day. The conversation was nothing special, just exchanging a few pleasantries about summer vacation which had just recently ended, but every relationship had to start somewhere, right? Today they spoke about summer vacation, tomorrow they could talk some more and Dylan began to make a mental list of topics of conversation... their teacher, stupid math questions that seemed to go on forever, favorite television shows... Maybe he would even get up the nerve to ask for her cell phone number. Then he could text her and maybe, just maybe even ask her to hang out after school or on a weekend one day soon.

Dylan's mind was completely preoccupied with thoughts of Keisha so when he entered the wooded trail in the forest that was only two blocks from his house, he failed to notice the older boys sitting on a large rock at the entrance to the path. Dylan and the dogs were walking at a leisurely pace since Dylan knew he still had over an hour before he needed to be home, and he was so absorbed with daydreams of this girl, who he was sure would become his first ever girlfriend, that he still didn't realize when the three older boys were just steps behind him. It was only when he felt a hard shove to his shoulder that he became aware of their presence, and Dylan spun around quickly to face whoever had pushed him. Dylan recognized the three kids as they went to his school, but they were in a higher grade and he had no idea what their names were. But whatever their names, they were clearly looking for trouble, based upon their aggressive stances and the smirks on their faces.

'Well, well, who do we have here?' sneered the largest of the three boys. His arm muscles bulged out from his black t-shirt. *How is it possible that a kid can have biceps the size of a professional wrestler???* wondered Dylan, feeling a sense of dread at what was to come.

'What's your name, kid?' snarled the same boy. 'When I ask you a question, I expect an immediate answer.'

'I'm Dylan. Dylan Dover,' replied Dylan hesitantly trying to look around for an escape route.

'I'm Dylan, Dylan Dover, hit me, shove me, knock me over,' taunted one of the other boys who then spat a huge glob of slimy spit right at Dylan's feet.

'Knock him over? Not a bad idea, unless of course, he is independently wealthy and can buy his safety. Hear that Dover knock me over, pay up or we're going to knock you down so hard, you won't be able to get up for a week!' jeered the third boy.

Halle and Oliver growled at the three attackers and Dylan saw the boys all take a step back. Dylan knew that Halle and Oliver were usually as gentle as baby lambs, but clearly the animals sensed the threat being made against their best friend and were ready to defend him. Dylan saw this as his only hope, so he dropped the dogs' leashes and took off, running deeper into the forest. He heard the dogs growling and barking behind him, and then one of the boys started screaming curse words.

Probably one of the dogs made contact and bit him, thought Dylan as he continued to run.

It didn't take long though before he heard the boys and his dogs fast on his heels. *They are catching up,* panicked Dylan. And he found within himself a burst of extra speed. Dylan could hear when the dogs captured one of the boys and took him down but the other two didn't stop to help their friend, rather they kept on coming after Dylan.

The pounding of their feet became louder, and Dylan knew that they would soon overtake him. To his right, Dylan saw his only chance of escape. There was a stream running through the forest that looked like maybe he could clear it if he got enough height on a jump. *I have no choice,* decided Dylan and sprinted off the path, running at full speed towards the water.

When he was only steps away, he realized his mistake. There was no way he would be able to jump far enough to get to the other side, but he had no choice but to make the attempt. He was already too close to abandon the plan. With a huge burst of energy, Dylan leapt and to his amazement and delight, he felt like he was able to fly right over the stream and landed far on the banks of the other side. He took the briefest moment to glance back and saw the two remaining boys standing on the opposite side, shaking their fists at him. Then the boys approached the water and started to wade in. Dylan knew he had no option but to keep running. Hopefully with his head start, he could find a decent hiding place and wait it out. The boys surely would give up soon enough.

I need to call for help, decided Dylan as he continued to run, and he pulled his cell phone out of his back pocket. But before he could dial, he saw the perfect place to hide. Just up ahead was a fallen log. The trunk was so huge that the tree must have been over one hundred years old. The log was covered in moss and wild mushrooms surrounded its base. Not hearing the boys, at least not yet, Dylan slowed his pace as he approached the old, fallen tree. He peered into its hollowed-out core and decided that being cramped and uncomfortable was better than being pummeled. He could make his urgent call for help from inside the hiding spot. Dylan got down on his knees and crawled inside.

Less than ten minutes later the two boys were standing exactly where Dylan had stood only minutes before. There was no sign of Dylan.

'I'm exhausted,' stated one of the boys and moved towards the fallen log. He sat down heavily and panted as he tried to catch his breath.

'You're in terrible shape, dude. My grandmother has better stamina than you!' but despite his insult, this boy too sat down on the log to recover from the chase.

'Hey, did you see how far that Dover kid jumped when he went over the water? It was totally insane. He must have jumped thirty feet!'

'He didn't jump that far, idiot. He's not Superman. He can't fly! But he did jump pretty far. I wonder where he went. There's no sign of him.'

'I don't know, maybe he is Superman and he flew back to Krypton.'

'Dean…'

'Yeah?'

'You really are an idiot. Maybe we better go back and check on Ron. We left him behind when the dogs pulled him down.

I hope he's okay. Those looked like some killer dogs.'

'Wait, we don't have to… listen,' replied Dean.

They could hear Ron's voice calling for them, and they could also hear the dogs running and barking at the same time.

As Ron came into view, he shouted for his friends to help him. 'Get – these – dogs – away – from – me!'

It was clearly evident to the other boys that if the dogs wanted to catch him, they could in a heartbeat. The dogs were right next to Ron and could have easily taken him down.

'Those are some well trained dogs,' muttered Dean.

When Ron reached the spot that his friends were standing, the dogs' behavior changed dramatically. Both animals started whining, almost like they were crying. The dogs approached the log and the boys jumped up from where they were sitting to back away. But the dogs didn't pay the boys any attention. They were frantically pawing at the log. One dog started going crazy and ran around the log from one side to the other, over and over and over again. The other dog cried out loud howls into the sky.

'Let's get out of here, now!' said Ron, 'while the dogs are preoccupied.'

'But what about the kid? We lost him,' replied another.

'Who gives a crap about the kid. He must be hiding from us. He'll come out and go home when he's ready. But tomorrow in school, we will find him and finish conducting our business with Dover knock me over,' stated Ron. 'Now let's go!' And with that, Ron took off as fast as he could go, heading back towards the entrance of the forest where the trail began. It only took a moment before his friends began running right behind him. The dogs stayed where they were, crying for their missing friend.

At 6:00 p.m. exactly, Dylan's mother turned off the oven and waited for her very responsible and always punctual son to come through the door. At 6:05, Dylan's father, Mike, sat down at the table for dinner. At 6:10, Olivia put the hot food on the table and checked the clock again for the twentieth time in the last ten minutes. At 6:15, Olivia began to call Dylan's cell phone but got no response. She hung up, waited for one minute and called again. At 6:30, after having called her son fifteen times, she burst into tears.

'Livy darling, I'm sure he's fine,' soothed Mike. 'He's just late. It was bound to happen at some point. He must have run into a friend and they are probably talking. He just lost track of the time.'

By 7:00 p.m., with still no sign or word from Dylan, Olivia called the police. An hour later, a small search party consisting of two police officers, Olivia and Mike started to look for Dylan in the immediate area around the house. By 10:00 p.m., the search parties were ramped up and over a dozen officers were now involved; several of them were dispersed to the forested area.

At approximately 10:20 p.m., Olivia, Mike and several police officers stood at the fallen log where Dylan was last seen and watched in dismay as the two dogs continued their vigil for their beloved Dylan. The dogs cried and whined, looking forlorn and completely devastated. One of the police officers, who understood a little bit about animal behavior since she too was the owner of a dog, got down on her hands and knees and entered the same hiding spot that Dylan had occupied several hours previously. She moved her flashlight slowly from side to side looking for evidence, anything that might indicate that Dylan had been there. She saw no sign of him but just to be sure, she crawled her way forward. She continuously swept the beam of light back and forth in front of her and up the sides of the log. She even inspected the tree trunk above her head. She saw nothing except for the aging wood, and she exited the other end of the log without having discovered any clues.

Olivia saw the police officer gesture that she was empty handed. It was at that exact moment that Olivia knew without any doubt that something terrible had happened to Dylan. He was gone.

CHAPTER THREE

Dylan felt horribly sick to his stomach and dizzy as the world spun around him. He felt like he was experiencing a combination of a fun house with those crazy mirrors that made everything look distorted and a looping, twirling, spinning roller coaster at the same time. Bright bursts of color flashed and made his head swim. He felt like he was moving fast but at the same time, he didn't think that he was going anywhere at all. He tried closing his eyes to see if that brought any relief, but it didn't help.

He groaned out loud, and vaguely wondered what was happening to him. But his precise location was not nearly as important to him at that exact moment as the horrendous way that he was feeling. He knew he would not be able to last much longer without throwing up. He moaned out loud again and called pitifully for his mother. Even though he was twelve years old, he was not beyond wanting his mother's comfort when he felt this sick! He couldn't hold it in any longer and his body began to retch. But he had nothing in his stomach since he hadn't eaten in many hours and nothing much came out of him except for some foul-smelling liquid that bounced right back into his face. Dylan had never in his entire life felt so wretched before and after what seemed like several hours but may have actually been much longer or much shorter, Dylan mercifully blacked out.

'What is going on here?'

Dylan could hear the words, but he was not able to open his eyes to see who was talking. He felt something nudge at his side and prod him rather uncomfortably especially since his stomach was still unsettled, but Dylan could not find the strength to respond.

'Carl, I need some help here. Looks like a 2280, can you come?'

Within an instant, Dylan felt but still could not see that another individual was now standing right next to him.

'Hmmm… it's been a while since we had a 2280. Who is he?' said the second voice.

'I don't know. He didn't register on the identifilizer5000, and that's supposed to be foolproof. His identify just doesn't register. I don't even know what faction he comes from. But he appears under age and he's in a restricted zone. We're going to have to report this, and I bet that means a long night for us. The boss won't let us go home until this is wrapped up.'

Dylan felt another push against his side and he heard the second person, who he now knew to be named Carl reply 'I guess we had better get him into secure custody until we figure this out. He can't just lie here in the middle of everything.'

Dylan's eyes were still shut, and despite his best efforts, he just couldn't get them to open. And then he felt the strangest sensation. It seemed that he was elevated off the ground and floating. He couldn't feel the floor beneath him anymore, but he also didn't sense anyone holding him up. It almost felt like he was drifting on air currents, but how could that be possible? He heard the two males talking about him as he silently glided along beside them. They were saying that he was a security breach, but Dylan didn't know what that meant.

The two voices were suddenly interrupted by a third person who seemed to appear out of nowhere. Dylan had not heard this person approach. One minute there were two people next to him and then out of the blue, there was now a third.

'Oh dear,' purred this new voice, 'what a situation we seem to have.'

'Clearly a 2280, sir. And his identity is unknown and not registering with the identifilizer5000. We were moving him into secure custody, and then we would have contacted you, sir. As soon as we got him there,' sputtered the first person who had found Dylan. He was clearly uncomfortable thought Dylan. *I wonder why?*

'You should have contacted me immediately, Vamsonberg. There is no excuse for your incompetence. And that goes for you too Wizman,' barked this man who was clearly their boss.

'But I shall deal with you two later. First, I must attend to the situation at hand. You two, get back to your posts. I will handle the 2280.'

'Yes, sir!' both men uttered with a trace of fear in their voices. Dylan could feel the rush of wind against his skin as the two individuals took off at a run.

'Now,' whispered the superior's voice into Dylan's ear, 'let us see who we are dealing with.'

Dylan felt hands aggressively probe his body in various places. He felt cold fingers skimming over his face and running down his arms. When the strange hands reached his right wrist, he felt the man flip his arm over and to Dylan's surprise, he heard this person inhale sharply and breathlessly exclaim 'This can't be.'

The cold fingers traced his birth mark – the strange group

of three little dots that Dylan had been born with. This man spent what seemed to be an unusual amount of time examining the markings and touching each of the three dots over and over and over.

They must have finally reached their destination for Dylan could hear the sound of a door sliding open and the next sensation he had was that he was resting on some kind of stretcher. He desperately wanted to know where he was, and as his wits were returning, he was aware that his parents would be dreadfully worried about his disappearance. He mustered up all of his strength and successfully managed to open his eyes.

Dylan found himself staring at the most unusual looking person (*was it even a person?*) that he had ever seen. Based on the voice he had heard, Dylan had been expecting a large, overbearing male but instead, Dylan was confronted with a man, yes, but he was no taller than the average six-year-old child. If Dylan had been standing upright, this individual would likely have only come up to his chest. The man had long, silver hair that hung to his shoulders, but Dylan could see the tips of his ears slightly protruding. His eyes were a brilliant blue, brighter than any that Dylan had ever seen, and they seemed to glow unnaturally in the yellow tinged light of the small room that they were in. The man's nose was tiny to match his small frame and Dylan could see the tip of his pearly white teeth. It looked like he had far too many teeth for such a small mouth.

Dylan cleared his throat and the stranger turned his mesmerizing eyes onto Dylan's face.

'So you have awakened, I see,' said the man with forced sweetness in order not to frighten Dylan. 'Not to fear boy. I will take care of you from here.'

'Do you know me?' asked Dylan with surprise. 'Can we call my parents to let them know where I am and to come pick me up? I want to go home now. Please…' Dylan whispered with tears prickling at the back of his eyes. He was trying so hard to be brave, but he didn't know where he was, and he still wasn't feeling very well. All he wanted was to see his parents' loving faces and to feel the warm comfort of his bed.

'We have never officially met, but I know who you are,' replied the stranger who was so intimidating despite his small stature. 'How did you get here?' the man demanded. 'Who showed you the way? Who came for you?'

'I, I d-don't know what you are talking about,' stuttered Dylan no longer able to conceal his fear. 'I don't even know where I am.'

'Don't lie to me, boy. The consequences will be much worse for you if you do. Now tell me, who came to retrieve you and bring you here?'

'I told you – I don't know what you are talking about!' cried Dylan.

The stranger stared into Dylan's grey eyes, now clouded with terror, the color of storm clouds. To Dylan's surprise, the man's demeanor suddenly changed, and he laid a hand gently upon Dylan's forehead.

'I believe you. We have lots of time to work this out. I am Reus. You will be coming with me.'

'But my parents!' shouted Dylan anxiously.

Just then, the door to the room slid open and Dylan heard the familiar voice of the first person who had found him.

'Sir, I knew you would want me to follow proper protocol, so I contacted D3W3. They are sending someone right away.'

'You what???!!!' screeched the man in charge.

'I – I thought that was what I was supposed to do,' came the trembling reply.

Dylan could not take his eyes off the person who had found him. His skin was pure white, as if he had no blood pumping through him. Even from several feet away, Dylan could see his eye teeth were razor sharp. He wore a uniform, like a guard, thought Dylan. *Where am I,* he wondered? The man's irises had no color. His eyes were like clear glass, completely translucent.

'Get out!' roared Reus. 'The boy is coming with me. I will take care of this. Now call D3W3 and tell them that I am handling the situation. They are not to come here!'

'Too late, I'm afraid Reus,' a singsong voice stated. Dylan's eyes shifted to the doorway. There stood a female that Dylan would best describe as looking like the tooth fairy's grandmother. She had white hair pulled back in a bun, and a kindly old face with wrinkles that crinkled as she smiled at Dylan. Her voice was soft and sweet and yet she spoke with authority. But most curiously, were the two wings on her back that fluttered softly as she moved.

'I'm so confused,' muttered Dylan.

'Oh child, I'm sure you are,' crooned the woman (*woman or whatever she was,* thought Dylan). 'Now, let us start at the beginning. I am Marianne Fairshefsky, but you can call me Mary. And you are?'

'My name is Dylan Dover.'

'Lovely, so we do know your identity, somewhat at least. I was told that your identity was unknown.'

'He doesn't register on the identifilizer5000, Ms. Fairshefsky,' said the guard.

'How curious. What faction are you Dylan? I'm guessing either wizard, witch, or warlock from the looks of you. You clearly aren't a vampire, elf or fairy. Definitely not a giant and too handsome to be an ogre. Perhaps you are a shapeshifter?'

Dylan stared at her blankly. 'I, I...I don't know what you are asking me. I live at 29 Park Lane in Upstate New York with my parents Olivia and Mike Dover. I have no idea where I am, or who you think I am, but please, I just want to go home.' Dylan's voice quivered with worry and exhaustion.

Dylan saw Mary and Reus exchange a strange look, and he blinked in confusion, not understanding what was happening.

Mary came closer and stood right next to Dylan. 'Can you sit up, my dear?' she asked.

'I can try,' replied Dylan. And he slowly was able to sit upright on the stretcher.

'Now Dylan, you are clearly of one faction or another, or you wouldn't be here. So we must discover which one you belong to, in order to determine who will be assigned to your case. I work for D3W3, so you may not be within my jurisdiction.'

'Pardon me for asking, but what is D3W3?' asked Dylan timidly, somewhat afraid to find out.

Mary laughed like little bells tinkling and replied 'The Department of Displaced or Delusional Witches, Warlocks and Wizards. Now my sense tells me that you are one of those, but we must make inquiries to be sure. Do you have any recollection of how you got here?'

'I don't even know where here is,' responded Dylan.

'Oh my. Well, you are in secure custody at the border crossing between the world of immortals and the world of humans. Immortals are not allowed to enter the human world without the Minister's permission, of course. You were found by a border officer, whose job it is to ensure that nobody enters or leaves without proper authority,' explained Mary.

Reus interjected then in a commanding voice. 'And as supervisory officer, I am in charge of the entire operation. So Mary, you have my permission to leave. Young Mr. Dover here will remain in my custody until we determine what is to be done with him.'

'My dear Reus, I am very sorry but I must remind you that once D3W3 is involved, we cannot relinquish our duty to anyone, so long as the child is within our jurisdiction. So unless Mr. Dover here is not a wizard, witch or warlock, then I must inform you that he will be coming with me.'

'Now, Dylan,' Mary continued, 'You talked about your parents. Can you show me a picture of them?'

'No, I don't have a picture with me,' replied Dylan, completely forgetting about all the pictures stored on his cell phone.

'If my suspicions are correct, you don't need one. If you want a picture to appear in your hand, just use your mind and make it so,' instructed Mary.

She's insane, thought Dylan. *Either I'm dreaming, or I have gone literally crazy. This makes absolutely no sense!*

'Just try, Dylan,' coaxed Mary in a soft, persuasive tone.

Here goes nothing, Dylan thought to himself. He screwed his eyes shut to focus completely on what he was being asked to do. In his mind, he imagined his parents and concentrated as hard as he could to envision a photograph of his family. He thought of every little detail that he could remember about his parents, their eyes, their smiles, their body shapes and posture.

The image was so clear, so vivid that he almost believed that he could see them standing right in front of him.

Dylan soon heard hands clapping. He opened his eyes and was greeted by Mary enthusiastically applauding his efforts and praising him. Dylan looked down and to his amazement he saw a crystal-clear image of his parents smiling up at him from what sort of looked like a photograph in his hand, but he knew it wasn't a photograph. He wasn't actually holding it either; the image shimmered around his hand. A holograph! That's what it was. As Dylan gazed delightedly at what he had accomplished, his two dogs ran into the image, wagging their tails and pawing at him, as if they wanted to reach out and touch him. Dylan blinked and lost his focus, and when he opened his eyes a split second later, the holograph had disappeared.

'Well done, Dylan! I knew my instincts were correct. A warlock through and through. No wand and no spells required. Therefore, you are of the highest faction, that of a warlock. That's one mystery solved. Now we just have to find where you belong and how it is that you were in the human world. I have never in my hundreds of years of service, heard of any case like yours. You my young friend, will be coming with me.'

Mary turned to Reus. 'Thank you, Reus. You have performed your duties most efficiently. But as you can see, clearly Dylan is a warlock and therefore, I am taking him into the care of D3W3. Your services in this matter are now concluded.'

Dylan saw Reus narrow his eyes, but his face remained passive and his voice stayed calm. 'Of course, Mary. I trust that you will keep me informed of Mr. Dover's progress.'

Mary laughed again. 'Oh Reus, you are funny. You know that there are laws of confidentiality. But I assure you that Dylan will be well cared for and that we will ensure that the proper place is found for him. But I do appreciate your concern for our young friend. We shall be leaving now. Dylan, do you wish to walk or to fly?'

'Fly? I don't know how to fly,' replied Dylan.

'Oh, but you do, perhaps you just don't know it yet. Very well, let us walk for the time being. I want to get you to our offices and then we can begin to sort things out. You will be much more comfortable there and we will be able to speak more freely, yes?'

'If you say so,' responded Dylan still as confused as he had been since he woke up. 'Can we call my parents when we get to your office?'

Mary looked at him with a puzzled expression. 'I think finding your parents will definitely be at the top of our agenda,' she agreed but unbeknownst to Dylan, she was not referring to his human parents.

'Come along then, Dylan. Goodbye Reus,' Mary sang as she escorted Dylan out of the little room where he had been held.

Dylan walked next to Mary through the long corridors lined with many boarding crossing guards. As they walked, Dylan's mind whirled at all that he saw. Creatures that he had believed were only in fairytales were all around him. Magical beings, some so large that they towered above his head and if they knelt down on their knees, would still be taller than Dylan. Others were very tiny and flew around him faster than he could fully make out their little, pixie-like faces. Some were easily identifiable as vampires – it was simply impossible to mistake their deathly white complexions for anything other than what they were. Yet others who he passed by did not have any physical traits that gave away their identities. They looked just like any other person who he would see at home.

'I must be dreaming,' he muttered.

'No, Dylan,' replied Mary as she squeezed his hand. This is not a dream, but together, we are going to figure out your history and your future.'

Dylan looked into her shining eyes and immediately felt safe. He trusted her, whether he should or not, he didn't know. But he certainly was happy to be taken care of by this grandmother looking fairy, rather than that guy Reus who scared him for reasons he didn't fully understand.

Down the hall, Reus watched Mary take the boy away from his control. *My master will not be happy about these circumstances,* thought Reus. *But he must be informed of the boy's return. I am quite certain that he did not arrange for this, or he would have had me intercept the child's arrival before being spotted by those moronic guards. So how is it that the boy ended up in the vortex from the human world if Baltazar did not plan for it to be so? It's a good thing that Baltazar placed me here years ago. He must have known that there was a chance the boy would cross over on his own. We will see what he wants me to do now. I feel that my position at the border is about to be changed and that he will have other plans for me.* Reus, with a quick snap of his fingers, disappeared in search of Baltazar.

CHAPTER FOUR

Dylan and Mary exited the building and Dylan looked around at his new surroundings. It was dark, but bright lights high above illuminated the darkness so that it was easy see. But upon closer inspection, Dylan could see that these were not ordinary street lights like back home. These were balls of light that shifted position in the sky. And when Dylan stared to get a better look, he could just make out what appeared to be wings flapping at an impossible rate of speed. They reminded him of the wings of a hummingbird, but these were definitely not any species of bird that he had ever seen. Dylan drew in a breath of excitement and froze in awe as one of them landed softly on his shoulder. Dylan turned his head slightly to gaze at this ball of wonder and gasped when his stare was returned by two, bright yellow eyes. The creature had no limbs, but Dylan could make out the translucent wings that shimmered like diamonds. It was perfectly round and the size of a baseball, but it wasn't smooth as Dylan had first thought. Up close, he could see tiny projections coming off its body that radiated the light he had seen from below.

As Dylan continued to gape at this unknown creature, its eyes changed color from yellow to pink to orange to blue and finally to grey – a color so familiar because it was just the same as Dylan's own. As Dylan looked deeply into the creature's eyes, he could see himself running away in a panic from the bullies and hiding in the tree stump – his last memory before waking up in this strange new world. Then he saw his two dogs pawing frantically at the ground and racing around and around the tree from which he disappeared. The next image Dylan saw was that of his parents. His mother sat on the ground and leaned her back against the tree, sobbing while his father tried to console her with tears coursing down his own cheeks.

Dylan couldn't help it. He tried to choke back his own tears, but he wasn't able to keep his feelings hidden anymore. He began to cry.

'There, there now, dearie,' Mary crooned softly. 'I see this fireball has taken a liking to you. That is very unusual. They don't often form such a bond with those outside of their own kind. But you will find that fireballs are the most loyal of creatures. She will be your gateway to the home that you have known. She will show you all that you want to see. Treat her with kindness and you shall never be lonely for she will always return to you. Now, we really must be going. My office is waiting for our arrival. Are you ready?'

'I guess so,' replied Dylan hesitantly.

'Excellent. Then hold my hand, tightly now, don't let go. You probably won't be able to fly on your own quite yet.'

Mary grabbed Dylan's hand and he gripped hers tightly in return. The fireball's eyes seemed to smile at Dylan and in an instant, the glowing light was gone.

'Away we go!' cried Mary, and Dylan felt himself rising up from the ground. There was nothing solid beneath his feet anymore and when he looked down, he found himself quickly gaining altitude. The first thirty seconds were terrifying, and he squeezed his eyes shut in fear.

But then something happened. It's like his brain was being

rewired. He was no longer scared, he felt…brave and weightless and in control. He opened his eyes and saw a world he didn't know streak by him as he flew through the dark sky. But he knew that he could take control of his destiny and that he would have to be strong if he was going to find his parents again.

He let one finger uncurl from Mary's hand, just to test how that felt. Then he let go with another finger and then another and another and another until he was not holding on to her at all. Mary smiled at Dylan and shouted in a loud voice so that he could hear her over the wind rushing past them. She called out: 'Use your mind to control your body. Concentrate on what you want, and it shall be!'

Then with a slight nod of her head, Mary let go of Dylan too. For an instant, he lost his concentration and he felt himself tumbling downwards, hurtling towards the ground that was so far beneath him, he couldn't even see it.

Concentrate!!! His mind screamed at him, *Fly, dammit, fly!!!*

His deathly downward descent abruptly ceased, and Dylan's body surged upwards. He laughed out loud to feel the wind against his skin, and the purest sense of joy he had ever experienced. He swooped and soared and cartwheeled through the sky. Well, they weren't perfect cartwheels, but he didn't care!

He saw Mary, hovering above him, watching his antics with her arms crossed over her chest but a grin on her face. Dylan could tell that she was in a hurry to get to her office and she was therefore just a little bit exasperated with him but at the same time, she was clearly enjoying the show he was putting on. Dylan could have kept it up for hours, but sensing Mary's growing impatience, he flew over to her, as fast he could, and pulled up just short of slamming into her with full force.

'Very nicely done, Mr. Dover!' exclaimed Mary. 'And all that without any formal training. Very impressive. But now we really do need to go. They are expecting us. Come along, dear.'

Dylan and Mary flew side by side the rest of the way to Mary's office. Dylan could have gone a lot faster, but he didn't know where he was going and he felt it would be impolite to ask for directions and take off on this person, well, person-like creature, who had been so kind to him. So he restrained himself and glided alongside his fairy guide.

The little fireball that had disappeared before once again made her presence known and darted between Dylan and Mary to join them in their journey. The glowing ball of light had no facial features other than its mesmerizing eyes which at the moment seemed to radiate a happy burst of yellow light on Dylan.

The three flew wordlessly and Dylan was able to pay closer attention to his surroundings. Some things reminded him of home. He saw what appeared to be houses beneath him, although they were certainly very different looking than the homes he was used to, in odd shapes and sizes and none of them had fenced backyards like at his human home... just wide-open spaces. But the closer they got to Mary's office, the closer the dwellings became. Until, and Dylan wasn't sure at first that his eyes weren't playing tricks on him; he flew past a house hovering in the sky. And then he flew past another house. And this time he was sure that his eyesight was accurate, because he actually saw someone inside through a window. Soon, they had to slow down a little in order to dodge all the homes that were stacked up one on top of each other in the sky.

'What the heck is going on? Do people live here?' asked Dylan.

'Well, not people my dear, immortals. Humans couldn't live like this!' Mary laughed at her own joke. 'As our population increases, we need to find additional room to house everyone, at least for those who wish to have a residence such as these. Some prefer to dwell below the ground, while others prefer to live above. Some want to live inside a structure; others prefer to be free from such encumbrances. To each his own, I always say!' responded Mary in her singsong voice. 'The closer we get to downtown, the more crowded it becomes. It seems like most magical beings prefer to live where all the action is. Only a few like the peace and quiet of the periphery. I am one of the few, but it makes for one long commute to the office! That however is a choice I happily make. Oh look, you can see my office now.' Mary pointed a wrinkled finger at a building that was substantially lower than the surrounding properties and was actually on solid land.

As they flew closer and closer to their intended destination, they started their descent. The ground looked like it was coming up pretty fast.

'Landings can be the hardest part,' Mary warned as they zoomed ever closer downwards. 'Try to keep your knees slightly bent, and your head up. When I say, stretch your legs down to try to touch the ground. Ready... steady... NOW!'

Dylan stretched out his legs, tried to keep his knees slightly bent and his head upright, but clearly something went wrong for instead of landing upright, he tumbled over and over until he finally came to stop, and lay panting on his side to catch his breath. The little fireball buzzed over Dylan's head, its eyes now worried, deep black as the night itself.

Mary hurried over. 'Dylan, are you okay? Are you hurt? Should we summon the healer?'

Dylan flexed one foot. Then the other. He wiggled the fingers on his hands. And then he opened his eyes. 'I'm fine,' he replied. 'Guess I need to work on my landings, huh?'

'Oh, I'm so relieved. You will have lots of time to perfect your flying and landing techniques. Now, let's get you inside!'

Dylan, Mary and the fireball that refused to leave Dylan's shoulder, walked into the D3W3 offices. It looked pretty much like every office Dylan had ever been in before – the doctor, the dentist, the principal's office (not that he was there very much!). A reception desk was in one corner, and a bunch of chairs were stationed in front of the other walls. A low table with magazines was right in the middle and an aquarium was in the far corner. Dylan took a quick glance at the cover pages of the magazines: 'Top Ten Ways to Wiz Up Your Wizardry'; 'Darkest Secrets of the Werewolf Revealed'; 'Battle of Ogres versus Giants – Will The Giants Win the Title Again?'

'Have a seat, Dylan. Let me go find my boss. He is expecting us,' Mary stated and hurried off, leaving Dylan and the fireball alone in the reception area. Dylan wandered over to the aquarium but what he saw was not what he was expecting. 'These don't look like any fish I have seen,' he exclaimed. 'What are these?'

Dylan stared, completely mesmerized by the creatures that clearly lived in water, but looked like aliens. They had fish-like bodies in all different colors and each had multiple heads, with human-like features that stared back at him. It was like looking at human bobble heads on a fish body! 'This is so creepy,'

Dylan murmured.

'Maybe you're the one who's creepy!' someone snapped. The voice sounded muffled but angry.

'Who said that?' asked Dylan, looking at the fireball.

'I did!' replied the voice. Dylan looked around but didn't see anyone.

'In here, stupid!' instructed the voice. Dylan looked into the fish tank. Sure enough, one of the little fish people had its human - like nose plastered to the wall of the aquarium and was staring angrily at Dylan. Its irritated voice rose through the water in a bubble and when it reached the surface it popped, revealing the message. 'You're bothering me, now get lost!' ordered the creature.

'I'm so sorry. I didn't mean to offend you. Goodbye,' replied Dylan and quickly moved as far away from the fish tank as he could.

Just as he was about to settle into a chair to wait, Mary returned with an ancient looking, crinkled up old man. He even had more wrinkles than Mary! He had a long white moustache that twirled down from his nose and was braided at his chin. The braid hung down past his knees. While his face was all withered with lines, his eyes were bright blue and sharp, conveying both his kindness and his intelligence.

'Well, well, so you are the cause of all the trouble, that rose me out of my bed so late at night,' the man said, but his words rang with laughter and not with condemnation.

'Yes sir. I'm Dylan Dover and I'm terribly sorry for the problems I have caused. I am really not sure how I got here or even where I am. Quite frankly sir, after spending some time with Mary, I'm not even sure *what* I am. But I just want to contact my parents and go home. Please, I know that they will be awfully worried about me.'

The old man approached Dylan and sat down in the chair next to him. He looked directly into Dylan's eyes and said: 'Dylan, I'm not going to lie to you. We cannot contact the people you call your parents. They are in the human world, and you have crossed into the world of immortals. I don't know how that came to be, but here you are, and so we must move forward. We need to determine your magical roots, for clearly, you were born of Warlocks despite the fact that no record of your delivery exists. We will do everything we can to figure out your history and I promise we will also ensure that you are well taken care of here. I will do everything within my power, which is quite extensive if I do say so myself, to make sure that you are happy.'

'But my parents...' Dylan's voice trailed off miserably.

'Your *human* parents,' the man repeated softly. 'I am sorry, Dylan. We cannot make contact with them.' He placed a gentle hand on Dylan's shoulder and let Dylan cry softly for a few minutes, understanding that he was still just a boy, far away from the only home he had ever known with no way to return.

The little fireball hovered close to Dylan's face and nudged Dylan every minute or two, concern clearly evident in its large eyes. After several long minutes, Dylan sniffed and found the inner strength to pull himself together. He rubbed his eyes and then looked to the stranger sitting next to him.

'Forgive me for failing to introduce myself sooner. I am Warrentree Warwickonis. Quite a name my parents chose for me, wouldn't you say?' he chuckled. 'I am the Director of D3W3 and as such, am directly responsible for your care until

46

we find your biological parents or until you come of age. Since you seem to have connected so nicely with Mary, I will assign her as your case worker. Now, it is far too late to do anything about your situation today, so I have called my assistant to come in to arrange lodging for you simply for tonight. Tomorrow, we will see if we can find more long-term accommodations for you. My assistant should be here any time… she wasn't too happy that I woke her up, but she knows that it's all part of the job!'

Just then, what was clearly an elf bounded in through the front door. She was small, less than three feet from the top of her head to the tips of her toes. She had long fair hair tied back in a ponytail, exposing her pointed ears. She had a tiny round nose, and perfect cupid bow lips. She was actually very pretty, thought Dylan… for an elf. She stood in the doorway with her hands on her hips and her violet eyes opened wide when she saw Dylan sitting on the chair.

'Oh my. Oh my, oh my, oh my!' she exclaimed in child-like voice.

'What is it Farah, my dear?' inquired Warrentree.

'He is the spitting image of my neighbor's son. If you hadn't told me that this kid sitting right in front of me was found wandering in the border security zone, I would have sworn it was my neighbor's boy.'

Farah took several steps forward and paused. Her hands were still on her hips and she leaned forward to get a better look. Not satisfied, she came closer still. But that wasn't close enough for her either. Farah took a graceful leap forward until she stood directly in front of Dylan. She cradled his face between her little hands and tilted his neck this way and that to look at him from all angles.

'The only thing that I can see is different is the color of his eyes,' she declared with certainty. 'Aside from that, I can assure you that the two boys are completely identical.'

'Are you sure?' asked Mary incredulously.

'Really, Mary... have I ever been wrong before? Of course, I'm sure.'

'What are the names of your neighbors?' asked Warrentree.

'Maggie and Ben Warston. Their son's name is Jeremy, but I believe that they all call him Remy.'

'Oh lovely,' Warrentree clapped his hands delightedly. 'I know Ben. He works for the Ministry, Department of Spells and Hexes, as I recall. I believe he is an adjudicator. Yes, yes, a very nice man indeed. We shall have to contact him and his wife right away. But perhaps it is too late tonight. In the morning might be soon enough...'

'No, no, sir. It must be tonight. This boy is clearly theirs for there cannot be another explanation for having two boys so completely identical. If they have been separated for this long a time, then they must be reunited at once. No time like the present, sir. Shall I contact them right away?' The little elf tapped her foot impatiently as she waited for her boss to confirm her plan.

'Alright, Farah. I suppose you are right. You may contact the parents immediately.'

'I told you, I am always right. Have I not proven myself after all these decades? I don't understand why people always question me. Well, perhaps we can all remember this the next time I am doubted. In any event, let me contact Maggie and Ben. I am sure that they will want to come right away!'

Farah danced her way to the reception desk and sat down in

the chair. She closed her eyes and mumbled some words that Dylan could not make out. Then she sat perfectly still, her eyes remained tightly shut, and they all waited. Suddenly, she sprung out of her chair and in one long leap she stood before her boss and Dylan once again.

'They are on their way, sir. Estimated time of arrival, three minutes and thirty-six seconds. And, you're welcome! I will take care of the paperwork tomorrow. For now, I am going back to bed. I need my beauty sleep, you know! Bye bye!' she called over her shoulder as she flew out the door.

Warrentree chuckled. 'She always fares a little on the dramatic side, but she is very efficient,' he informed Dylan.

Three and a half minutes later, just as Farah had predicted, Maggie, Ben and a third individual rushed through the doors at the offices of D3W3. In amazement, Dylan stared into the exact image of himself, except for the eye color. While Dylan's eyes were shades of grey, his counterpart had eyes of green. The two boys stared wordlessly into each other faces. Ben's face lit up in a huge smile. Maggie Warston dropped to the floor in a dead faint.

CHAPTER FIVE

'Maggie, Maggie?' called Ben, hovering over his wife's body and patting her face to try to rouse her. He shook her body with a little more force, but she remained out cold. Ben looked up at the others who had gathered round his wife and said, 'She must be in shock.'

'Give her a little breathing room,' replied Warrentree in a kind, but authoritative tone. *Clearly he is someone that is listened to,* thought Dylan. Everyone just stood there, waiting for the woman on the floor to wake up. The minutes passed and still nobody did anything. Dylan was so confused. Not that he had much experience with people fainting in front of him but on all the TV shows that he had seen, when someone passed out cold, people did *something*.

'Shouldn't you elevate her head, or her feet, or turn her to the side, or call 9-1-1?' inquired Dylan after staring at the woman still unmoving on the floor.

'What's 9-1-1?' asked the boy who looked just like Dylan. 'And why would we ever do any of those things you suggested?'

Dylan turned his head to respond, but when he gazed into the face that was so much like his own, he forgot what he wanted to say.

'Not to worry, Dylan. She will be fine. If she doesn't wake up soon, we will move her to her own bed where she can recover more comfortably,' stated Warrentree. Hearing another voice snapped Dylan out of his stupor.

'You aren't concerned that she passed out and is still unconscious?' questioned Dylan.

Warrentree chuckled softly. 'No, my boy. Maggie is a warlock, just as you are. It takes a lot more than a shock to cause any real harm to an immortal. And we don't want to use magic to rouse her prematurely. She will wake up, when her mind has had time to process what she has seen.'

Ben stood up then and came to stand right next to Dylan. 'My son,' he breathed. And then his stance wobbled, and it looked like he was going to pass out too! But he regained his balance quickly and reached out a tentative hand to touch the top of Dylan's head. 'My son,' he repeated in wonder.

Just then, Maggie sat up and called out 'Where is he? Where is he?' Her head whipped around from one side to the next until her eyes met Dylan's gaze. Dylan could see tears spill down her cheeks as she slowly rose from the floor. She took tentative steps, with her right hand outstretched, and silently approached Dylan.

Dylan reached out his hand in response and when she grasped his fingers, he was enveloped by a feeling of something he could not describe. He felt loved, he felt at peace. He felt home. He sensed without question that this woman had given birth to him, and that in itself did not shock him, since his mother, his human mother, had always told him that he was adopted. But as he let himself be pulled into a giant bear hug by the female warlock, his mind whirled with questions. Ben couldn't resist, and he threw himself into the hug as well. And then Dylan felt a third set of arms encircle his body. His identical twin joined the embrace too.

When everyone finally let go, they all began talking at once.

51

Warrentree immediately held up just one finger and the room fell into silence. 'I know we all have many questions, and there are many mysteries here for us to unravel,' he said. 'But perhaps Dylan is tired and would prefer to go home now. We can talk more about this tomorrow.'

'Home?' questioned Dylan. 'What home? You told me that I couldn't go home.'

'Our home,' said Maggie lovingly. 'Your home. Where you belong.'

Dylan didn't know what to say. He desperately wanted to see his parents – his human parents, but he also realized that Warrentree was not going to let him be reunited with them. At least not yet. Dylan's emotions were so conflicted. He was excited to find his birth family and to discover that he had a twin brother. The idea of being in a magical world and knowing that he had some kind of superpowers was also pretty cool and a little bit scary too. But he was deeply saddened and missed his parents and his dogs and his house and his bed and …He felt tears threaten to overwhelm him again and his shoulders sagged. An intense feeling of exhaustion began to invade his body and he felt his eyelids droop. It was suddenly an effort to stay awake.

'I think young Dylan has reached both his physical and emotional limit for today,' said Mary. 'Time for bed, young man. We can reconvene in the morning.'

Mary wrapped Dylan in a comforting embrace. He felt as if he were floating in a warm bubble bath. His eyes closed gently, and then Dylan fell into a dreamless sleep.

CHAPTER SIX

Dylan was awake for some time before he opened his eyes. He was so perfectly relaxed and at peace that he didn't want to move. He just wanted to lie in his bed a little bit longer. There was a soft flapping of wings in his ears that began to irritate him and invaded his perfect blissful state. He swatted at the sound, thinking it must be some sort of insect, but the dratted noise came back a moment later. He brushed at his ears again and the buzzing stopped but only for a second. When he whacked at his ears a third time, the tips of his fingers connected with something prickly that gave him an uncomfortable but not quite painful electric shock. This time, Dylan opened his eyes and when he saw what was hovering around his head, he let out a shriek of surprise.

In an instant, Dylan was even more terrified as he stared into a face that was identical to his own. Dylan's eyes darted around the unfamiliar room and tried to make sense of what he was seeing. Then everything came rushing back into his mind. It wasn't a dream. He wasn't in his house on Park Lane in Upstate New York. His dogs Oliver and Halle were not lying on his feet as they usually were when he woke up every morning and his parents Olivia and Mike would not be there to greet him with a cheerful good morning, a hot breakfast and kiss on his cheek. Dylan had thought he was getting too old for those parental kisses, but what he would give at this moment to have his mother planting a big wet one on him right now!

The glowing object continued to dance around Dylan's head, and from its erratic behavior, it was clearly distressed about something. Dylan quickly realized that he was the cause. The floating ball of electricity thought it had hurt him. Dylan reassured the creature, *the fireball* that he was fine, just a little disoriented.

Then Dylan turned his attention to his brother, who stood poised next to his bed. The two boys smiled tentatively at each other and then the one standing sat down gingerly on the edge of Dylan's mattress.

'So,' he said to Dylan.

'So,' Dylan replied.

'I'm Jeremy, but everyone calls me Remy,' he informed Dylan.

'I'm Dylan.'

'I know,' he responded with a mischievous grin. The boys laughed a little awkwardly. After all, what do you say to your identical twin who you never knew existed?

In his mind, Dylan contemplated how similar they were. *I wonder if he has the same birthmark that I do*, he thought.

'I have a weird marking on the inside of my right wrist,' said Remy. 'Three dots in a diagonal line.'

Dylan stared at Remy incredulously. 'I didn't ask you about a birthmark.'

Remy flushed. 'Oh sorry, I thought you did.'

'No, at least not out loud. But I was thinking it.'

'Can I read your mind?' asked Remy utterly astonished at this revelation.

'It appears so. Can I read yours?' inquired Dylan. And then, Dylan heard Remy's response loud and clear in his mind. 'If you can, repeat this: My brother Remy is going to be the greatest warlock in history.'

Dylan grinned and said out loud: 'My brother Remy is going to be the greatest warlock in history. But that's only because he had a head start. Maybe we will be the greatest warlocks together, if you can catch me up!'

Remy laughed, and the two boys delighted in their new-found discovery of each other.

'I wonder what the story is with you.' Remy inquired. 'I mean, how did any of this happen? Mom and Dad never even mentioned a twin.'

'I have no idea. My parents, I mean my other parents always told me that I was adopted but I don't think they knew about any of this warlock stuff. I thought I was just a regular kid whose birth parents had to give me up because they couldn't take care of me. But do you want to know something that is also really strange, that just came to me now?' Dylan whispered to his brother. Remy nodded and, in his head, Dylan could hear Remy encouraging him to continue. 'The person, well, not person exactly, but the individual who came to interrogate me at the border yesterday, he didn't know my name, but he knew who I was. He didn't want me going with Mary. He wanted me to go with him and he was really pissed when Mary took me away.'

Remy contemplated that for a minute and then he murmured, 'Maybe we should keep that information to ourselves for now. It might freak out Mom and Dad and I think that they might be freaked out enough already!'

The boys then decided that any information that they thought should be kept away from their parents, at least for now, could only be discussed through their minds. *No sense in risking being overheard,* both boys agreed silently. *Great minds think alike,* they both thought at the exact same moment. *Stop that!* Both boys began to giggle, and the giggle shortly turned into a laugh until soon Remy and Dylan were laughing so hard that they fell back on Dylan's bed, holding their sides with tears streaming from their eyes.

Maggie and Ben burst into the room and smiled happily to see their sons, reunited and bonding together. The proud parents looked at each other and reached out to join hands. Ben squeezed Maggie's fingers gently and pulled her closer to him. But their happiness was not entirely complete, for they both knew that there was still one son missing. And if one missing son could miraculously reappear in their life, then there was still hope of finding the third one. Hope that had never existed before bloomed wildly in Ben and Maggie's hearts. Maybe, just maybe their third son was still alive.

CHAPTER SEVEN

'So Dylan, what do you like to eat at the start of your day?' asked Maggie of her newly found son.

Dylan realized how hungry he was. 'I'm pretty easy. I like most things. Pancakes and waffles with warm maple syrup, scrambled eggs and bacon really crispy, oatmeal if it has lots of brown sugar on top, toast with jelly but not jam – I hate fruit lumps on my toast. Or in a pinch, I'm good with most cereals but my mom likes to make sure that I use 2% milk because she thinks I'm too skinny and need the fat content.' Dylan's voice came to an abrupt halt. 'I'm really sorry, I mean my other mother. I- I -I don't know what to say…'

Maggie's face never lost its smile as she approached Dylan. 'That's okay, sweetheart. This is sudden for all of us, and I can see how much you love your human parents. Ben and I can't ever replace them, and I can't tell you how grateful we are that they clearly raised you so well. We thought you had died during delivery so having you back with us is the most incredible, wonderful, most amazing thing that could have happened to our family. But we know it will take time for you to adjust. For all of us to adjust really, since our family is now grown. But the most important thing is that we are all together now.'

Maggie's words made Dylan feel loved and welcomed into his new family, but he still couldn't help but feel sad about the parents he was not able to see, or even to contact. He knew that his human parents would be worried sick and that they must have been looking everywhere for him. Dylan wished that there was a way for him to at least send a message to the Dover family that he loved to let them know that he was safe, even if he couldn't come home, at least for now. Dylan decided that he would raise the issue again with his new parents, as soon as the time felt right.

'Mom,' Remy interjected. 'Why did you think that Dylan didn't survive the delivery?'

Maggie and Ben exchanged a pointed look, and Ben gave his wife a slight nod.

Maggie sighed and said, 'Let's figure out these foods that Dylan talked about and then Dad and I will explain to you while we eat.'

Maggie grabbed Dylan's hand for support and together they flew out the door. In the next instant, Dylan found himself in a different room that he had not been in before. He sat on a large stool as did the others, with Remy right next to him and his birth parents across from them. While Dylan would have expected a table, none existed here. As he glanced around, he noticed several things at once. First, the stools that they were sitting on were not on the floor but rather hovered in the air. Second, there was no floor! Literally – no floor at all – he could see straight down to the ground which must have been hundreds of feet below him. There were walls that surrounded them with huge windows which gave him a clear view of the outside. And what Dylan saw made his jaw open with shock. Outside the window he saw what he assumed to be the sky in the most brilliant blue color and floating in that beautiful sky were other houses, well, what looked to be house-like although very different from any houses he had ever seen at home. His human home. Dylan looked at his new family members who seemed delighted with his discoveries. Dylan also witnessed strange floating balls, dozens of them in all different colors blowing between the houses. With surprise, he realized that these mysterious objects were fireballs, but without the fire – they didn't glow with light the way he had seen them before. Remy heard his thoughts and sent back a message that the fireballs only lit up in the dark.

'I guess this isn't what you're used to, huh,' grinned Remy. Dylan could not find words, so he just nodded his head in agreement.

'Now then, food,' said Maggie with authority. 'Let's see what Dylan was talking about. Dylan, I need you to concentrate on the foods you want us to eat. Show me what they look like. Think about how they taste. Imagine the texture and how they feel in your mouth,' Maggie urged. Dylan closed his eyes and concentrated as hard as he could. It only took a moment before images of his favorite breakfast foods were hovering in front of him. Dylan's eyes widened in amazement as he stared at the holograms that clearly he had created. Maggie's eyes lit up in happiness at her son's discovery and then narrowed in concentration. A wide smile spread across her face. She snapped her fingers and a table miraculously appeared before them. On the table was every food that Dylan had mentioned with little labels on each dish identifying what they were.

'How's that?' asked Maggie of Dylan, hoping for his approval. 'Did I miss anything?'

'N-no, you didn't miss anything.'

'So what's the matter, sweetheart? I sense that something is not right…'

Dylan hesitated. Maggie prompted her son again. 'It's okay, Dylan. You can tell me.'

'Well, it's just that I don't eat all this at once. There is enough food here to last a month.'

Everyone laughed. 'Don't you worry about that, Dylan. Here when you get hungry, you just have to imagine what you want and it will appear. I was able to create these foods from the images that you had in your mind. We haven't ever eaten any of these foods so it will be a new adventure for us,' replied Maggie.

'That's not entirely true, Mags,' quipped Ben. 'I have had some of this kind of food back when I did my service for the Ministry OTV.'

'OTV?' asked Dylan.

'Outside the vortex,' replied Ben.

Dylan shook his head in mild confusion. There was a lot he still had to learn. Soon everyone was eating the human food that Dylan loved, and there was clearly agreement that everyone was enjoying it as much as he was. Remy kept ramming pancakes into his mouth as if he would never eat his fill. Ben closed his eyes and savored the crispy bacon while Maggie seemed to like everything equally and just seemed happy to be surrounded by her family. Nobody was able to talk with their mouths stuffed with food but as soon as everyone's appetites were satisfied, Remy and Dylan simultaneously looked to their parents and said, 'Now tell us the story of our delivery.'

'It's okay, Mags. They deserve to know. Do you want me to tell them?' asked Ben.

Maggie nodded her head, too choked up to speak.

Ben leaned forward and in a conspiratorial soft voice, he began the story, which started long before the boys' delivery.

'Remy, you already know some of this from school but Dylan you first need to understand the history of immortals for you will see that your delivery is very much a part of our communal past.

Centuries ago, immortals lived alongside humans. There was no world just for us, like we live in now. There was just the one world where we cohabitated – immortals and mortals living side by side. Of course, immortals had secrets that could never be revealed to humans, they could not know of our powers for surely, they would try to kill us if they ever discovered what we could do. And while we are certainly more powerful than they are, humans could still bring about our destruction, if they knew the ways to kill us. Being immortal does not mean we are indestructible.

Some of us looked too different to be seen by humans without causing problems, so these creatures hid in places that the humans would not find them. Under the sea, high in the mountains, deep in the forests. Sometimes a human would get a glance at one of these immortal beings, but no human was ever able to actually find or capture one of these immortals, so they were safe to continue their existence even though they were in such close proximity to humans. But some immortals were better able to blend in with the human population. Warlocks, witches, wizards, vampires and shapeshifters – we all looked human enough to live amongst them, in their towns and cities. We had to be very careful to not use our powers in ways that would be detected. The vampires especially had a difficult time for unlike the rest of us, they would sometimes kill humans and on occasion, even change them into one of their own. Shapeshifters too sometimes caused human deaths, but usually out of fear and in self-defense. Shapeshifters rarely kill humans for sport. Warlocks, witches and wizards rarely posed any threat to humans. We were content to exist in their midst without causing any harm.

For many decades, when a human died at the hands of an immortal, the death would be explained by natural factors such as an illness or accident. But then a shift came to immortal culture. There were many who began to resent having to remain in hiding and felt that immortals should dominate the shared world. These beings believed that humans should become slaves to the immortals and those who resisted should perish. But there was also resistance to this idea. There were also those who did not want humans to serve us, nor for the people to be killed. These immortals wanted our co-existence to continue in the peaceful manner that had been enjoyed for so long.

Conflict erupted within the immortal societies and soon conflict escalated into a civil war. This war was between immortal beings, but the battles were waged in the open where humans became both witness and victim. Immortals were killing other immortals but posed as humans to make it look as if mortals were doing the slaying. Horrific methods of death were imposed publicly as warning for other immortals. Some were burned at the stake or quartered and hung then displayed on pikes for public viewing. Unfortunately, some innocent humans were also caught in the wrong place at the wrong time and murdered in this manner. These innocents were seen as casualties of war.

The war progressed and in an effort to wipe out larger factions of immortals, deadly spells were cast which made creatures, both human and not, die by the thousands. Human history books today tell the story of plagues that spread like wildfire through human populations, and it's to our benefit that the mortals believe disease to be the causes of so many deaths as our secrets remain protected.

After many, many years and countless deaths, a truce was finally reached by the immortal leaders who led the two sides of the war. It was decided that a new world would be created, one for only immortals, where all creatures could live in the open and there would be no secrets. Each of the two leaders would become members of the Ministry that would govern the new world, and each would appoint one deputy as their closest adviser. Remy, I'm sure you know this already, the leaders are Atticus Warsimon and Callista Wargreen, and both are warlocks. Atticus appointed Baltazar Vamremicus, a vampire as his deputy and Callista chose Alexia Wizcharm, a wizard as hers.

But the immortals could not fully disconnect from the human world. The vampires needed to have some interaction with humans. They would always desire human blood, even though it was not necessary for them to survive, they felt strongly that they should not be made to suffer without. And of course, if vampires ever want to grow their population, then humans must be changed.

Others too wanted to have contact in the human world. Some had already formed relationships with humans which made them particularly vulnerable for their secrets to be discovered. Some even created children with mortals who therefore were partially immortal. Nobody knew if the half-blood children would have access to the immortal world but there was too much resistance to kill them outright.

And so, it was decided that some immortals would remain in the human world. They would serve as guards to watch the vortexes which linked our new world with that of the humans, and also to monitor children who were born with immortal blood and report back to the Ministry of any concerns that arose.

Now, when the Ministry was created and the two leaders each chose their deputy, a council was also formed. You know that the leaders were both Warlocks and that one chose a vampire as his deputy while the other chose a wizard as hers. But other types of immortals were concerned that their interests would be forgotten or ignored, so the council was created to allow for representatives of each type of immortal to be present in the Ministry – elves, ogres, giants, fairies, witches, werewolves, wizards, warlocks, shapeshifters…Everyone would be given a surname with the preface of their faction. That way everyone would be easily identifiable. And so, our new world was born.

The Ministry then began to pass doctrines to govern the immortals. They borrowed the idea of law making from the humans and created rules to maintain peace and harmony. We are not allowed to use our magic to impersonate other immortals. We are not allowed to use our magic to steal powers from other immortals. An immortal is able to gain the powers from another only if the powers are explicitly and voluntarily gifted from one immortal to another. If magical powers are given from one immortal to another, the exchange of powers can be reversed by the Ministry if it is later determined that the powers were only transferred under duress. There are certain creatures and objects that we are not allowed to possess because they have been deemed by the leaders to be potentially dangerous to our kinds. But probably one of the most important rules we have is to prevent immortals from entering the vortex and crossing into the human world, without permission of the Ministry. Only select individuals are permitted such access and only if there are legitimate reasons for entry.

Here is where our history begins to link to your delivery but what I can tell you from this point on is only based on rumors. Nobody seems to know the truth of this matter, and I can't even tell you where this gossip started. I can tell you that for a while, these ideas spread like wildfire, but the Ministry was very quick to put an end to it. We are not ever supposed to repeat this, but I think it's important that you know, since it connects to the circumstances of your birth.

Soon after our world was created, one vampire had to be destroyed by the Ministry. As I recall, he was rebelling and even killed another immortal. His actions were clearly unacceptable, and the Ministry had no choice but to punish him. Rumor has it that this vampire before his death said something that frightened the leaders of our realm. Apparently, the vampire before his execution foretold of a future for immortals that would lead to the destruction of everything and everyone in the immortal world. This prophecy apparently says that four siblings born at the same time will either save our world or allow for its complete destruction. And the sign to demonstrate that these siblings have arrived is something to do with stars, which we don't even have here, so it must be referring to the human world where they do. From the information that I have heard, the rebellious vampire was believed while he was still human to have the unusual ability to foresee the future, which is why the leaders were so concerned.

That is all I have ever heard about the vision and the Ministry released a public statement when the information first got out that denied any concern for the destruction of our world. But I can tell you this, soon after this whole scandal with the prophecy becoming public and then squelched by the Ministry, a new mandate was passed.

All births of immortals must be immediately registered with the Ministry. And all deliveries must be reported in advance of the delivery date. A representative from the Ministry would be sent to record the birth and personally register the identities of the infants.

We of course knew that your mother was expecting multiples – we were so excited about that! Originally, we wanted to have a home delivery, but once we learned that there was more than one infant, we were told that there were likely three of you, we decided it was too risky to deliver without assistance. Immortal pregnancies can be tricky when dealing with multiples – the babies' magic sometimes hides additional fetuses. Most deliveries of immortals are relatively risk free for both the mother and child; however, having three of you at once posed some concerns and to ensure everyone's safety, we decided that we would need the help of a Master Deliverer. We reported the expectation of an exceptional birth to the Ministry as required and eagerly anticipated welcoming three babies into our family. This requirement of reporting anticipated births to the Ministry seems to me that it may be connected to the prophecy.

The day of your delivery came, and I clearly remember your mother lying on the stretcher in the birthing chamber. The process seemed to start without any problems but very quickly, things seemed to go wrong. I remember the Master Deliverer was panicked. He clearly knew that there was a problem. He got the first child out quickly and handed the baby over to us. That was you, Remy,' Ben said with a smile towards his first- born son.

'But after that, things went horribly wrong, very fast. The Master Deliverer was chanting so quickly that I couldn't make out his words, but clearly, his magic wasn't strong enough, for he soon held up two more infants, both baby boys, that didn't survive. We had only the briefest moment to look at their tiny bodies before they disappeared.

And I will never forget the words that the Master Deliverer said to us at the time. His words have both haunted and comforted me for the last twelve years. He told us our other two children were gone – that he couldn't save them from their fate. And then I clearly recall that he advised us to focus on our living son and that while our other sons will always be in our hearts, we must move on without them. I remember him telling us to cherish the son we had and that you, Remy, were destined to do great things. I hear those words in my mind every night before I fall asleep.

Except last night was different because last night I knew that we were lied to and now I am left with so many questions. Dylan is clearly alive, he survived the delivery. So is our other son, your brother, also alive somewhere? Why were we deceived in this way? And by what miracle has Dylan been returned to us?'

Ben, overwrought with emotion, began to cry. His head slumped onto the table and Maggie reached over a comforting arm to caress his shoulders. 'Shhh, shhh, it's okay darling…' she crooned repeatedly. Remy and Dylan sat perfectly still but their minds were whirling in synch. *What is going on here?*

Where is our brother? Why were we separated? Is our birth some-how connected to the prophecy???

And at that moment, both boys subtly turned their right arms, underneath the table so that their parents could not see what they were doing. They each saw on the underside of both their wrists the three small dots in a diagonal line. Neither knew anything about star constellations in the human world, but they both instantly realized that these birthmarks were not a coincidence.

Ben's tears soon dried up and he smiled at his boys in apology. 'Sorry, guys. I'm just a bit emotional with everything that's going on. Forgive me.'

'Ah, Dad,' exclaimed Remy. 'All good. Now, let's talk about some more about this prophecy and what exactly is the connection between that vision and us.' Remy wanted to hear more about this vision that the Ministry outlawed, to try to discover how it might relate to them, but his mother had other plans.

Maggie bolted up from her stool and flew over to hover between the two boys. 'You listen to me,' she said fiercely, 'You two have nothing to do with that prophecy. The Ministry representatives attended and recorded all deliveries, not just yours. You are just two brothers that were separated by some bizarre mistake and that's all there is to it. Some error was made, which your father and I intend to correct, but that's it! Got it?'

Dylan and Remy nodded simultaneously, but in their conjoined minds, they knew that that was not it at all. There was much more going on than their mother wanted to believe, but they also knew that contradicting her at this point was just going to lead to more problems. So they silently agreed to keep their thoughts to themselves.

CHAPTER EIGHT

Reus approached the entrance to Baltazar's residence, unsure of what to expect. And this greatly worried him. Baltazar was one of the most powerful immortals, second in command, and so not only was he an immensely powerful vampire, but he wielded heavy authority as one of the two deputies of the Ministry. If Baltazar desired Reus' death, he would have lots of options. Kill him now in the privacy of his residence and make an excuse later to justify his acts or have him arrested and then executed by the Ministry on the basis of Baltazar's command. But Baltazar could also provide Reus with great rewards, if he was so inclined. Some of these benefits could potentially help Reus achieve his ultimate purpose which could never be revealed to Baltazar. And Reus just didn't know how news of the Dover boy coming through the vortex would be received by his master.

The entrance to Baltazar's residence would be easy to miss, if one didn't know what to look for. Baltazar had designed his underground castle deliberately in that way. He did not want others to know where to find him, unless he desired himself to be found. Reus had been his private servant for centuries, and thus was privy to many of the secrets that Baltazar prized, but even Reus only knew what Baltazar wished to reveal. There were secrets that went far beyond the knowledge that Reus had.

The ground surrounding Baltazar's castle looked relatively barren. There was grass, artificial but a fairly decent replica of the real thing, which the immortals borrowed from the human world. There were a few small, somewhat gnarled trees scattered about. These trees had sharp limbs that protruded from the trunks, which seemed to reach out as if to catch something or someone, in its grasp. And that was precisely the purpose for which Baltazar had placed them there. These trees were the first line of defense to Baltazar's residence. Nobody could get to the entrance without first passing by the tree guards. That is, unless you knew what to expect and therefore, how to bypass the trees from snatching you up and capturing you in their relentless hold.

But Reus knew how to get around the tree barrier. Just before he stepped into the range of the first tree, Reus came to complete stop. Then with a snap of his fingers, he began to float straight up and over the tops of the small trees. Reus looked down with his sharp eyes for the marker that was very familiar to him but would never be noticed by others. When he saw the small indentation on the ground, he knew that he was directly over the entrance to Baltazar's private world.

With a second snap, Reus plummeted straight down. But instead of crashing, the ground split open, as if the ground had opened its mouth and devoured Reus. Reus' descent continued and for several minutes, his body remained on its downward journey deeper and deeper below the surface. The air rushed past his face, and the only thing Reus could see were the dark, crumbling walls as he raced past at a speed unknown to humans.

Finally, Reus felt his body slowing down and he landed softly on the floor. Baltazar's castle while underground looked very much like a place that royalty would live in, and that was no coincidence. While living in the mortal world, Baltazar had come to appreciate the luxuries that the human kings and queens enjoyed and so when it came time to create his personal space in the world of immortals, Baltazar simply emulated what he had seen by the royals.

His castle was vast, with many corridors and large rooms filled with ornate furnishings. There seemed to be an infinite number of windows which looked upon absolutely nothing but the darkness of the dilapidating walls of earth which surrounded the structure. There were numerous rooms to sleep, but Baltazar as a vampire had no need of sleep. There were dozens of rooms to entertain guests, but as far as Reus knew, Baltazar did not ever have guests, aside from official business of the realm. There was even a grand ballroom for dancing, but in the centuries that Reus had known Baltazar, there had never been an occasion where Baltazar had danced even a single step. Reus could not even recall a time when he had heard music of any kind being played in Baltazar's presence. Reus knew Baltazar probably better than any other immortal with the exception of one other, and so when he landed on the beautiful tiled floor in the main entrance of the castle, he knew just where to look to find his master. If Baltazar was not there to meet him, for surely Baltazar would have seen his impending arrival, there would be only one place where he would be instead and that was the secret library.

Baltazar protected his secrets fiercely, and even though his castle was well hidden, disguised from view, and buried hundreds of feet beneath the ground's surface, even that was not enough to ensure his privacy. Baltazar had constructed within the protected walls of the castle, a library that itself was magical. As a vampire, Baltazar himself did not have the ability to create such a place, but he entrusted one other immortal, the most powerful warlock in their world, to construct it for him. That warlock was none other than the male Minister who was the co-leader of the realm named Atticus, and he had Baltazar as his closest adviser.

Baltazar's library was not fixated in the castle, but rather it could move anywhere within the vast walls of the residence. At Baltazar's request, Atticus had placed powerful magic through-out the subterranean castle that blocked all other supernatural powers from being utilized in Baltazar's residence. To Reus' knowledge, only Atticus' powers remained intact while inside this hidden domain. Reus' powers could therefore not be used to locate the library, so knowing that he would find Baltazar there, Reus had to wait until Baltazar sent for him. Reus knew without a doubt that his master was aware of his arrival, but he didn't know how long it would be before he was summoned. Reus worried that Baltazar was making him wait intentionally, to allow time for his fear to escalate, which it was doing monu-mentally each second that passed.

Finally, after what seemed like hours, a sudden noise caused Reus to turn around and face the circular staircase that rose gracefully upwards towards the second floor of the castle. The beautiful golden pickets and engraved railings of the staircase were rattling harder and harder. It almost looked like the entire spiraling structure was going to collapse, but of course, that didn't happen. Instead, a small door appeared under the first curve of the stairs, and Reus knew what to do.

He walked towards the doorway and stretched out his hand to turn the knob. The door opened. The entrance was so small that even Reus, an elf, had to duck his head in order to be able to pass through. As soon as his second foot cleared the doorway, he felt his body twisting and turning as it hurtled through the passageway. In an instant, he landed directly in front of Baltazar. His master sat in a high - backed chair that looked very much like a royal throne. In between Baltazar and Reus was a massive, black desk that shone in the dim light of the room.

Reus was not surprised to find himself in the magic library, but he was impressed about the doorway under the stairs. It seemed that every time he was summoned to this room, Baltazar had a new way of transporting him, and that isn't easy to do after hundreds of years. Reus tried to gage the mood of his master by looking intently at his superior's face. Baltazar's appearance never failed to intimidate Reus. Like all vampires, Baltazar's eye color reflected the amount of blood he had recently consumed. When full of blood, their eyes would be black as the darkest onyx, but today, all he could see of Baltazar's eyes was the silver rim of his iris. His eyes were completely translucent which alerted Reus to the fact that Baltazar had not consumed blood for quite some time, and that would not likely improve his mood.

Baltazar in his human life must have been viewed as extraordinarily handsome, thought Reus. He still maintained his former attractiveness, with his shock of dark blond hair, almost the color of toffee. He had a strong, square jaw and a pleasant but cunning smile, when he chose to use it. Baltazar was always impeccably dressed and today was no exception. His white button- down shirt was open at the collar, revealing his perfect deathly pale marble-like skin, which Reus knew if touched, would be cold and smooth, like stone.

Baltazar showed no emotion at Reus' appearance, and Reus did not have any idea how to interpret the blank stare that he received. Baltazar did not seem either angry or happy to see him, and Reus braced himself for what his master was going to say.

'So Reus, it's been a little while since you were last here,' began Baltazar in a calm, but cold sounding voice.

'Yes, Master. But I trust you have been receiving my reports. I always send them daily, as you instructed. I have never missed a day. And I assure you that my information is both accurate and complete…'

Baltazar waved his hand impatiently. 'Yes, yes, Reus. I am not concerned about the quality or quantity of your reports. But tell me this,' Baltazar leaned forward on his chair and pointed an accusatory finger at Reus. His voice changed from calm and cold to fiery with intense anger. 'How is it possible that the boy came through the vortex? You were placed at the border specifically for one purpose and one purpose only. To guard the entrance to the vortex and prevent this very thing from happening. And yet, now not only has the boy come through the vortex, but you lost custody of him. And I am informed by *others* that he is now reunited with his birth parents!'

Reus quivered at the rage in his master's voice. 'I – I didn't know that the child was placed with his parents. The last I saw of him, he was taken by D3W3.'

'You didn't know?' roared Baltazar. 'How did you not follow up? Did you not think that the boy's location would be of the utmost importance?'

Reus didn't have a response. He looked down at his feet and

clenched his hands tightly together waiting for what would come next.

Baltazar let him wait. He sat in silence for many minutes, while Reus continued to stand motionless, hoping that the next words he would hear would be ones of forgiveness.

Finally, Baltazar spoke. 'You *will* bring that boy to me. Now that they are together, the threat they pose is closer than ever. They must be separated, immediately! But Reus, hear me well, the boys must remain alive! In the interim, I will remain solely responsible for the third one, since it is now clear that you can no longer be trusted to keep him apart from the others. If you fail me this time, then Reus, I promise that will be the end of you.'

'Yes, of course master. You can trust me. I won't let you down again,' gushed Reus with relief washing over him that he was not to be destroyed. At least not yet. He could redeem himself. He knew that he must remain in Baltazar's favor. Baltazar had the power to ensure either his demise or his survival, and if Reus was obliterated…well, the consequences would be dire and not just for Reus himself. There was too much at stake for him to fail, more so than even Baltazar realized.

'Well then, get out of here. Go to those boys and fetch me the one from the human world without delay!'

'How will I manage that, master? I can't just ask him to come with me…'

Baltazar cut off his words. 'I don't care how, just do it. Do whatever it takes. Figure it out or face the consequences!' Baltazar could not feel the blaze of warmth that emanated from the small stone that lay against his numb skin, but the voice in his mind was clear. Reus could not fail.

And with that, Reus felt himself once again tumbling through the passageway, but this time instead of returning him to the main entrance of the castle, Reus was catapulted out of the underground lair. Reus landed awkwardly on the hard ground and sighed wondering how he was going to pull off this job. When he regained his balance and once again stood firmly on the ground that hid Baltazar's residence below, Reus suddenly had an intriguing idea.

He was ready to begin his new mission, but in order to follow Baltazar's orders he was going to have to defy one of the Ministry's most sacred doctrines. *Let's hope Baltazar approves of this plan,* Reus thought, for if not, that could mean the end of everything.

CHAPTER NINE

Back in the Warston residence, the tense mood created by Maggie's outbreak was instantly lightened when the little fireball that had become so attached to Dylan bounded into the room. It danced around the shoulders of all four family members, clearly excited to be part of the group. The glowing ball's eyes flashed in happy colors, first yellow then pink then green then blue…until it finally landed on Dylan's shoulder, its translucent wings tickling his neck. It nuzzled up under his chin and everyone laughed.

'Looks like we are going to have a pet,' quipped Ben.

'He needs a name,' Remy replied eagerly. 'How about Marvin?'

'Marvin?' said Dylan incredulously.

'Marvina?' laughed Remy, delighted with his brother's reaction.

'Well, I don't know how to recognize what gender it is. Can you?' asked Dylan.

'No idea,' replied Remy. 'Why don't you ask it?'

'Hmmm, hadn't thought of that. Okay,' Dylan said turning his eyes once again towards his little lit up friend. 'I'd like to know what gender you are and find a name that you will like. So…are you a boy?' The little fireball just stared into Dylan's eyes, reflecting back the grey of Dylan's irises. 'Are you a girl?' The ball of light began to flash, throwing rays of rainbow-colored light around the room, like a disco ball.

'That solves that issue,' smiled Maggie. 'So, what will you name her, Dylan?'

Dylan looked down at the non-existent floor for a moment, focusing on the landscape that spread hundreds of feet below him. When he looked up, there was a trace of wistfulness apparent in his eyes.

'If you don't mind, I would like to name her Via.'

The fireball's eyes shone a brilliant, happy yellow indicating her contentment with the name Dylan had chosen.

'Our little fireball friend seems to like the name you picked, Dylan. Why do you think I would mind?' inquired Maggie softly.

'Because that is my mother, my human mother's nickname. I know that I'm not allowed to be with her, but naming the fireball after her will be a reminder for me. But I don't want to upset you, so if you prefer, I can name her something else…'

Maggie floated around the table and wrapped her arms around her new-found son.

'I think it's a beautiful name. And I'm not upset. You miss your other parents terribly. I understand.'

Dylan nodded solemnly, fighting back tears and Via's eyes turned dark. When Maggie looked into the face of the little fireball, she was transfixed by what she saw. Deep in Via's eyes, Maggie could clearly see the face of a man and a woman. Both of them were frantic, looking for something. The woman's long hair was wild about her face. Her eyes were tormented with fear. The man looked haggard and his shoulders slumped down, dejected and in despair. Maggie knew that the ball of light was showing her Dylan's human parents and she knew what had to be done.

Maggie enveloped Dylan in a tight embrace and rocked him gently back and forth for several minutes while Ben and Remy looked on, not knowing what to do to help. Finally, Maggie released Dylan. She didn't have words to comfort her son, and she knew that any attempt would fail to reassure him. So she didn't even try to speak. She just let her love radiate around him and hoped that she would be able to bring her child a little bit of peace.

Remy, sensing how difficult the situation was, interjected by asking Dylan if he wanted to go hang out upstairs. Dylan quickly agreed. Once the boys had left the room, Maggie told Ben that she had an errand to attend to right away. He saw her resolve and didn't question her further. He simply nodded and agreed to check on the boys every so often. Maggie gave her husband a gentle kiss in silent appreciation for his understanding and then flew out the door.

The boys went into Dylan's room. Remy wanted to show Dylan some of the cool stuff that he could do with his magical powers. They both wondered if Dylan would be able to do the same. Remy sent objects flying around the room, just using the power of his mind. He made himself become invisible and then re-appear an instant later somewhere else in the room. He levitated the furniture. He even made the room flip upside down so that the floor became the ceiling and the ceiling became the floor!

'Make it rain inside the room,' cried Dylan excitedly, hoping to feel the splash of water on his skin.

Remy immediately turned to Dylan and said, 'I can't do that.'

'Oh, you haven't learned how to do it yet?'

'We aren't ever allowed to control weather. It's one of the Ministry doctrines and anyone who even tries will immediately be transported to Gehenna. Only the Ministry is allowed to control the weather, and they have decided that everyday shall be the same, except for days that are declared as sacred. On the anniversary of the start of the civil war, the sky is black, the air is freezing and we get pelted with rain all day long. It is a day to remind us of the destruction that could have happened if a truce had not been declared. The Ministry requires everyone to sit outside in the cold and be miserable. We aren't even allowed to talk! We have to remain silent the whole time, otherwise you will be punished. They set up holding rooms for small children to go to on that day, supervised by Ministry officials, because the little kids can't keep quiet and would ruin the effect that the Ministry is trying to achieve. You're lucky; we just recently had that day, known as the Day of Atonement. The day that celebrates the peace treaty starts with a quick but massive rainfall, to wash away the pain caused by the war, followed by an intense brightness that we never see at any other time. It doesn't get dark at all on that day. There are parties outside and everyone dances and sings. That one is called the Day of Reconciliation, and it's coming up soon.'

'What's that place you mentioned, Gehenna?'

'It's the place where immortals are sent if they violate Ministry doctrines. We are taught that it is always dark and damp. There is never any light. The immortal is stripped of all their powers before they enter and at the mercy of the guards until they are released, if that day ever comes.'

'Wow that sounds awful. What other doctrines are there that have to be followed?'

'Not too many really. Dad mentioned them earlier. You

cannot change the weather. You cannot impersonate others. You cannot go into the vortex without Ministry permission and if you do enter the world of humans, you must maintain our secrets. You cannot steal someone else's powers and you cannot use your powers to destroy other immortals – only the Ministry is allowed to order the destruction of an immortal. That's about it really.'

'If everyone here is immortal, then how would someone be destroyed? Isn't the point of being immortal that you can never die?'

Remy laughed. 'Is that what humans think about immortals?'

'Some humans don't believe that there are any such things as immortal beings. They believe that stories about things like vampires and witches are just made up. But there are people who do believe that immortals exist. I always thought immortal meant that you couldn't be killed.'

'Well, your understanding was wrong. Immortals can be destroyed. It might not be easy to kill one, not like humans that are so frail, but immortals can be put to death…if you know their vulnerabilities and how to break through their powers. We can also be severely injured, although it happens very rarely. And regular magic cannot heal anything except superficial wounds. We have master healers who have exceptional powers to help an immortal who suffers from a serious injury.'

Dylan stared wordlessly at his brother, his jaw slightly open in fear.

'Don't worry Little Bro,' said Remy. 'We aren't allowed to destroy other immortals, so none of us even know how to do it. Only a select few, chosen by the Ministry are entrusted with that knowledge.'

Just then, Remy spied a small, shiny object peeking out from under Dylan's bed. 'What's that?' Remy said reaching over to pick up the rectangular item. He had never seen anything like it before in his life.

'Oh, that's my cell phone,' replied Dylan.

'What's a cell phone?' asked Remy.

'It's a way of communicating with other people. I can call them or text them or send an email.'

Remy looked at his identical brother with a blank expression on his face. 'I don't get it,' he said.

'Well, let's say I wanted to tell my mother that I was at the park. I would dial her phone number into my phone and then talk to her. Or I could just send her a written message by text or email…' Dylan could see his brother was still confused. 'Okay, let me show you.'

Dylan took the phone from his brother and clicked on the phone icon. He could see the list of his recent incoming and outgoing calls, but when he clicked one of the numbers, nothing happened. He tried going into his text messages and could see the messages that he had not yet deleted, but they were all frozen and he was not able to do anything more than show them to his brother and try to explain how it worked. Remy was mesmerized by what he saw as a primitive way of communicating with others. In the immortal world, if he wanted to tell his mother something, he simply thought about the message he wanted to send, and it immediately transported to her. The note would appear instantly in her hand. Other immortals communicated with others in different ways, but all of them had an instantaneous method that did not rely on some strange handheld device that may encounter technical glitches. They even had a system for immortal mail which some supernatural beings preferred, especially the really old ones!

But Remy was interested in looking more closely at this cell phone object, to see the symbols up close. Dylan heard his brother's thoughts and passed it over. Remy was first faced with the password screen. He read his brother's mind and immediately entered the numbers required. Then he began clicking on the different icons. Dylan was content to lie back and let his brother play with his phone. Remy seemed especially delighted with some of the games that still worked - the ones that did not require Wi-Fi! And then Remy hit the photos icon.

As Remy looked at the photos Dylan had stored, he could see in his own mind what Remy was seeing. Dylan got up and went to sit next to his brother. He explained who everyone was – his parents, his friends, his dogs… Remy felt his brother's pain twist his own insides. It was as if he and Dylan shared one body. Remy took his brother's right hand in his own and gently turned it over so that the strange birth mark was showing. Then he placed his own arm directly next to his brother's, also with the three little dots facing up.

'I understand,' Remy whispered softly. 'Your pain is my own. We are inseparable now. You will always have me. We will figure everything out together… our delivery, you being taken and put in the human world, our missing brother… all of it.'

Dylan did not need words to respond. The two boys stared at their upturned wrists and wondered how their delivery was connected to the prophecy and what that might mean for their futures. All they knew instinctively was that the vision that nobody was allowed to talk about definitely had something to do with them and the brother who was yet to be found.

CHAPTER TEN

Maggie arrived at the offices of D3W3 and hoped that she would find who she was looking for. She entered the front door and was immediately greeted by her neighbor, Farah Elrich. Farah always had a smile for Maggie, who she liked immensely, and was quick to offer her a seat in the waiting area.

'Is everything okay with the boys? Is Dylan adjusting to your family? I certainly hope that everyone is doing well. We really didn't expect to see you quite so soon...'

'Yes, Farah. Everything is fine but thank you for your concern. I just have a small matter to discuss with Warrentree, if he's in. Nothing of great importance, just a *tiny* issue that I was hoping to work out with him.'

Farah cocked her tiny head to the side and placed a finger under her chin, trying to assess the truthfulness of Maggie's remarks. Farah didn't like to be left out of important information. Sensing that she wasn't going to get anything more out of her neighbor, she smiled brightly again and agreed to locate Warrentree. Farah jumped out of her seat and sprinted behind a closed door to find her boss. Only a few minutes later, and she returned with Warrentree trailing right behind her. Warrentree sauntered confidently into the waiting room and immediately went up to Maggie. He took both her hands in his and pulled her gently so that she was standing before him. He noticed her smile, but it didn't quite reach her eyes and he knew something was up. He also knew that his assistant was just a tad nosy, and that this would not be the place to hear what Maggie wanted to tell him.

'Farah, Maggie and I will be in my office. Please ensure that we are not disturbed.'

'Yes, boss,' she quipped in her twinkly bell-like voice. Although truth be told, she was very disappointed to be left out of the discussion.

Maggie followed Warrentree back to his office. Once she was settled in her chair, the giant door gently closed, and the latch settled into its place, thus securing the office from any prying eyes or ears. Warrentree sat across from Maggie behind his desk and steepled his fingers under his chin. His eyes were warm and concerned, as he asked Maggie the reason for her visit.

'Warrentree,' she began hesitantly. 'Having Dylan returned to us is a dream come true. I never had any idea that any of my boys, other than Remy, survived the delivery. So his arrival is a miracle that we never even hoped for! We loved him instantly and are doing everything we can to make him happy. And Dylan too is trying so hard to please us. He is such a good boy…' her voice trailed off sadly.

'So what is the problem, my dear?' inquired Warrentree in soft, gentle tones.

Maggie sighed heavily. 'He misses his human parents, and while I do think he understands that he cannot be with them, he worries a great deal about them. He knows that they are frantically looking for him, consumed with fear about his disappearance. I desperately want to bring my son some peace of mind. I want to deliver a message to his human parents to assure them that he is safe and loved, even though he cannot return to them. Please Warrentree, I have tried to imagine what

I would feel like in their position. I have their son; the least I can do is let them know that he is well. Can you help me?'

Warrentree closed his eyes. He had not expected this problem to arise but then again, he had never dealt with any situation like this before in all of his centuries working for D3W3. This was a unique circumstance, and he decided that since the issue was unprecedented, he would have to make an executive decision based upon his own judgment and instinct. He opened his eyes and saw Maggie sitting on the edge of her seat, waiting for him to speak.

'Maggie, you know I cannot let you enter the vortex,' he saw Maggie's eyes fill with tears as she was told that she would not be able to deliver her message. 'But I can do it for you.' Maggie blinked in surprise and smiled widely at the solution. 'You create the message, and I will deliver it for you. But Maggie, I hope you understand that the content must comply with Ministry doctrines. You will have to be careful in what you say.'

'Of course, Warrentree. I understand completely. I can create the message here, in your office, so you can be sure that you approve of it.'

'Maggie, I trust you. I don't want you to think that I need to be present. I am quite content to give you some privacy.'

'No Warrentree. That will not be necessary but thank you. Please, I want you to see the message, and perhaps you will be able to tell me their reaction once you return?'

Warrentree nodded in assent to both requests. Maggie adjusted her hair slightly and brushed the tears off her cheeks. Then she began to speak.

'Mr. and Mrs. Dover. We have Dylan. He is with us, safe and loved. He cannot return to you, but please know that he loves you and talks about you all the time. Please be assured that he is well. I will try to send you updates, if I can in future days. You will not be able to locate him, and I am so sorry for your pain and loss. He is a wonderful boy and we are so thankful for what you have done. I promise that you do not need to worry about him. He will never forget you and we will always be grateful that you took him in and raised him as your own. Be at peace. Your son is well loved. Goodbye.'

The words Maggie spoke flew together in a whirlwind, spiraling together in a tunnel formation and then finally collapsing upon themselves into a small, square shaped object that landed softly in Maggie's outstretched palm. She handed the small, solid object over to Warrentree and thanked him for agreeing to deliver the message on her behalf.

Warrentree smiled in approval at the words she had spoken but did not know whether it would help Dylan's human family to overcome the loss of their only child. He hoped that the message would bring some sense of reassurance to the humans, but in his heart, he knew that nothing would ever compensate for the disappearance of their son. Knowing that Dylan was alive and safe might bring them some peace, but the thought that he was out there somewhere, would mean that they would never have closure. Warrentree wasn't sure that sending the Dovers a message was the best course of action, but he understood both Maggie and Dylan's concern for the humans. At least they would learn that Dylan was alive and being well cared for, he thought.

'Do you know what these people look like, Maggie?' he asked. Maggie waved her hand and an image of two peoples' faces appeared hovering over Warrentree's desk. He nodded in thanks and made mental note of what Dylan's human parents looked like, to be sure that he delivered the message to the correct individuals.

Maggie left Warrentree's office with a lighter heart, and a promise that he would advise her of the Dovers' reaction, as soon as he returned. Warrentree gathered his official documents, told Farah he would be gone for the rest of the day and transported himself to the border security zone.

Warrentree was one of the few members of the immortal realm who had Ministry approval to travel outside the vortex into the human world. He had been a trusted member of the Ministry for centuries in various capacities and would often be sent on missions to check on immortals who were still living amongst humans. He was well recognized at the border and a perfunctory glance at his documents was all that was required by the guards before waving him through. The border officers did not even ask about the small square object that was tucked into his pocket.

Warrentree walked the familiar path to the vortex entrance, where he was greeted by the final checkpoint officer. It was Carl Wizman, one of the guards that had been on duty the night that Dylan was found in the security zone.

'How is the kid doing? The one that came through the vortex the other night?' Carl asked. 'Have you figured out who he is yet?'

Warrentree thanked him for his concern and simply replied 'We are working on it. Confidentiality prevents me from saying more, as I'm sure you understand, but rest assured, the boy is doing well.'

'That's good news,' replied Carl. 'Reus will be happy to hear that.'

'Reus?' questioned Warrentree. 'Reus has been asking about him?'

'Oh yes. Frequently at first. He was really peeved at me for calling D3W3, and then he kept showing up here to see if we had heard anything. But come to think of it, I haven't seen him here at all today.'

Warrentree wasn't sure what to make of Reus' interest in the child raised by humans, but he stored the information away having some inkling that it might be important. Carl waved Warrentree through and into the vortex chamber. An instant later, Warrentree felt the familiar sensation of spinning through space. He had travelled through this gateway thousands of times so the motion did not cause him any distress. He simply closed his eyes and hummed a favorite melody to himself while he hurtled through the tunnel.

Sometime later, he felt the ground solid beneath his feet. He looked around to see where the portal had deposited him. It was clear that he was in a forest, there was no doubt about that, but he could not ascertain anything more about his precise location. He hoped that the vortex had delivered him within close range of his targeted destination, otherwise finding the human home of Dylan Dover might take a while. Warrentree was hidden by the thick branches of trees that enveloped him, but he looked around to ensure that he was alone. Satisfied that there were no humans anywhere in the vicinity, he let his mind envision where he wanted to be – 29 Parklane, the home of Olivia and Mike Dover. Only the birds were witness to the fact that one moment Warrentree was in the forest and the next, he had vanished.

Warrentree was one of only a small group of immortals who

could transport themselves in this manner. Creating a transport portal to move from one place to another almost instantaneously was a feat that few immortals could accomplish. Warrentree could travel between locations that were a short distance apart but anything beyond a few miles required greater powers than what he possessed. In fact, to his knowledge only the leaders of the immortal realm, Atticus and Callista, and perhaps to a lesser extent the deputy Reus, had magic powerful enough to do that. Fortunately for him, the Dover residence was close by and Warrentree could sense that his transport portal would deliver him exactly where he wanted to be.

Warrentree could not just appear in the middle of a human street, that was clearly too risky, so he used his magic to remain invisible, at least for the time being. Warrentree observed the house that Dylan had grown up in, from behind a large oak tree that stood on the opposite side of the street. He was able to decipher that at least one human was home. He could see the lights on in the house and the silhouette of a person moved past one of the main floor windows.

Just then, the front door opened, and two large, white dogs bounded out of the house and straight towards Warrentree. A human female stood in the doorway and shouted for the dogs to come back. But the dogs raced at full speed across the street to where Warrentree stood secure in the knowledge that he could not be seen. The dogs stopped at his feet and immediately sat down. Warrentree looked into their eyes and knew that these were no dogs. These were shapeshifters and they were able to sense his presence. The woman in the doorway kept calling for the dogs and when they refused to return, she came after them. Warrentree knew that this was Olivia Dover and she was presenting him with the perfect opportunity to deliver Maggie's message.

'I'm going to distract her,' Warrentree instructed the dogs. 'When I do, you take off into the forest. I will meet you there, okay?' The dogs cocked their heads in understanding and waited for the moment to arrive.

Warrentree waved his hand and caused the front door of the house to slam loudly. The woman turned back around, startled by the noise and when she did, Warrentree made himself visible. By the time the woman had once again turned towards the dogs, Warrentree was there, with each one of his hands resting lighting on the dogs' heads.

'Oh, I'm so sorry. I didn't see you there,' the woman said to Warrentree as she walked over to where he stood. 'The dogs won't hurt you.'

'I am not afraid of your dogs, ma'am.' Warrentree looked closely at Olivia Dover. She was small in stature, but he could tell that she was not frail or weak. But she did look tired, as her eyes were rimmed in red and she had black smudges under her eyes from lack of sleep. Her hair was pulled back into a messy ponytail and her body carried a sadness about her that Warrentree understood completely. He hoped with all his heart that what would come next would alleviate some of her despair.

'Ma'am, I have a message for you.'

'How do you know the message is for me? We don't know each other,' she replied.

'You are Mrs. Olivia Dover,' Warrentree said softly.

'I guess that gives you the advantage since I don't know who you are,' she responded with sharpness grating her usually gentle voice.

'I know that to you I am a stranger, but I do have an important message, one that I think you will want to receive.'

'Fine,' she replied. 'So give me the message.' She stretched out her hand to receive what she anticipated would be a letter of some sort. She looked surprised when Warrentree dropped a small square object, unlike anything she had ever seen before, into her outstretched palm. The object started to shake and quiver before it exploded in a small burst of light and an image of Maggie floated in front of Olivia's shocked eyes.

Warrentree nodded at the dogs, who silently took off at full speed, without being noticed by Olivia who was too distracted by the vision before her. Olivia watched mesmerized as Maggie delivered her heartfelt words, and Olivia reached her arms out before her to try to capture the image. But as soon as Maggie's message was complete, the holograph shimmered slightly before it dissolved and fizzled away.

Olivia stood perfectly still for a moment, trying to make sense of what she had seen and heard. Thoughts whirled through her mind and she was dumbfounded as she processed the fact that her son was alive but somewhere that she could not reach him. And then Olivia crumpled to the ground and began to weep. Warrentree felt dreadful and wished that he could bring some comfort to this poor woman. He placed a gentle hand on her shoulder and that caused her to snap her head up.

'Who are you,' she cried. 'And where is my son?' She stood up, grabbed Warrentree by the shoulders and started to shake him. 'Where is he?' she kept repeating. Warrentree just stood there, accepting her physical assault until she stopped yelling out of sheer exhaustion. He cradled her in a gentle embrace and whispered softly into her ear.

'I cannot tell you. But rest assured, I will watch over him. Take comfort that he is alive and well. Goodbye for now, Olivia.'

Warrentree released Olivia from his grasp and she again fell to the ground. As she lay there reeling from what she had been told and from seeing images that had no logical explanation, Warrentree made his escape. He silently walked away, until he was sure that Olivia was not watching him. Once he was out of her range of sight, he again waved his arms to protect himself in a veil of invisibility.

He was not quite ready to return home, so he glided silently over the city streets and thought about what he would tell Maggie. The truth, he supposed, was the only option. Maggie deserved to know. He also vowed to watch over Olivia Dover and to do whatever he could to help alleviate her pain. He would have to return to the human world again soon. Finally, he went back to the forest and found the shapeshifters waiting for him.

The sky was starting to turn dark, and the forest was empty of all humans. Warrentree transformed himself to be visible once again and instructed the dogs to also change back to their usual form. The large huskies immediately began to quiver. Their limbs started to elongate into human looking arms and legs. Their snouts shrank from long and pointed to short human noses. Their pointed ears curled up to form whorls of carti-lage. And within a minute, the transformation was complete. Standing before Warrentree were two human-like beings. A male and a female. Both had light blond hair and eyes in the most unusual color – neither green nor blue. Their irises were a brilliant shade of turquoise. They shared the same shaped nose and the same pointed chins. They were both completely naked. Warrentree waved his hands and covered the creatures in clothing. The shapeshifters smiled in delight.

'We haven't worn clothes in twelve years!' exclaimed the male.

'Unless you count the doggie sweaters that Olivia bought us for Christmas that one time,' quipped the female. 'But more importantly than clothing, how is Dylan?' she asked eagerly.

'He is fine. Reunited with his immortal family,' replied Warrentree.

'Can we see him? Our purpose here is done, since Dylan is no longer in the human world,' responded the male.

'What was your purpose here? Who sent you?' probed Warrentree, knowing that this information was essential in figuring out the mystery of Dylan's separation from his original family.

'Our purpose was to protect him, which we did until he disappeared,' said the female defensively. 'I don't know who ordered us here. Those were the directions given to us by the Ministry official.'

'Oh, it was the Ministry that sent you here?' Warrentree tried to make his voice sound calm but he couldn't believe what he was hearing. If someone in the Ministry sent the shapeshifters here, then that meant Dylan was placed with a human family by someone in authority. *What is going on here,* he thought to himself.

'Do you remember the name of the Ministry official you dealt with? The one who gave you your orders?' asked Warrentree pleasantly, not letting his true emotions be revealed.

'Not me. Do you sis?' replied the male. 'It was so long ago.

I don't even know if I remember how to walk on two legs!'

'Nah, I don't remember either. Can we please return now to the immortal world? I would really like to see Dylan again and then get resettled in our real home,' sighed the female

'Oh, me too,' said her brother.

Warrentree nodded. 'Of course. It appears your mission is complete. Well done you two. You did an exemplary job keeping Dylan safe and now he is returned home. We can all leave immediately. Into the vortex we go.'

Warrentree didn't know what he was going to do with this information, but he decided that he would have to investigate further, and he had better keep this knowledge to himself, at least for the time being.

CHAPTER ELEVEN

Reus knew he would have to act fast. He was about to violate one of the Ministry's most sacred doctrines, and he wanted to finish the job as quickly as possible to avoid being detected. He recognized that Baltazar would see his report and know what he had done. Reus just hoped that his master would be forgiving of this transgression. Baltazar did say to him to do whatever it would take to deliver the boy alive to his underground castle. As a Deputy Ministry and second in command of the realm, Baltazar was supposed to be a strict enforcer of the rules. Reus determined, however, that his master's desire to have the boy in his custody would outweigh his responsibility to punish Reus' deviant behavior. At least, he hoped that would be Baltazar's interpretation of what he was about to do.

In the immortal world, creatures lived openly without having to conceal their secrets as they did living alongside humans. This meant that darkness was not necessary as the immortals did not have to hide in the shadows. But as with many other human conventions, the world of immortals borrowed the concept of day and night, simply as way to mark the passage of time. The Ministry controlled lightness and darkness in their world, and the skies changed from one to the other at the same moments every day. There were no sunsets or sunrises like humans enjoyed, for day and night were not caused by the rotation of the earth. It was rather like the Ministry flicked a switch to either cast the skies into darkness or to return brightness to their world. Immortals with their many powers could not be fooled by darkness, so trying to hide one's rule breaking behavior by waiting until nightfall would not be of any benefit. And of course, many immortals did not have need of sleep. Even those who did could get by with only short spurts of slumber if they preferred. Reus therefore had no reason to wait until darkness to execute his plan and so he decided to brazenly commit this most sacred rule infraction in the middle of the day. As he prepared, he tried to convince himself that it made more sense for him to do it now anyways. After all, the creature he was about to impersonate would more likely visit the home of the Warston family in the middle of the day. *Wouldn't she?*

In the privacy of his own home, a cozy but very comfortable abode cut into the side of a cliff, Reus decided that he needed one more piece of information before he could put his plan into action. He needed to know where *she* was right now, to be sure that they would not cross paths – that would be a disaster! In his hand, Reus held a blank piece of paper. He then snapped his fingers and magically, an image appeared on the paper. Reus could see that she was in her office, working diligently at her desk. He would be safe, at least for the moment.

Reus mentally ran through what he would say when he encountered the boys. When he knew word for word what he intended to say, he stood in front of a mirror, closed his eyes and snapped his fingers. He immediately felt different – lighter, less attached to the ground. He opened his eyes to see what his magic had accomplished. Instead of seeing an elf staring back at him from the mirror, the reflection showed him exactly as he had hoped. He had transformed into a fairy. But not just any fairy. Staring back at him from the looking glass was a perfect replication of Marianne Fairshefsky, the D3W3 caseworker assigned to Dylan Dover. *Perfect,* thought Reus. *Perfect, but very dangerous. I must act quickly. Who knows how long she will remain in her office,* he thought to himself.

Reus needed one more essential item before he was ready to leave. Hidden deep in the cliff walls was the object he had secreted away so long ago. Reus walked through his small home to the back wall which lay directly on top of the cliff behind it. He lay down flat to find the notch he was looking for, which was just a tiny indentation where the wall met the floorboards. With his little finger, he pressed firmly on the notch and a square section of the wall, no more than three inches wide, began to protrude outwards. Reus was then able to grasp the small area and pry it away. Behind that piece of wall, lay his secret treasure nestled in the frigid embrace of the cliff.

The small oval shimmered like a pearl, frozen all this time since he had stolen it from right under the Ministry's watch decades ago. Although Reus also had a sense that Baltazar was well aware of what he had done and allowed his transgression to remain hidden. Reus had protected this prize carefully and hidden it where it would never be found. But now he was ready to release his treasure from its frozen state and beckon it to life. He lifted the object out of the nest he had made to cradle it gently while time passed. Reus held the small oval carefully in his hand. Its shell glimmered in his palm and inside the delicate exterior he could just make out the shadow of the creature that lay within. Reus snapped his fingers softly, so as not to startle the unhatched creature. The magic he performed would ensure that once born, his wishes would be carried out. He carefully wrapped it in soft cloth to protect it and to begin the warming process, and then he placed it gently in his pocket.

Taking a quick peek outside his front door, Reus was not surprised that there was nobody in sight. He didn't get a lot of visitors and he didn't have any neighbors close by. Using the wings posed only a minor setback. He flew around in circles a few times to get the hang of them but found to his delight that he quickly mastered the art of fairy flying. Once he was confident in his abilities to pass as a fairy, he took off at full speed for the Warston residence. He knew exactly where they lived and if it weren't for the fact that Reus recognized that if he was caught he could be put to death, he would have enjoyed the excursion. Flying with wings was rather enjoyable, and a nice change from just snapping his fingers to transport himself from place to place.

He arrived at the Warston house, high in the sky, within a matter of minutes. Reus cleared his throat and then without further hesitation, he lifted the door knocker and let it fall heavily to announce his presence. The door knocker awoke from its nap when it was lifted and dropped, and the eyes of a cat-like creature stared at Reus.

'Why does my sight seem to deceive me,' asked the door knocker of Reus. 'I see what appears to be a fairy, and yet your eyes tell me otherwise.'

Reus was speechless. He had not anticipated this problem.

'Well…' probed the door knocker.

Just then, Ben Warston opened the door and smiled delightedly.

'Mary, how good of you to come see us. Are you here to check on the boys?'

'Wait just a minute,' interjected the door knocker. 'You appear to know this fairy and yet a fairy she is not.'

'Oh door knocker,' replied Ben. 'Of course this is Mary. She is Dylan's case worker. Maybe it's time we took you in for some slight adjustments. Now Mary, please do come inside.'

Reus sighed in relief. That was one problem overcome and clearly Ben was fooled. Would he be able to trick the rest of them as well?

'Why don't we sit down somewhere comfortable where we can talk, maybe without the boys to start?' asked Ben. 'I'm so glad you stopped by. There are some things we wanted to talk to you about. Maggie,' he called. 'Come downstairs. We have a guest.'

Maggie floated into the room, and smiled at Mary, well at least who she thought was Mary. Ben and Maggie settled themselves on a plush sofa, while Reus sat across from them on a high-backed chair. Reus, remembering that he was supposed to be Mary, crossed his legs the way that he thought a female fairy would sit and waited to hear what they had to say. He was anxious to see the boys and hoped that this little talk would not take too long. He wanted to do what needed to be done and get out of there as quickly as he could. He did not want to be in Mary's form for too long. Every minute put him at greater risk of detection.

Reus cleared his throat nervously. 'So...' his voice came out sounding too much like a male elf. He pretended to cough and cleared his throat again. 'So...' this time, the sound was much more female fairy-like, but he decided to speak as little as possible. Luckily for Reus, that one word was all that was needed to encourage Maggie and Ben to start talking. Reus, as Mary, pretended to be interested as they told him that Dylan seemed at times to be homesick and was missing his human parents. Reus faked concern by nodding his head at what seemed to be appropriate moments in the conversation. It seemed like they were going to talk forever, thought Reus anxiously. Finally, he could take it no longer and he interrupted them.

'Perhaps, I could speak with Dylan. Alone?' Reus inquired, thinking that was quite a reasonable request for Mary as the caseworker to make. It would also conveniently give him a chance to finish the final stage of his plan and get out of there!

'Yes, that would be so helpful, I think. Thank you,' replied Maggie gratefully. 'Come with me and I will take you to his room.'

Maggie delivered Reus to Dylan's door and knocked. 'Dylan, sweetheart? Can I come in? Mary, your caseworker is here to see you.'

Dylan opened the door and gave his mother a wide smile. 'Hi mom. Hi Mary. Come on in.'

'Well, I will leave you to it then,' said Maggie. But before she left, she pulled Dylan in for a fast hug. Dylan didn't resist, and in fact, it made him feel safe and protected. Just the way his human parents had also made him feel. He invited Reus into his room, thinking that this was Mary.

Reus started to walk around the room, pretending that he was admiring everything there. He ran his hands over the various pieces of furniture and picked up several objects, as if to examine them. Dylan sat on a chair and watched intently. *Could he tell something was amiss?* wondered Reus. Regardless, Reus knew what he had to do next. Turning his back towards Dylan, he reached into his pocket and gently wiggled the small oval out of its protective cloth. He held it lightly in his hand, still concealed inside his pocket. Reus then approached the bed and sat down on its end. Reus, using his closest impersonation to Mary's voice then asked Dylan how he was adjusting. Dylan cocked his head to one side and gave Reus a penetrating stare. Reus sat frozen, not sure what to do next. He might have to abort his plan and get out of there immediately, but then, to Reus' relief, Dylan's eyes softened, and he began to speak about how much he liked his new family even though he wished he could see his human parents again, just to let them know he was okay.

While Dylan spoke, Reus maintained solid eye contact with him, to ensure that Dylan would not see what Reus was doing. As Dylan talked, Reus planted the shimmering oval under the covers at the foot of Dylan's bed. It would be warm and safe there, as long as it wasn't disturbed for about six hours, thought Reus. And by then, Dylan should be asleep in bed and it would be too late for anyone to help him. Reus was confident that the creature would follow his orders exactly and he was certain that it wouldn't be long before Dylan was in his custody. Once the deed was done, Reus just wanted to escape from the Warston residence and transform back to himself. Reus hastily interrupted Dylan with an assurance that everything would be okay.

'No need to see me out, Dylan. I will be back to check on you again soon. Bye for now,' chirped Reus in his best fairy sounding voice. And then without wanting to delay a moment longer, Reus using his fairy wings, flew out of Dylan's window and streaked across the sky as fast as he could. As soon as he was back in the privacy of his secluded home, he immediately snapped his fingers and grinned as his elf form instantly re-appeared.

'I hope you are satisfied, master,' said Reus, knowing that this report would be delivered to Baltazar within minutes. Now he just had to hope that the rest of the plan would work.

CHAPTER TWELVE

At dinner that night, Dylan got to try some of his brother's favorite foods. Dylan enjoyed the crispy, sweet taste of fried gumagos, for which there was nothing even remotely equivalent in the human world, and the slightly nutty taste of something that resembled noodles which were called Savamichy. He was still getting used to his feet dangling off the stool with the open air beneath him. Floating around in this home high in the sky was definitely cool but was certainly an adjustment!

'So Dylan,' said his father. 'What would you think about starting school tomorrow? Your mother and I think that it might be good for you, and Mary seemed to agree as well when she was here earlier today.'

'Yeah!' shouted Remy. 'That would be awesome. You won't have to worry, Dylan. I will introduce you to everyone. It will be great having you at school with me.'

'You have school here? I was kind of hoping that maybe immortals didn't have to go to school.'

Ben and Maggie laughed. 'Oh Dylan, you are very funny,' replied Maggie.

'The concept of school is something that our world borrowed from human society. When the immortal world was created, there were lots of ideas we took from the humans. Humans might not have our powers, but that doesn't mean that they aren't intelligent beings,' added Ben.

'Okay then. I will start school tomorrow. But let me ask

this, do you guys have winter break? Spring break? Best of all, summer vacation?'

Remy looked at Dylan with a confused expression on his face. 'I don't know what those things are,' confessed Remy.

Dylan's eyes opened in amazement. 'You mean you go to school and don't have time off? The school doesn't close to give students a break? Not ever?'

'Well of course, school isn't open all the time, honey,' soothed Maggie. 'We also borrowed the concepts of days and nights, weeks and months from humans too, although time passes differently in our world. You only go to school five times a week, just like you are used to, and there will be some extended periods when the school is closed. But I think Remy was more confused about your reference to winter, spring and summer. We don't have seasons here, and perhaps he has forgotten what he learned in school in his Human Culture and Societies classes.'

Remy giggled. 'I bet you will ace that class, Dylan!'

'Yes, I'm sure he will be able to tutor you, Remy. And I hope you will help him in the other courses. Dylan has a lot of catching up to do,' said Ben.

'Duh, dad. Dylan knows that he can count on me. He will be caught up in no time. Can we please go upstairs now?'

'Sure, boys. But I don't want you going to bed too late tonight. We have had a lot of excitement here since Dylan arrived but now it's time to get back into a routine, okay?' Maggie responded.

'Yes, mom,' the boys said perfectly in synch, and then laughed.

Once upstairs, Dylan and Remy hung out in Remy's room.

Remy was showing Dylan some more things he could do with his powers and was encouraging Dylan to try.

'You just have to think about what you want to happen, Dylan. But the trick is to make sure that you picture all the little details in your mind, otherwise, your magic won't work so well.'

Dylan started with simple things. First, he tried to use his powers to show Remy another favorite food – chocolate ice cream. Dylan pictured the cone in his mind, with the chocolate ice cream on top, but he forgot to think about how cold ice cream is so when the ice cream appeared in Remy's hand, it looked perfect but only for a split second. Then the whole thing melted all over and dripped down Remy's arm. Remy laughed and licked the delicious treat off his skin.

'Even melted, it tastes great,' he declared.

Dylan tried again, and the next time, his ice cream was a success! 'I could get used to this!' exclaimed Dylan, thinking of all the ice cream he could conjure up using his new-found powers.

'That's a great start, Little Bro,' said Remy. 'Tomorrow, I will help you start working on harder magic. But I think we should stop for now. I'm kind of tired. Do you mind if we go to sleep now?'

Dylan yawned. 'I'm tired too. See you in the morning.'

'If you need anything, you know how to find me,' said Remy.

I just have to call you with my mind, thought Dylan in reply, and Remy nodded having heard Dylan's thoughts.

A few minutes later, Dylan was ready for bed and climbed under the covers. Via, his sweet little fireball, settled softly on his pillow. Dylan used his powers to make his room dark and smiled that he was successfully able to accomplish that goal. He snuggled down deep into his blankets and within moments, was fast asleep.

At the foot of his bed, the shimmering oval object began to quiver. It made a light tapping noise, but the sound was muffled by the heavy blankets. The shell cracked, and a small head poked itself out of the casing. Only a second later, a second head appeared. And then the shell fell away as the creature slithered out from its embryonic home and into Dylan's bed. The serpent was 'V' shaped. Joined at the bottom to make it one, but two distinct bodies and two separate heads. It was only the size of Dylan's little toe at the moment, but this creature would double its size every few minutes until it reached its full length, which would easily stretch longer than Dylan's full body.

In his own isolated home, secluded in the cliffs now covered in darkness, Reus waited anxiously. *Any time now,* he thought. *The sleeper serpent has surely hatched. It shouldn't take long before it entwines itself around the boy. And once the creature has him in her grasp, she will return to me, her master, to deliver the prize. Baltazar will be pleased and I will be one step closer to completing my mission.* Now all he had to do was wait.

CHAPTER THIRTEEN

Dylan was dreaming of his past life. His human parents were laughing as they watched him playing with his dogs on the front lawn outside their house. Dylan was rolling on the grass with the dogs when all of a sudden in his dream, the dogs started growling. They barred their teeth and snapped their jaws furiously at some unknown threat that Dylan couldn't see. He also heard a strange buzzing sound, almost like a bee flying around his head, but he couldn't see precisely where the noise was coming from. Dylan tried to stand up, but his legs wouldn't work. He was trapped. Something was holding him down and he couldn't move. He tried to thrash around but he was pinned to the ground. He felt something squeeze his chest and it was hard to breathe.

Dylan's eyes flew open and he panted in fear from his nightmare, but for some reason, the pain in his chest did not disappear with the dream. Dylan's body was covered by blankets and he couldn't move his arms to pull them off. He briefly saw Via, fluttering anxiously about his head, her eyes flashing in the darkness an angry red color. She was making a weird sound that he immediately associated with the buzzing in his dream. Via was distressed but he couldn't help her, and she too was helpless to come to Dylan's aid.

Help me, Remy! Dylan called out in his mind.

At that moment, the head of a snake slithered out from beneath the blankets and stared Dylan straight in the eyes. The snake had only one eye like a cyclopes, but it was giant and it seemed to pulsate light in a rhythmic pattern as it continued to gaze unblinkingly at Dylan. It took only a second, before Dylan was under a trance set by the sleeper serpent. As the one head maintained its unwavering gaze, the other segment of the creature continued to wind its scales up higher on Dylan's body. Soon Dylan would be fully engulfed by the serpent. His shoulders, his neck and in a moment, his face would be entrapped within the serpent's hold. The serpent was careful not to squeeze too tightly. She knew her master wanted this child delivered alive. She also knew that if she did well she would be rewarded, and both tongues flickered excitedly at the feast that would be provided to her once she returned the boy as instructed. When the creature had Dylan fully wrapped within its scales, the serpent would escape into the night and bring the child, unharmed and alive, to her master. The task was almost complete, and the two-headed creature prepared to depart.

Just then, Remy burst into the room. He immediately saw Via moving fast and erratically over Dylan's head. With the light she illuminated, Remy also could make out something that was about to smother his brother. *Light,* he thought and the full brightness of the room exposed what Remy had not been able to see clearly before.

Remy was momentarily stunned. *It can't be!* His mind raced as he stared incredulously at something he had only heard about in school. It was a sleeper serpent, one of the most dangerous creatures in the immortal world. Remy knew that these snake-like creatures had two heads, two bodies and hypnotic eyes that put its victim into a trance and made easy prey. He also knew that there had not been any sightings of sleeper serpents in decades. They were so deadly that the Ministry had hunted them into extinction – at least that's what Remy had been taught.

Remy knew he had to act fast to save his brother, but what could he, a young warlock do? He could call out for his parents but that would put them in danger too, and he didn't want to risk their lives, so Remy acted on impulse. He ran towards the creature intending to use his powers to try to electrocute it. Even if he couldn't kill it, maybe he could at least get it off of his brother.

When he reached the bed, he immediately could see one serpent head staring into his brother's eyes, holding Dylan in its unwavering, hypnotizing gaze. In an instant, the second head whipped around to stare at Remy. But no matter how long it glared at Remy, its pulsating eye had no effect on him. Remy was immune to the sleeper serpent's deadly stare.

The serpent was angry and both its mouths hissed threateningly towards Remy, exposing pointed fangs that dripped with venom. The serpent knew its orders were to return the boy alive, but this second child confused it. The creature did not know whether it could kill this second, identical looking boy or not. Without clear directions, the serpent could only act on its innate instincts.

The head that was not hypnotizing Dylan, lashed out and sunk its teeth into Remy's arm. Its venom poured into Remy, rapidly spreading throughout his body. But rather than weakening and killing him, the venom had the opposite effect. He felt power surge through his body, and he pointed his index fingers towards the deadly creature.

Die sleeper serpent, his mind commanded. *DIE!*

Waves of electricity came shooting out of Remy's hands and attached themselves to the serpent, all along its scaly bodies. Remy's eyes narrowed in concentration as he kept up a steady stream of power to obliterate the creature. He watched as the serpent convulsed as the electricity penetrated its body, and then its scales began to blacken. The creature began to shrivel up and fall off of his brother's body.

But even when the serpent lay dead at his feet, still Remy's power did not relent. He kept blasting its motionless body with his magic until all that remained was a pile of ash. But even still he did not stop. Dylan watched with wide eyes as his brother used his powers until the pile of black soot burst into flames and disappeared in a whirl of smoke. Only then, did Remy lower his hands and collapse exhausted onto Dylan's bed.

'You saved my life,' Dylan whispered into his brother's ear.

'I know. You would have done the same for me,' replied Remy earnestly.

'I don't think I would have known how to do what you just did.'

'I don't know how I did it either. And I don't know how a sleeper serpent ended up in your room.' Remy telepathically conveyed everything he knew about sleeper serpents into his brother's mind.

'What should we do now?' asked Dylan, fear quivering in his voice.

Remy put a comforting arm around his shoulder. 'I don't know, Dyl but I have a feeling that this has something to do with the prophecy. And I don't think we should tell mom and dad. It will just worry them. We need to figure this out ourselves.'

Dylan nodded in agreement. 'Okay, but we need to get on this. Someone or something must be after us. Based on what you told me, this is no coincidence. Extinct creatures don't just randomly appear out of nowhere. Something is going on.'

'I think you're right. Do you want to share a room, at least for a little while?'

'You read my mind,' replied Dylan with a little smile. And then trying out his powers again, he conjured up a second bed, right next to his own.

'Not bad, Little Bro,' complimented Remy. 'But next time, you have to remember to include the dimensions in your thoughts. They both laughed as they stared at the perfectly formed, but completely miniature bed that Dylan had created. It only took one more attempt before it was perfect. The two boys fell asleep with Via perched between them and shared dreams of where to start their investigation the next day.

In the meantime, Reus sat wide awake, staring out of the window into the empty darkness beyond his house. His creature had returned to him, in accordance with the orders he had magically directed before he planted it in Dylan's bed. But instead of a vibrant double bodied, two headed sleeper serpent with the boy firmly encased in its scales, all Reus held in his hands was a tiny smudge of black ash. Wisps of blackened smoke swirled softly out of his palms and then disappeared into oblivion.

Reus snapped his fingers and watched again the images of what had transpired in Dylan's bedroom. His anger built until finally he could stand it no longer and he lashed out at the holograph with his fist, shattering the picture into a thousand shards. But magic cannot be defeated by fists, and within moments the picture reassembled itself.

Frustrated and enraged, Reus snapped his fingers again to make the disbelieving image disappear. *How could one warlock, so young, so untrained, be able to defeat a sleeper serpent? And if one of the boys had special powers, then what does that mean about the other two?*

Reus wasn't sure what he was going to do next, but clearly something had to be done. And in the meantime, Baltazar was going to have to be appeased...somehow. His existence depended on it.

CHAPTER FOURTEEN

Dylan and Remy opened their eyes at the exact same moment the next morning. *This identical twin thing is really weird,* thought Dylan. *Yeah, but in a good way,* responded Remy through his mind. The boys grinned at each other and Via bounced excitedly between them, wanting their attention.

'Okay, Via. We see you,' laughed Dylan, giving her an affectionate pat. He felt a slight tingle from her electrical current, but it didn't hurt.

Just then, there was a knock at Dylan's door and when Dylan called out that it was okay to come in, their mother opened the door and stepped into Dylan's room. Maggie was surprised to see the second bed pushed up right next to Dylan's. Both Remy and Dylan had been raised as only children to this point. She had assumed that they would want to have some privacy by keeping separate rooms. Maggie felt badly that she had obviously made such a wrong assumption, but she also felt a surge of happiness that her two boys were so clearly becoming close in just a matter of days.

'You boys decided to share a room?' she asked.

Remy and Dylan shot each other a subtle glance and Remy's mind reminded Dylan not to let her know about what happened last night. The boys gave their mother an identical sheepish look. Maggie smiled broadly at her sons as she contemplated their similarities. Their bangs flopped in their faces, the cowlick they both shared sending their longish hair into an endearing part right in the middle of their foreheads. The shape of their facial features was the same. Even their mannerisms, how they held their heads slightly to the side as they indulged her staring at them was the same.

The only obvious difference was the color of their eyes. Remy's right now were a deep, dark green, and while Dylan's eyes were also dark, they were an unusual shade of grey. Maggie, who was always very observant, wondered if something was bothering the boys. Their demeanor was playful, but the darkness of their eyes suggested something else was going on.

'Everything okay with you two?' she asked.

'Yeah, of course. We're great. Right, Dylan?'

'Absolutely. I'm just a little nervous for school, I guess.'

Well, that's a plausible explanation, thought Maggie. *Dylan is anxious about starting school and Remy is worried for him.* That settled all of Maggie's uncertainty and she came over to ruffle Dylan's mop of hair.

'Everyone gets the first day jitters. But by the end of the day, I'm sure you will be feeling much more comfortable at your new school. Now, what can I get you to eat before you head off?'

'Mom,' Remy said. 'I think Dylan should try to conjure up his own food. He can practice using his powers.'

'I think that is a great idea,' she replied enthusiastically. 'Get dressed and then come downstairs and let's see what Dylan comes up with!'

Remy and Dylan pulled on their clothes quickly then flew down to the main floor and settled themselves on the stools. Ben and Maggie were already there, nursing hot drinks.

'Okay, Bro, you're up. What are we going to eat?' prodded Remy.

Dylan thought for a moment. 'French toast,' Dylan decided.

'Never heard of it,' quipped Remy. 'But I hope it's as delicious as those pancakes from yesterday! Now remember, you have to envision all the details – the size, the texture, the smell.'

Dylan nodded his head and concentrated. He pictured steaming hot French toast sitting on a plate. The yellow egg coating turned slightly brown by frying in the pan. The thickness of the bread. Crispy outside but soft and tender inside. The stickiness and sweetness of the maple syrup. The dusting of the icing sugar. And then, poof! Before them all sat a plate with thick pieces of perfectly made French toast, dripping with maple syrup.

'This smells amazing!' gushed Remy and he stuck a fork and knife into the steaming hot food to take a bite. But when he picked up a generous piece off of the plate, they could all immediately see Dylan's mistake. While the top side of the French toast was fully cooked to perfection, the bottom side was just a gooey mess of a raw egg, dripping onto the plate. Everyone looked to Dylan to see how he would react, concerned that he might be disappointed in his results, but Dylan just laughed. He laughed so hard that tears poured out of his eyes. Maggie, Ben and Remy couldn't help it – they started to laugh as well. Once everyone was back under control, Dylan concentrated on the bottom side of the French toast and was able to successfully fix the problem of the uncooked breakfast. Soon, everyone was savoring this popular human food, which they had never tasted before.

Once everyone was finished, Maggie waved her hands and the dirty dishes were magically clean and disappeared from sight. 'Okay boys, time to go,' she said. Maggie gave both of her sons a quick kiss on the tops of their heads and prodded them towards the front door.

'Have a great day, guys! Can't wait to hear about it later. Love you both!' called Ben from where he still sat perched on his stool.

Dylan and Remy stood at the threshold of the house ready to leave, but Dylan was frozen in place. Remy looked at his brother with a confused expression. Maggie stood slightly back and also wondered what was causing the holdup. She didn't want Dylan to be late on his very first day.

'Look down,' whispered Dylan. Remy glanced down and saw the ground hundreds of feet below, which for him was nothing new, but for Dylan, it was going to take some getting used to.

'Not to worry, Little Bro. We are going to fly, remember? You are already floating in the house. There aren't any floors on this level, and you have been just fine.'

Maggie rushed forward. 'Maybe Dylan isn't ready yet. Dylan, honey, do you want me to take you to school? You don't have to fly on your own if you don't feel up to it yet. I understand – there's a big difference between floating in our house and flying out the door.'

Dylan had two thoughts at the very same time. First, he could think of nothing worse than his *mommy* taking him to school, as if he were still a little kid. And second, he remembered flying with his caseworker, Mary when he first arrived in this strange new world. *I can do this,* he thought, and Remy nodded his head in agreement.

'I will be right next to you, Dylan. I promise I won't let you fall. And even if you did, nothing much would happen. Warlocks are hard to break!' Remy laughed.

Dylan screwed his eyes shut and focused. He remembered Remy's advice to think about *all* the details. He pictured himself soaring through the air, and with his eyes still closed, took a tentative step forward. Then he took a second step, then a third. But he didn't feel anything different.

'Uh Dylan?' asked Remy.

'Yes…'

'You're still just floating. Are you ready now to fly?'

Dylan slowly opened his eyes and saw that he was no longer inside the house, but rather was hovering just outside the front door. *I can do this!* he admonished himself and with that, he inhaled deeply and then with a surge of power, took off and soared into the blue sky. Dylan could hear Remy laughing behind him and soon they were flying side by side. Remy showed off a little, doing some loops and even a couple of insane nose dives. Dylan didn't feel quite up to performing those tricks yet, but he was quietly pleased with his flying ability, which while not fancy, was certainly respectable.

The more Dylan flew, the more comfortable he became. Soon, he was able to control the motion of his body in the air without having to think about it quite so much. Instead, Dylan was able to marvel at the sights of the immortal world. The landscapes changed abruptly and often, from almost barren in places to lush and green. There were hills, there were valleys. There were spaces where the land was flat and others where it was rocky. Some buildings were on the ground, while others floated at all different levels in the sky.

He saw immortals walking on the ground, so human like! And others were in the air. Not everyone flew like he was. Some were on broomsticks – must be witches, he thought to himself, so cliché with the broomsticks! Others had wings and flew like birds. Remy heard his thoughts and responded by telepathic communication. *Some immortals technically don't have to fly. There are a few who have such strong powers that they can transport themselves anywhere they wish to go through a portal that they create. We have been learning how to do this in magic class at school, but I don't think I will ever be able to do it. That's okay though, since most of us don't have these powers I don't feel so bad about not being able to do it myself. And I still prefer to fly. It's so much more fun!*

All too soon it seemed the boys were approaching the school. *Ready to land, Dylan?* Remy inquired with his mind. Dylan took a deep breath, remembering his first attempt. *Okay, here goes nothing,* Dylan thought. He lowered his body closer to the ground and reduced his speed. *Knees flexed, body position more upright,* he instructed himself. He hoped that nobody would be watching him – this could be embarrassing! Dylan kept his eyes opened and tried to gauge the exact moment when his legs would reach the ground. *Concentrate, concentrate* and then…a perfect landing! Remy touched down next to Dylan and congratulated him on his execution.

'Considering your lack of experience, you seem to be a natural! You clearly have impressive talent when it comes to flight, Dyl!'

Dylan beamed at his older brother but before he could respond, the two boys were surrounded. Clearly, a new face in the school courtyard was bringing out the crowds. Dylan grew anxious, not sure that he liked having so much attention focused on him, but he was relieved to see that the faces staring at him were friendly, although somewhat also puzzled. They were clearly surprised to be meeting someone who looked identical to Remy. Dylan quickly scanned the group of students and noted that they were all wearing what appeared to be almost identical looking black sweaters with buttons that ran up the front. Each sweater had two crests -one on each side of the upper chest. Colored bands were on the sleeves, but some students had different colors than others.

'What's the story here?' one of the kids called out above the others.

'Hey guys, this is my long lost but now found twin brother, Dylan. It's a long story, but we have to get him registered at the office, so we will all talk later, okay?' responded Remy.

Dylan found himself the recipient of many welcoming slaps on the back, and quick introductions. Remy assured him that he would have lots of time later to meet his friends again and he ushered Dylan towards the school administrative building.

As the two brothers walked together, their steps in perfect synchronization, Dylan saw something dark soaring towards them from across the courtyard. It almost looked like a bird with wings outstretched from each side. The wings flapped up and down quickly and then settled into a gliding position. But the flying object had no head and as it came closer, it became very apparent to Dylan that this was not an animal at all. As the unknown entity approached them, Dylan inhaled sharply in fear. Remy, hearing his thoughts just laughed and extended his right arm. And then it became very clear to Dylan what the item was. A black sweater landed on Remy's arm and draped itself over his elbow. Remy held the object out for Dylan's inspection before pulling it on over his shirt. What Dylan had thought were wings were not wings at all. They were sleeves!

Dylan noted the same two crests he had seen on the other kids, one on each side of Remy's chest, but he had no idea what the symbols meant. The bands on Remy's sleeves were purple and shiny. There were two of them on each side. Dylan leaned in closer to inspect the sweater. He didn't recognize the images on the uniform at all. Up close, he was also able to notice a small, dime size shimmering disk embedded in one of the crests.

'What's the little silver thing on your jersey?' Dylan inquired pointing to the shiny object on the sweater.

'Oh, that's just the ITIS,' Remy explained. 'They will tell you about it when they give you the sweater.'

'ITIS? That sounds like a disease,' Dylan laughed but Remy didn't understand the joke.

'You know, ITIS,' Dylan responded. 'Like appendicitis?' Remy shook his head in confusion. 'I forgot, you don't get sick here they way humans do. Never mind, I will explain it to you later,' said Dylan.

'You'll get a uniform too, Dylan. You have to wear it all the time while you're here, but it never leaves the school grounds. And it's made just for you. Nobody else can ever wear it. Each one is created only for its owner. It even grows with you as you get bigger,' Remy explained. Dylan nodded his head, amazed at the new discoveries he kept making in this strange new world that he now called home.

When they stepped into the office, the secretary Mrs. Witsmith was eagerly awaiting their arrival. 'Oh boys, I'm so glad you made it early so that we can get Dylan his schedule and his uniform with plenty of time to make it to his first class on time. Now, your parents let us know yesterday that you would be enrolling so we were able to already make pre-arrangements, based on what they told us about you, Dylan.' She muttered some words, too low for Dylan to hear, and then a small book appeared in his hands. Dylan closed his fingers around its pages, but the book shook violently to escape his hold. Once Dylan's grip loosened up, the book flipped open to the first page.

'That's your schedule, dear,' Mrs. Witsmith instructed. 'We placed you in the advanced Human Culture and Societies course. Your parents told us that you have extensive knowledge in that particular area of study. We also put you in the regular class for Warlock Education since we don't have any other options. But for all your other courses, based on your lack of formal education, we are putting you in remedial. At least for now dear, but if you work hard, you can always move up to the advanced classes.'

Dylan looked at his list of courses. History of the Immortal World, Cross-Faction Perspectives, Politics and Doctrines of the Ministry, Magical Warlock Education, and Human Culture and Societies. *Interesting,* he thought. *No math, no science, no geography, no literature. What kind of classes are these?*

'Now dear, let's go see Mr. Fairshelf. He's expecting you,' the kindly secretary said to Dylan.

Dylan was ushered into what looked exactly like any principal's office in the human world. There was a large desk in the middle of the room. A couple of chairs that didn't look overly comfortable sat in front of the desk. He sat in one of them while Remy perched on the other. There were lots of framed pictures on the walls. One of the most prominent was a certificate in a large, gold frame that read:

To Alvin Fairshelf, in recognition of a century of outstanding service to the Ministry.

The bottom of the document had a seal that looked like one of the crests on Remy's sweater. Dylan continued to look around the room. Another picture immediately caught Dylan's attention. It showed a gathering of immortals from all different factions, looking happy. The slogan said: 'Ask not what the Ministry can do for you, but what you can do for the Ministry'. Dylan had to suppress a giggle. *Isn't that a kind of plagiarism?* he wondered. From his earliest memories of school, Dylan could recall his teachers emphasizing the importance of American history, especially specific events and people that made significant contributions to their country. Certain quotes had been drilled into their minds from the earliest days of school. Quotes like the one from JFK, and Martin Luther King Jr. were as ingrained in his memory as his own address. Dylan speculated for a moment whether his course on history of the immortal world would be similar to studying American history. Just then, a fairy flew into the room, his wings beating quickly as he tried to hurry. He visually assessed the two boys, quickly noting their identical features, with the exception of their eye color, just as their parents had described.

'Hello Remy, and you must be Dylan,' the fairy said in greeting. He came over to shake Dylan's hand. 'We are so happy to have you join us, Dylan. I spoke with your parents briefly yesterday, so now it's just a quick formality to issue you your school uniform and then you can be on your way. Remy, you can go son. I want to speak with Dylan alone, I'm sure you 'remember having the same talk when you started school.'

'Yes sir, Mr. Fairshelf. Bye, Dylan,' said Remy and then he left the room, shutting the door behind him.

'So, Dylan. I understand that you have experienced, shall we say, some unusual circumstances?'

'Yes, Mr. Fairshelf. That would definitely be an accurate statement.'

'Indeed,' Mr. Fairshelf chuckled. 'Let me explain to you about the school uniform. A personalized uniform will be created and issued to every student upon entry to the school. The uniform belongs solely to the student and will not be able to be transferred or shared with anyone else. The same uniform will be with you throughout your education. It must be worn at all times while at school and during school events. It will grow with you and will not allow itself to be worn by anyone other than yourself.'

'What do you mean by that, sir? It's a sweater. How can it choose who wears it? What if I put on Remy's by mistake?'

'That is impossible, Dylan. The uniform will not allow itself to be on any individual other than its assigned owner. Your uniform will find you whenever you enter school property. It will also leave you before you exit the school grounds. Let me show you the elements of the uniform.' Mr. Fairshelf whistled once, a loud, shrill noise and a moment later, Dylan heard a loud bang on the office door.

'Whoops,' the principal muttered and with a wave of his hands, the office door swung open briefly before it clattered shut again. A black cardigan sweater sailed into the room and landed on Mr. Fairshelf's desk. He picked up the uniform and held it out for Dylan's inspection.

'Here on the left, you will see the crest of the Ministry. You can see the emblems which represent our leaders Atticus and Callista, and the symbol of unity that ended our civil war and brought peace to all immortals. On the right, this is the crest which belongs to all warlocks. Each type of immortal has its own crest. While it is true that warlocks have the greatest powers of all types of immortals, it is essential that warlocks do not consider themselves superior to others. Our world is based on co-operation and harmony between all groups, so while powers may differ between factions, we are all seen as equal in the eyes of the Ministry. The warlock crest serves as a reminder of this to all warlocks.'

Dylan peered closely at the warlock emblem. It was unlike anything he had ever seen before. A fierce looking dragon was in the middle, a grimace that maybe was supposed to be a smile on its lips. Wisps of smoke curled out from its mouth. The creature's wings extended outwards, which dominated most of the crest. In each claw, the dragon clutched a golden rope and attached to the end of the rope on each side was a disk, which was also a shiny gold color. Dylan suddenly realized that the images weren't random, but rather the dragon was holding a scale in its hands, and the creature itself was the fulcrum. Dylan smiled when he remembered the word fulcrum from science class last year – the point at which something is supported or balanced. On the disk suspended from the dragon's left hand there was one large flame that burned brightly in bursts of red, orange and yellow. On the disc that was located hanging from the dragon's right claw, there were many smaller flames, but all equally as vibrant and colorful as the other side. The scale was perfectly balanced.

'You see, Dylan. One warlock may have power greater to many other immortals, but in our world, we do not function as individuals. Rather, we are part of a larger collective and when considered as a whole, our importance, our value, our powers, are all equal contributors to the success of our society. Do you understand?' Mr. Fairshelf inquired of his newest pupil.

Dylan nodded his head solemnly.

'The colored stripes on the sleeves indicate both your faction and your academic progress. The color purple signifies that you are a warlock. A single band, like yours, designates that you are still in the beginning stages of your academic career. As you achieve certain goals which are monitored closely by the Ministry, you will be awarded additional stripes. In order to be deemed ready to graduate and assume your place in the adult world of immortals, you must achieve four bands.'

'How long does it typically take for someone to earn all four bands?' asked Dylan, as he silently compared the human school system that had a defined ending, with this potentially endless scheme of education.

'Well Dylan, each individual is different and will make progress at their own pace. We don't measure academic growth in terms of time. And keep in mind that each of us has unique talents and strengths that can be used to serve our society in different ways. Some of us may have abilities that are, shall we say, more pronounced than others. Those with exceptional powers will leave here and continue their development in other, more specific areas. Master healers, for example. Or educators, like myself. Others may find that their formal education ends after they complete their learning here and they will be placed into roles that best suit their capabilities. There are certain fundamental requirements that the Ministry insists upon for graduation which is reflected in the bands that are awarded as students attain those expectations. But beyond that, each individual is assessed on their own merits in determining where they go from here. And of course, the Ministry will consider an individual's personal preference. There are always choices available, one's gifts and abilities will dictate what the options are. Do you have any more questions at this point?'

Dylan shook his head.

'Good, then let us move to the final feature of your uniform and get you on your way,' Mr. Fairshelf stated with a grin. Once again, he waved his hands and a strange, unfamiliar looking object appeared on his desk.

'This Dylan is the technology for the ITIS, the most essential element of your uniform. ITIS stands for Iris Transmission Intelligence System. We are going to use the device to scan your eye. The machine will register a precise imprint of your iris, which is unique only to you. It will then generate an exact replicate of your eye scan on to the ITIS, which will then be embedded in the uniform. The ITIS records everything you think, everything you learn in school. This will allow the Ministry to monitor your progress and determine when to award you additional bands and ultimately, when you are ready to graduate. They usually review a student's ITIS every few months. The scan doesn't hurt, and it only takes a moment. There will be a bright flash of light, but that's all it takes to register your eye imprint. Are you ready?'

'I guess so...' Dylan replied. The machine looked harmless enough and he knew that everyone had it done.

'Excellent, just lean forward then. Place your elbows on

my desk and rest your chin in your hands,' instructed Mr. Fairshelf. Dylan did as he was told and Mr. Fairshelf pushed some buttons on the machine, Dylan assumed to program it, then placed the device, which looked kind of like binoculars but only had one side, up to his left eye. Just as he had been told, there was a burst of bright light and then it was over.

'Hmmm....' said Mr. Fairshelf, closely examining the device. 'I think we have to try again, Dylan. The technology cannot find any birth records for someone with your delivery date who has not been accounted for already. It's supposed to match your eye scan with your identity. I'm quite certain I put in the correct date – it's the same as Remy's so I know I have the information recorded accurately. Perhaps I did something wrong. One more time, if you don't mind,' he said, once again re-programming the technology.

Dylan repeated his previous actions and a second attempt was made.

'I don't understand it, Dylan. This machine has never failed before, but it cannot find any record of you to match with your ITIS. I'm so sorry there must be a problem with the device. I will have to call the Ministry to order a new one or have this one repaired.'

'The problem might not be the machine, Mr. Fairshelf. When I first arrived after coming through the vortex, the border guards couldn't find a record of me either.'

'How strange. I've never heard of that happening. Ever,' stated Mr. Fairshelf. 'Well, for now we will just have to issue you the uniform without the ITIS. Once we figure out what's going on, we can just do it again.' Mr. Fairshelf handed the sweater, without the shiny disk, over to Dylan. 'Welcome to our school, son. I know you will be very happy here. If you ever need anything, my door is always open, figuratively at least!'

'Thank you, sir,' replied Dylan sincerely.

Just then, there was a sharp knock and a small figure pushed through the doorway. Dylan peered down into his face and knew that he had seen this miniature creature somewhere before. The little face was definitely familiar. Dylan could immediately tell by his stature and pointed ears that the creature was an elf. His face was older, etched with lines. His eyes were a piercing blue. He had long silver hair that was tied back behind his head. But where would he have encountered him previously? The elf shuffled over to stand directly next to Dylan.

'Oh lovely, what perfect timing,' smiled Mr. Fairshelf. 'Dylan, meet Reus. He is going to be your teacher for all your remedial subjects.'

Reus stared into Dylan's grey eyes and gave him a slow smile. The elf's teeth were pearly white and there seemed to be far too many teeth for such a small mouth. And that's when it hit Dylan where he had seen this Reus guy before.'

'I remember you,' sputtered Dylan. 'You were in the security zone when I fell through the vortex.'

'Yes, yes, of course that was me,' he replied steadily. 'And now the Ministry has reassigned me to be your personal teacher. It is my duty to ensure that you are properly educated and that we make up for lost time as rapidly as possible. So, I hope you are prepared to work hard, for we have much to accomplish. You will be spending the mornings with me and then you will rejoin the others for lunch and again in the afternoons for your Magic and HCS classes. Let's be going then, Dylan. Mr. Fairshelf, we will be leaving you now.'

'Yes, of course Reus but before you go, did you say that you met Dylan upon his arrival when he came through the vortex?'

'Yes, I was there. I wasn't the guard who found him, but I was called in soon after Dylan's unexpected homecoming.'

'Maybe you can help me then. The ITIS cannot match an identity with Dylan's eye scan and Dylan mentioned that his identity also didn't register then either. I'm not sure who to report this to… the technology has never failed before.'

'Hmm, I understand the problem. Leave it with me, if you will. I'm sure that the two incidents will require the same solution. I can take care of reporting this for you.'

'Wonderful!' exclaimed Mr. Fairshelf, clapping his hands. 'That's one less item on my list of things to do. Thank you, Reus. That is a very welcome offer and I happily accept! Now, if you want to be heading off to class, I have some matters to attend to.'

Reus nodded his head solemnly and beckoned Dylan to follow him with a gnarled finger. Dylan was worried. His new teacher did not appear to be overly pleasant. With a final glance back at the kind- hearted Mr. Fairshelf, Dylan reluctantly followed Reus out of the office.

'Our classroom is down this way,' Reus pointed past a row of buildings. 'Then when we reach the games field, we will turn right, followed by a left and finally one more right. Now, my expectation is that by the end of the week, you will be able to fly at least part of the way.'

'Fly? Oh, I can do that already,' boasted Dylan. And without having to put much thought into it at all, Dylan rose up gracefully from the ground, and flew off, leaving Reus standing stunned as he watched his pupil fly as if he had been doing it his whole life. *I wonder what else he can do,* thought Reus. He snapped his fingers to transport himself to the classroom. It simply would not do to have young Dylan arrive before the teacher!

Reus greeted Dylan at the door to their classroom. Dylan looked around the empty room.

'Where is everyone else? Shouldn't they be here by now?' he asked.

'You are my only student, Dylan. We shall be able to get much more accomplished since there will not be others to distract us.'

Dylan was disappointed and anxious. He did not want to be alone with this creepy little elf. But what choice did he have. He sighed and mentally prepared himself for what was to come. But just then, there was a loud crash as the door to the classroom was slammed hard against the wall. Standing in the entrance stood a girl with long, ebony hair and flashing dark eyes. She stood in a defiant pose with her hands on her hips and her feet spread apart. Dylan was mesmerized. He could feel his heart pounding inside his chest. His palms got sweaty. His face grew warm.

'Okay, I'm here. So let's get this stupid party started,' she growled.

CHAPTER FIFTEEN

'You must be mistaken,' snapped Reus. 'This is not your classroom.'

'No, *you* must be mistaken. This is exactly where the office told me to go. I'm not an idiot. I can read numbers on classroom doors. Look,' she responded in a harsh tone as she thrust a copy of her schedule into Reus' hands. Dylan was taken aback by her disrespectful attitude. In the human world, speaking to a teacher in that kind of manner would get a kid in trouble! But she didn't seem to be worried about offending Reus at all. She just continued to brazenly stand there while Reus fumed.

'I'm going to take care of this immediately,' Reus hissed. 'You two stay here and don't leave this room.' He snapped his fingers and disappeared.

The girl gave Dylan the once over before she curled her legs into the lotus position and floated on the air in front of him. 'My other teachers didn't like my attitude. Now that this new guy is here, I guess they figured that they could just foist me on him so they don't have to deal with me anymore. Well, except my HCS teacher. She loves me. I'm the head of that class. So, you must be the new kid that everyone is talking about. Remy's twin, right?'

'Um, um yeah,' stuttered Dylan. *I'm not making an overly impressive first impression* he thought. *Say something interesting,* he admonished himself. *She is the most beautiful girl I have ever seen, what should I say???*

'I'm Dylan Dover,' was what he finally came up with. *Dummy!* he thought to himself.

'Dover? What kind of last name is that? Dover is not an immortal last name,' she replied.

'Oh yeah, I guess I should use my new last name, Warston.'

'I still don't get it. Why would you have a new last name and an original last name that isn't recognized by the Ministry?'

'Well, it's a long story, but I guess the short version is that I was living with humans until just recently when I somehow fell into a vortex and ended up here. Then this agency found out that my immortal family was the Warstons and reunited me with them.'

The girl's stare was penetrating. Her eyes were shining with curiosity and so dark that they reminded Dylan of polished onyx. Dylan found that he couldn't look away. He felt an attraction to her unlike anything he had ever experienced in the human world. Dylan's mind whirled, trying to think of something clever to say but he remained totally dumbfounded. *She's going to think I'm an idiot,* he thought in a panic. But to Dylan's great fortune, she steered the conversation and he immediately relaxed.

'You lived in the human world until now? That's my dream… to live in the human world and get out of here! I have so much that I want to talk to you about!'

Well, this is great news, rejoiced Dylan silently. *She wants to talk to me!*

Just then, Dylan's daydreams were shattered when Reus popped back into the classroom. He glared at the girl and said, 'It appears that you will be joining our class after all, Miss Wiz. I am Reus. Now, we shall begin with the history of the immortal world, and since Dylan has no formal education, I will assume that we must begin with the basics. From what I hear about you, Miss Wiz, going back to the foundations will be to your benefit as well.'

Dylan thought he would have a difficult time concentrating on history lessons when the most gorgeous girl he had ever seen was only a few feet away, but to his surprise, Reus was a great teacher. And what Dylan was learning was so interesting! Reus started his lecture at the beginning of time, with the first immortal creatures to walk the earth. Dylan was astounded to discover that immortals existed even before humans, and that their history went back to pre-historic times on the human calendar.

The girl, whose first name he did not yet know, was definitely not stupid or ignorant. She too became engrossed by the lesson and soon her tough demeanor melted away. Reus sensed a change in her attitude and happily responded to the willingness of his captive audience to learn. After several hours, Reus paused and told his two pupils that they would have a twenty-minute break. He snapped his fingers and was gone.

'So, I didn't get a chance to ask you before. What's your name?' inquired Dylan of the girl that had him so enraptured. He got the words out without stuttering and was both happy and relieved at his successful attempt to make conversation!

'It's Althaea, but everyone just calls me Thea.'

'And your last name is Wiz? Is that unusual? I mean to have a last name that is just the prefix of the faction you are in? I haven't heard a last name like that here before. But then again, I haven't been here for very long.' Dylan realized that his question might be kind of personal and hoped that he hadn't offended her.

'It's just Wiz because I don't have a family name. My parents abandoned me when I was delivered. I don't know who they are. Apparently, they just dropped me off at D3W3 when I was only a few hours old. D3W3 determined that I was in fact a wizard, so they were able to take control of me. They put me with a family but for some reason that didn't work out. Neither did the next one, or the next one. I kept getting moved around until finally a few months ago I told them that I was going to take care of myself. I don't need anyone else to take care of me. I am completely independent. I was told that as long as I stay in school until graduation, and stayed out of trouble with the Ministry, that they would agree to me living independently. Some fairy named Mary checks up on me every so often but for the most part, they leave me alone.'

'Hey, Mary is my caseworker too!'

'Looks like we have something in common then.'

'So graduation… I don't really get it. The principal tried to explain to me that the Ministry decides when you are ready to leave school. Are people in school like, forever, here?'

'When you have completed all the Ministry requirements, you're done with school and then the Ministry will place you according to your aptitude, but we are told that we can also make certain requests. I heard of someone who graduated in less than five years from the time he started, but that might just be a rumor. Most people take at least ten years, some even longer than that. How does it work in the human world?' she asked with great interest.

'Well, we have grade levels based on your age. You have to write tests and complete assignments and at the end of each school year, if you pass, you move up to the next one. By the time a person turns eighteen, they are usually done school. Unless they want to continue their education but not everyone does that.'

'School based on age, that's interesting,' she replied. 'Age in the human world is probably pretty important, but here, age is pretty much irrelevant.'

'Age doesn't matter?' Dylan asked incredulously.

'Well, think about it. Immortals never die. Any of us who have magical powers can stop our physical aging process whenever we want. Well, except fairies who can only do it for others, since their magic can't be used to benefit themselves. Vampires are physically frozen at the human age when they made the change. Shapeshifters age very slowly but will never die of natural causes, same goes for the ogres and giants. So I guess age matters when you're young, like us, and don't have control over our lives,' Thea's voice sounded bitter. 'But once you graduate, age is of no importance. The Ministry places people based on ability, not age, and I'm going to prove to them that I am meant to serve in the human world. That is my only goal, so the more I know about humans, the better prepared I will be. You can help me with that.'

'Of course. I would love to help you! And I'm sorry about your parents. I know how hard it is to lose your family.'

'You can't miss what you never had. And you have a family, so why would you know what it's like to lose one?

'I have an immortal family, and they have been super nice to me. I already love my mom and dad, and Remy – well, he's the best. But I also have a human family. I'm not allowed to see my parents or my dogs… I'm not even allowed to let them know that I'm alright. They must be so worried about me, and I can't do anything to help them.' Dylan swallowed hard and fought to keep back his tears. He didn't want to cry in front of Thea.

She moved closer to sit next to Dylan and put a comforting hand on his shoulder. 'Maybe you will be allowed to see them again one day. Maybe they will let you return.'

'I mean, I don't fully know all the rules and stuff yet, but from what I have been told, and what you just confirmed is that immortals cannot cross into the human world without the Ministry's permission. I don't think that they would let me go back.'

'You don't know that. Maybe they will. Don't give up hope, Dylan.' The two were silent for a few minutes, each lost in their own thoughts.

'So, can I ask you some questions about the human world?' Thea inquired.

'Sure,' Dylan responded eagerly, happy to change the subject.

'Okay,' Thea said, 'so explain to me what are these things I have heard about called sunsets?'

CHAPTER SIXTEEN

The rest of the morning rushed by, with Thea and Dylan learning about the role of the Ministry. *Not nearly as interesting as history*, thought Dylan, *but important for me to know, I suppose, especially if I want to try to convince the Ministry to let me go back to see my human parents.* When the bell signaled the start of lunch, Reus gave his two pupils a genuine smile.

'I'm most impressed, with both of you. Dylan, you are showing great promise. Thea, I'm very pleased that I will be able to report that you too, are focused and engaged.'

'Perhaps I just needed the right teacher to inspire me,' she quipped back.

'Enjoy the rest of your day then. This afternoon you will rejoin your classmates for Magic and HCS. I will see you both tomorrow.' Reus snapped his fingers and was gone.

'You surprised me, Thea,' said Dylan with a grin.

'Why?'

'You came into the class and seemed, well, shall we say, less than happy to be here. But you clearly impressed Reus. He seems to really like you.'

'Do you think so? I hope you're right!'

'But why the sudden change of attitude?'

'When I first came in, I didn't know that our teacher was Reus, but once he told me who he was, well, that changed everything.'

'I don't get it,' replied Dylan still confused.

'Reus is well known in our world. He works closely with the Ministry leaders. Everyone knows that he is often placed on assignment by the Ministers and their Deputies personally. He's not just some unknown cog in the wheel; he might actually have some sway. And since I want to be chosen to go to the human world after graduation, he might be able to put in a good word for me. His recommendation could totally help me.'

At that moment, the door was flung open and Remy stood on the threshold with a big smile.

'So Little Bro, how was your morning with the creepy elf?'

'Not so bad, actually. In fact, it was interesting, and the elf isn't really so creepy.'

'Sounds like your morning was much better than mine. I almost fell asleep in my classes.' Remy then turned his attention to Thea. 'I didn't know you were in this class, Thea.'

'I was a last-minute addition,' she replied. 'Got a problem with that?'

'Nope, not at all. I was just making conversation,' Remy retorted. 'Ready to go to lunch, Dylan?'

'Sure, I'm starving. Do you want to come with us, Thea?'

Remy looked taken aback by Dylan's offer to Thea, but he didn't retract the invitation either. Remy looked rather surprised when Thea accepted. Thea had always kept to herself. She had never eaten lunch with anyone before.

'Do you mind if we walk this time?' asked Dylan. 'I wouldn't mind getting a better look around, and when I fly, I still feel that I have to concentrate too hard not to crash.'

'No problem,' Remy agreed without hesitation.

The three of them began to walk towards the building that housed the cafeteria. Remy and Thea pointed out various landmarks to Dylan to help him navigate the campus. In many ways, this school strongly resembled those that he was used to, and he commented on the similarities.

'I'm not surprised,' responded Thea. 'After all, the immortals borrowed a lot of ideas from the humans when they created our world. The whole idea of educating the young came from humans. And of course, with some immortals stationed in the human world, they report back to the Ministry about things that they observe which would benefit our own society. So as human school structures have evolved over time, ours have as well. They might not have powers like ours, but humans can be fairly intelligent,' Thea laughed, and Dylan thought it was the most charming sound he had ever heard.

The cafeteria was large, loud and really not so different from those at home, thought Dylan. With a few exceptions. There was nowhere to purchase food, no lunch line, no steaming trays of French fries or pizza slices. And while students sat in clearly delineated groups, the cafeteria did not have the typical organization of tables and chairs. Dylan looked around in amazement, still not used to seeing people hovering in mid-air. At least some kids were air bound. Others had planted themselves upside down on the ceiling. *It must be difficult to eat in that position,* thought Dylan. Remy laughed out loud, having heard Dylan's inner thoughts. Dylan was relieved to see that some students did in fact eat sitting at traditional tables and chairs and was even more relieved when Remy steered him towards one of those tables.

As they approached Remy's friends, Dylan was greeted with cheerful introductions that came at him far too fast to remember. There were six others at the table, and Dylan could easily figure out that one was a fairy and one was an elf. He also assumed from their extremely pale demeanor that two others must have been vampires. The other two, he wasn't able to tell just from their appearance, so he gathered that they would have to be either witches, warlocks, or wizards, although he wasn't certain. There were so many different types of immortals. The striped bands on their sweaters were red, but Thea's were blue. Clearly, these two were not wizards like Thea, nor warlocks like himself, thought Dylan. These two are probably witches, he concluded. Remy beckoned Dylan to sit next to him, and Thea squeezed in as well. Some of the kids gave her questioning glances, but nobody made any comments about her sudden change of heart to sit with them, even though she had always sat by herself before.

Dylan was carefully observing Remy's friends to see what they were eating, but he didn't recognize any of their food. The vampires just drank something out of dark bottles, and Dylan consciously decided not to think about the liquid that must have been in there. He watched Remy conjure up his own lunch, and Remy gave him a nod, prompting him to do the same. Dylan closed his eyes and pictured in his mind a slice of double stuffed pizza, dripping with cheese and smothered with pepperonis. He concentrated really hard to remember all the details to ensure that the crust was fully cooked, even on the bottom, and he even made sure that the pizza appeared on a plate to catch the crumbs and a napkin to wipe the sauce off his face. Then he visualized a can of cola, ice cold and sweet, with condensation droplets running down the side of can. When he opened his eyes, to his great delight, his lunch was in front of him, exactly as it should be. The other kids stopped talking and stared at Dylan, as stunned by his food as Dylan had been by theirs.

'What are you eating?' asked the fairy, who Dylan was pretty sure was named Monica.

'This is pizza with cheese and pepperoni. It's one of my favorite foods,' enthused Dylan. 'Do you want to try it?'

All of them immediately clamored to taste the foreign food that Dylan had created, so Dylan closed his eyes again to conjure up slices for everyone at the table, well everyone except the vampires. To his delight, he found it was much easier this time to get it right. He would have been so embarrassed if he messed up his magic, the way he had done earlier at breakfast. For good measure, he also had a can of icy cola accompany each piece of pizza.

'This stuff is unbelievable,' stated the elf, named Enderson.

The vampires turned up their noses in distaste.

'You don't know what you're missing,' said Enderson to his blood drinking friends, but with humor in his voice.

Thea was the one most taken with the food and drink that Dylan had brought forth. She peppered Dylan with questions about the ingredients, how to prepare the pizza and what a pizza oven was. She asked Dylan to show her visually what he was explaining. Dylan used his fingers to draw a square in the air, and in an instant, it was like watching a 3-D movie about how to make pizza. Dylan couldn't stop grinning as he became more comfortable using magic. And, best of all, the girl of his dreams was looking to him as an expert about a topic important to her.

The lunch period flew by, and Dylan found himself at the center of attention. He had been worried that he wouldn't be accepted by the others, not only because he was new, but because of his strange upbringing. But Remy's friends were all welcoming and made him promise to conjure up some more human favorite foods in the days to come.

Just before the end of the lunch period, Dylan felt a hard slap between his shoulder blades.

'Well, well, what do we have here?' drawled a deep voice, laden with disapproval.

'Just shut up, Traysik. Go find someone else to bother. We are not interested,' said Remy, defending his brother.

'Is that so? Well, I am interested. Interested to see how badly your identical twin here performs in magic class. It will be hard for him to be worse than you, but it should at least be entertaining to watch the two identical freaks make fools of themselves.'

'The only fool here is you,' growled Remy as he jumped up to confront the bully.

At that moment, the bell rang signaling the end of lunch. 'See you in class freak,' sneered Traysik before he took off and flew through the door.

Remy sighed, and Dylan could clearly hear his thoughts. Remy had been having some trouble in magic class recently. Traysik was the best of all the warlocks in school, and he was lording his accomplishments over others, especially Remy. Traysik never failed to flaunt his triple stripes, he was the closest immortal in the school to be declared ready to graduate, and he never let anyone forget it.

'Don't worry about Traysik,' one of the other kids said to Remy. 'He's just a jerk. We all know that. See you in HCS.'

All the kids from the table scattered in different directions.

'Where is everyone going now?' asked Dylan.

'Magic class is the only course that divides us by factions. We have to learn the magic of our own kind, but the Ministry doesn't like the fact that some of us have more power than others. All factions are supposed to be equal, but there is no way to deny the fact that some factions have greater magical ability than others. They separate us for this class in order to prevent negative feelings arising between the groups. Too bad it doesn't prevent negativity between immortals of the same kind,' sighed Remy.

Remy led his brother to their magic class, the class designed only for warlocks. They must have been the last to arrive, for the room was already full of other warlocks ready to learn more about how to harness their magical powers. Just after Remy and Dylan arrived, a small puff of purple smoke floated in from the doorway and travelled to the front of the room. The tiny cloud exploded with an ear shattering noise and scattered purple droplets all over the students, like confetti. The students all laughed with delight, except for Dylan, who was too shocked and frightened to laugh. Traysik caught the look on Dylan's face and shouted out to the class:

'Look at new kid, Remy's identical idiot. He must be scared of his own shadow. Is he a warlock or a war-wuss?'

Everyone laughed at Dylan's expense and he felt the hair prickle at the back of his neck in anger. Fortunately, the teacher heard the exchange and admonished Traysik for his behavior. She came over to personally introduce herself to Dylan.

'I am Delaney Warmaster, and I am your instructor of magic. I understand that your skills are undeveloped and certainly unrefined due to your exceptional circumstances, but with hard work and a positive attitude, I am sure you will soon become as proficient as your peers,' she said kindly.

'If by peers, you mean his brother, then it won't take longer than a minute!' jeered Traysik.

The teacher shot Traysik a menacing look, pointed her finger at his chest and softly muttered 'freeze'. That's all it took to stop Traysik in his tracks. He stood completely frozen, unable to move and unable to speak.

'There shall be no disrespect in my class, Traysik. You are frozen for the rest of this period and will have to make up the work on your own time. As for the rest of you, get into your groups and continue working on the assignment from last class.' Then she turned to Dylan and said, 'You may work with your brother. He will explain the task to you and I will come to check on you shortly.' With that, she turned away to help some other students.

'So what are we supposed to be doing?' asked Dylan.

Remy sighed again, clearly distressed about the task at hand. 'We are supposed to be learning how to create transport portals. If you can create a portal, you can transport yourself anywhere in the realm instantaneously. It is the fastest and most efficient way to travel. But if you get it wrong, the consequences can range from bad to truly terrible. You may just end up somewhere that you didn't want to go, but if you get it really wrong you could end up disintegrating yourself.'

'If it is so dangerous, then why do it at all?' asked Dylan with a slight tremor in his voice. This type of magic sounded too frightening for him. He would be happy to stick with flying.

'Mastering the transport portal is a sign of power. Only the best immortals are ever able to accomplish it, and for those who do, there are great rewards given by the Ministry. So far, Traysik is the only one who has gotten close. Last class, he tried to transport a fireball through the portal he created, and it came back in only a dozen pieces or so. Poor thing, but Ms. Warmaster took it to a master healer, and had the little guy fixed up in no time. We practice on other objects, you see. And only if we are successful, will we try it on ourselves. Most of us will never master it, but I think that out of everyone here, I am by far the worst. I can't even get a proper portal to appear.'

'Let's try it together,' suggested Dylan. 'Two minds are better than one! Teach me what to do.'

Remy closed his eyes and sent visual images to his brother, explaining step by step how to conjure up a transport portal. Once Dylan understood the process, they were ready to try. The two brothers turned to face each other and grasped each other's hands. In their minds, they went through each step of the instructions, one at a time. They were so focused that they were unaware of anything or anyone else in the room. Their minds worked as one as they used all of their powers to construct the portal.

'Oh my,' said the instructor, Ms. Warmaster, startling the boys out of their trance-like state.

Remy and Dylan opened their eyes and to their utter astonishment, a small swirling vortex hovered between them. The portal was definitely smaller than it should have been to transport a fully- grown warlock, but it was well formed and spinning quickly as it should be.

'Let's try it out,' suggested Ms. Warmaster. She retrieved from her pocket a red striped ball. 'Perhaps we will test it using something that is inanimate. No need to cause unnecessary harm to a living creature.'

She then threw the ball into the vortex and both the ball and the swirling portal opening immediately disappeared.

The boys continued to hold hands and stared at the space that the vortex had been. 'Now what?' whispered Dylan.

'I don't know. I've never gotten this far before,' replied Remy.

'Now we wait to see if the vortex and the ball return,' said Ms. Warmaster. 'I will be able to tell from the ball's appearance where it has been.'

'And if they don't reappear?' asked Dylan of his teacher.

'Then the transport portal failed, and we will be thankful that we only sent a ball into the abyss.'

The next minute passed in excruciating slowness. 'Keep your hands joined boys,' instructed their teacher. 'Your magic is clearly more powerful working together.'

As they continued to stare at the empty space between them, a crowd gathered round. Just when Dylan was ready to give up hope, there was a large popping noise that broke the silence around them. The vortex was back and an instant later, the ball came hurtling out of the portal and straight into the hands of Ms. Warmaster. She examined the ball closely before clapping her hands together.

'Well done, boys! You did it. A successful transport portal! You are the only ones in the class to have accomplished this goal. And not just this class, you are the only warlocks that I have ever taught in all my years who have successfully created a working transport portal. I hope you realize, Dylan, how incredible this accomplishment is to have achieved! There are only a handful of immortals in our entire world who have mastered the ability to create effective transport portals. Only the most powerful immortals have ever achieved this feat! Working together, you two boys have escalated to a unique and elite status amongst immortals. You have demonstrated a power that all of us wish to have, but so few of us have achieved. Now you can work on perfecting your transport portals. Concentrate to increase its size and strength to be able to move larger, more complex items, including yourselves. We won't have you try transporting yourselves any time soon. Based upon my experience, the fact that you created even a basic transport portal is extremely impressive and so now I will have to find someone with greater expertise than my own to further develop your skills. Even I have not been able to master this power. I'm very impressed! And on your very first day, Dylan! I cannot wait to see how you and Remy will continue to advance in your magical abilities working together! You are now at the head of the class!'

The frozen form of Traysik remained motionless but his unmoving eyes glared at Remy and Dylan, with deep malice and hatred. And the brothers knew that their newly found powers were not being as well received by the *former* head of the class.

CHAPTER SEVENTEEN

Maggie sat anxiously in Warrentree's office, waiting for him to arrive. She had shown up without an appointment, but she just could not wait any longer to hear about how her message to Dylan's human mother had been received. In the century that she had been with Ben, she had never hidden anything from him, until now, and her secret weighed heavily on her mind. But she knew that she couldn't tell her husband what she had done. He worked for the Ministry as a fairly high ranking official, and she was afraid that he would not approve. As a wife, she felt terribly about her lie of omission but as a mother, how could she let this poor human woman suffer needlessly, not even knowing if the boy she considered her own was safe? Maggie knew she had done the right thing, and she was hoping that the information Warrentree had for her would validate her actions.

Time seemed to pass slowly as she continued to wait. As she sat trying to be patient, she let her thoughts wander to the past several days. It was incredible how her entire existence had changed in such a short time. The re-emergence of one of her missing children filled her with such joy that she felt she would burst, but it also raised so many questions and she was determined to find out the answers. Warrentree must have access to their delivery records, and that's where she wanted to begin her search.

Finally, Warrentree bounded into the room, apologizing

profusely for making her wait. He gave Maggie a gentle pat on her shoulder before he sat down at his desk.

'No problem at all, Warrentree. I showed up unannounced. I am so grateful that you could see me.'

'Ahh Maggie, I am glad you came. I was planning on contacting you myself later today so you just beat me to it. I imagine that you want to know about the delivery of your message?'

'To start, yes. I am so hopeful that my message brought the poor woman some peace of mind.'

Warrentree nodded his head gravely. 'Well, to some extent yes, but as I'm sure you can understand, she was overwrought with emotion. Here, let me show you.'

Warrentree waved his hands and the image of Dylan's adopted mother appeared before Maggie. She watched the entire scene play out, and her heart broke as she not only saw, but genuinely felt the pain of the human who had loved and cared for Dylan his entire life. Tears fell from Maggie's eyes and she wished desperately that she could do something more to help ease the woman's suffering.

When the last image faded away, Maggie stared transfixed at the air, thinking about what she had seen.

'Warrentree, please can I send her more messages? Just to reassure her that Dylan is doing fine. Better than fine actually. I think it would help her.'

'Maggie, I know your request is a noble one, but do you really believe that continuing contact will comfort her? Perhaps additional messages will just make her more distraught.'

Maggie shook her head vehemently in disagreement. 'Warrentree, if I were in her shoes, I would want reassurances to know my child was safe and happy. As much as I would

150

miss him and want him back, not knowing would be so much worse. Please…'

Warrentree steepled his fingers underneath his chin in contemplation of her request. 'Okay, Maggie. The next time that I will be crossing through the vortex, I will deliver another message for you. I can carry it over when I will already be going there on other business. I don't want to raise awareness of what we are doing, so I think it's better to keep it inconspicuous. I will let you know when I will be going again, probably in a week or so.'

'Thank you so much, Warrentree. I can't tell you how much this means to me.'

'You're very welcome, my dear. Now, if that is all…?'

'No, actually. There is another matter we need to discuss.'

'Is there a problem with Dylan?' Warrentree inquired politely.

'No, not at all. Dylan is doing beautifully. He and Remy have already bonded and Ben and I couldn't be more thrilled to be getting to know our son again. He is such a wonderful boy. The problem is not with Dylan. But we do want to have an investigation started into the circumstances of his delivery. When the boys were delivered, only Remy survived, or so we were told. We saw the lifeless bodies of two other babies. We saw them disappear. So how is it possible that Dylan is in fact alive? And where is my other child?'

'Yes, Maggie. I agree that a full investigation must be conducted. I have already alerted the Ministry and the Records department will be sending over their delivery records. That is where we need to begin.'

'I agree,' replied Maggie. 'And I want to be involved in the investigation.'

'Maggie, you know that is not possible. But I will keep you apprised of any developments. I promise.'

Maggie's eyes flared in anger that she could not participate in the investigative process but when she looked at Warrentree's face and saw genuine concern in his eyes, her temper dissipated. She relaxed, having full faith that Warrentree would leave no stone unturned. The mystery of her sons' delivery would be revealed. She would just have to be patient. Maggie got up to leave.

'Oh Maggie, while you are here, there is one more small matter I would like to discuss,' implored Warrentree.

'Of course. What is it?' she replied.

Warrentree snapped his fingers and Farah, his assistant, immediately flew to her boss' office.

'What can I do for you, Warrentree?' Farah asked in her sing-song voice.

'Can you please ask Oliver and Halle to come to my office, right away please?'

'Of course, I will get right on it,' she replied before she flew off as quickly as she had come.

'I think you will want to meet these two, Maggie,' said Warrentree with a twinkle in his eyes.

Just then, two beautiful birds landed on Warrentree's window and began pecking at the glass. Their feathers were a brilliant white with streaks of grey, and their eyes were bright and the most unusual shade of turquoise that Maggie had ever seen. Warrentree walked over to the window and opened it wide. The two birds flew into the room and perched on the arm of Maggie's chair. They gazed at her for a moment before they fluttered down to the floor in unison and stood side by side.

Their small bodies began to tremor and shake; their wings outstretched began to expand. From beneath the feathers emerged fingers, then arms and shoulders. Their tiny bird legs started to grow longer and thicker. Their torsos contorted, and their necks elongated. And within the span of a few seconds, instead of birds standing before Maggie were two human looking naked immortals. *Shapeshifters, of course* Maggie thought. Warrentree quickly used his magic to clothe the two siblings who seemed perfectly at ease in their undressed state.

'You two must be closely related,' Maggie laughed as she took in their almost identical appearance.

One was clearly male, and the other female, but their facial features and body structures were so similar that there was no other explanation. Their hair was a soft gold, so light that it looked almost white with silver strands that practically glittered in the streams of daylight that came through the window. Their eyes were large and wide-set and maintained the unusual blueish – green color that Maggie had seen in the birds. Their bodies were lean, clearly agile and athletic, thought Maggie.

The girl spoke on behalf of them. 'I am Halle and this is my brother, Oliver. We were placed as protectors of Dylan when he was in the human world. We miss him and still worry about him. Our orders to watch over and protect him have never been revoked. We were hoping that we could come home with you to continue our duties. We won't be any trouble, we promise!'

Warrentree interjected, 'Halle, what do you mean your orders have never been revoked? You didn't tell me that you felt compelled to continue to protect Dylan.'

'Protect him from what? Who gave you the orders to begin with?' demanded Maggie.

It was once again Halle who responded. 'We don't know who gave the original orders. All we know is that the Ministry assigned us to go with Dylan when he was in the human world and to stay with him to watch over and protect him. When he disappeared through the vortex, we didn't know what to do, until Warrentree found us and brought us back with him. Oliver and I have decided that since we have never been told of new responsibilities, that we should continue with Dylan, until the Ministry recalls us.'

'Tell her the whole truth, Halle. She deserves to know,' growled Oliver at his sister. Halle glared at him.

'Tell me what?' begged Maggie, desperate to know more.

'Our instincts tell us that Dylan is in danger. We can sense it.'

'What kind of danger?' Warrentree demanded authoritatively.

Halle shrugged her shoulders. 'We don't know precisely but we can feel something is not right. We would feel better if we were close to him.'

'I'm sure that will be fine, to come home with me that is,' replied Maggie in a shaky voice. 'But I think we need to find out who placed you with Dylan to begin with and why.'

'I agree, Maggie. Let me start making some inquiries,' responded Warrentree as he ushered them all out of his office. 'I will be in touch soon.'

Maggie looked at the two shapeshifters and decided that they would be able to share all kinds of information with her about Dylan's first twelve human years of life. 'Let's go home,' she said, already thinking of the questions she would ask once they were settled, of course.

CHAPTER EIGHTEEN

Remy and Dylan moved on to their last class of the day, HCS – Human Culture and Societies. The boys were thrilled at their shared accomplishment of successfully conjuring up the transport portal, and they refused to let the menacing glare of Traysik diminish their happiness. They decided to walk to the next classroom, so that it would be easier to talk. Dylan still wasn't sure he could communicate all that well while he was flying. Even though the flying process was getting easier, he still felt more comfortable walking and talking at the same time.

'I still can't believe it,' crowed Remy triumphantly. 'I was never even close before, but with you, Little Bro, I felt so powerful.'

'I have nothing to compare to, but I know what you mean. When we were holding hands and working together, I felt... I don't know if I can even explain it... so strong, like I could do anything,' replied Dylan.

The two boys grinned their identical smiles and didn't need words to express what they were feeling. Their uncanny ability to read each other's minds made verbal communication completely unnecessary.

Thea spotted them and quickly joined the boys en route to the classroom.

'Hey Dylan, how was your first magic class?' greeted Thea, completely ignoring Remy.

'Incredible!' Dylan enthused. 'Absolutely incredible.'

'That's great,' she replied before looking at Remy. 'And what about you? Any luck today?' Remy's historic lack of success in magic was well known, much to his chagrin.

Remy smirked at Thea. 'My class was equally as incredible,' he said.

'Really? I'm shocked... you know, based on what I have heard about you in the past,' she responded.

'Well, for your information, today Dylan and I worked together, and we achieved something that nobody else has been able to do. Warmaster said we are the top of the class,' replied Remy with satisfaction. He hated his reputation for not doing well in magic and was feeling rather smug about his new -found success.

'What did you do?' Thea asked genuinely interested.

'You know we aren't allowed to talk about specific details from magic class with those outside our faction. You could get in big trouble just for asking,' Remy admonished.

'Oh please! Who would know if you told me what happened?'

'I don't know, Thea but I'm not about to take any chances. You will just have to believe me when I tell you that we were awesome! Right, Dylan?'

'We were definitely awesome,' agreed Dylan.

'That's interesting, don't you think?' said Thea addressing both boys.

'What's interesting?' responded both Dylan and Remy in complete unison.

'Well Remy, no offence but you sucked at magic before then along comes your identical twin and all of a sudden, you are at the top of the class. Doesn't that strike you as odd?'

The boys both pondered this wordlessly for a moment. Their

minds came to the same conclusion at the exact same instant. It was like firecrackers exploding in their heads as they came to the realization together. They looked at each other with wide eyes, green staring into grey. The color of their eyes deepened as their understanding of what had happened became more and more clear. Thea watched them closely and knew something was going on.

'What is it? Tell me, please...' she whispered just loud enough for the boys to hear. They all instinctively knew that an important discovery had just been made and that realization should remain secret, at least for now. Thea wanted in on it, after all, it was her comment that made the boys think about whatever it was! She grabbed each of the boys and yanked them to a stop. 'Tell me,' she ordered.

Remy clearly did not want Thea to know anything, but Dylan's thoughts tried to convince his brother that she could be trusted. *It's okay, Remy. I know I just met her, but I truly believe if we tell her to keep our secret, she will. Plus, she is so smart; maybe she will have some ideas about how to help us make our powers stronger. Please... I really like her.*

So that's really what this is about. You like her and want to impress her, right?

Well, yeah that's part of it. I can't hide that from you. But I really do think that she may be able to help us. Maybe she has heard about something like this before. She definitely knows a lot of stuff and we could use all the help we can get. What do you think?

It's against my better judgment, but if you want to tell her, I guess it's okay. But she has to promise to keep our secret. Until we figure out exactly how this works, I don't want anyone else knowing.

Not even mom and dad?

Especially not mom and dad. Agreed?

Agreed.

'Thea,' said Dylan. 'We will tell you, if you swear not to repeat this to anyone.'

'I swear with all my magical powers that I will not discuss this with anyone other than you two,' she replied with sincerity.

'Okay… after class or we're going to be late!' Remy cried, and sprinted towards their next classroom.

Thea glared at Remy's receding back and then Dylan brazenly grabbed her hand and pulled her forward. 'Come on, we can talk after school!'

Thea considered the situation for a second, and then she smiled. 'Okay,' she replied. 'We can talk after school.'

Dylan was thrilled that she didn't pull her hand away but as they approached the classroom, she let go. Dylan was disappointed as he guessed that Thea did not want others to see them holding hands, but then he perked up. After all, he had just met her that very morning and already the most beautiful, intelligent girl that he had ever met had held his hand, at least for a minute!

Remy called out to Dylan to come sit next to him near the back of the room. Thea took her place right at the front and Dylan stared wistfully at her as she sat down. Remy could read his mind and shook his head disapprovingly. *You don't like her?* Dylan inquired wordlessly of his brother.

I don't know her. Nobody does. She has no friends. Until today, she never sat with anyone at lunch or hung out with any of us, ever! I know she's gorgeous, but of all the immortals at this school, I don't see why you are falling so hard for her.

I can't explain it. But I feel this weird connection to her, like nothing I have ever felt before.

I know. I can feel it inside of you. But that doesn't mean that I understand it...

The boys' internal conversation was cut short as the teacher entered the room. She had very long brown hair that fell past her waist, with braids at the front that she tied behind her ears. Her eyes were the darkest black that Dylan had ever seen. Her face was very pretty but extremely pale, and she wore a long, floral skirt and a puffy blouse. She reminded Dylan of one of those 1960s hippies that he had seen on TV.

She stood at the front of the room and clapped her hands once. All talking immediately ceased. She smiled brightly at her students and said, 'I understand we have a new student with us. Dylan, why don't you come up here and introduce yourself to the class.'

Dylan really didn't want all that attention on himself, but the teacher smiled encouragingly at him and beckoned him with her hands. Feeling he didn't have much choice, he reluctantly walked to the front of the room.

'Welcome, Dylan,' the teacher said when he stood beside her. 'I am Vanessa Vamdercamp, the HCS teacher. As you can guess, I was human before becoming a vampire. I lived for 26 years as a human before my transformation, which on the human calendar, took place on Christmas Eve, 1966. I fell in love with a vampire you see, and he changed me so that we could be together for all time. He had been living in the human world but once I was changed, we both came here to live in the open. He thought I was too free spirited to fit in with the human world once I became a vampire, and he's probably right!

So, I have been teaching HCS ever since. That's my story. I am sure we are all very interested to hear yours!'

Dylan felt everyone's eyes staring at him, waiting for him to speak. He cleared his throat nervously, not really sure what to say. He decided to keep his story simple.

'I was raised by human parents and until a few days ago when I fell into the vortex by mistake, I didn't know that I wasn't a mortal. And now I have been reunited with my warlock family, and here I am.' Dylan moved to go back to his seat, but Ms. Vamdercamp placed a cold hand on his shoulder and stopped him.

'Dylan, your story is fascinating. Let's delve a little more deeply, shall we?'

'Well, Ms. Vamdercamp, I really don't know…'

'Nothing too personal, I promise. Now, when you say you didn't know you were a warlock, did you not notice that you had certain non-human abilities?'

'Well, I didn't have any special powers in the human world, if that's what you mean.'

'Of course, you had such powers. You obviously just didn't realize it. Think back… was there ever a time when you did something exceptional. Something that you couldn't explain?'

'You mean like wishing for something that came true?'

'Well, perhaps, but as I'm sure you are learning, wishing is not the same as magic. A wish is just a thought, but magic requires details and structural foundations.'

'Yes, I am definitely learning that,' replied Dylan wryly thinking about his magic food disasters.

'I'm referring to exceptional abilities, things that humans simply cannot do.'

Dylan thought hard for a moment. 'Right before I fell into the vortex, I was running away from these bullies who were chasing me, and I jumped over a wide stream of running water that I didn't think would be possible. It was like I flew over it.'

'Oh yes,' Ms. Vamdercamp cried delightedly. 'That is precisely what I was talking about. You see class, immortal powers can never be suppressed even if they are unknown. Just like what we discussed last class! Thank you, Dylan. That was most helpful!'

'You're welcome,' Dylan mumbled somewhat confused. 'Glad I could help.' Ms. Vamdercamp patted him affectionately on his back and permitted him to return to his seat.

'Now class, we will continue our discussion from last week...' Ms. Vamdercamp was interrupted by a hand going up from one of Dylan's classmates.

'Ms. Vamdercamp, could we, just for today at least, take a little break from the curriculum and ask Dylan some questions?'

Ms. Vamdercamp paused for a moment in thought. 'Hmmm, I don't know Sammy. Dylan – how would you feel about that? Do you feel comfortable answering some questions about the human world? I know that everyone is curious and since you have just come from there, and I haven't been back since my transformation, I think it would be very beneficial if you could share your knowledge with the class? But only if you feel up to it, of course.'

Remy nudged Dylan. 'Go on, it will save us from the boring lecture she was giving last class. And look at how excited Thea appears at the prospect,' whispered Remy to his brother.

Dylan sought out Thea with his eyes and was rewarded by her smile and nod of encouragement.

'Okay,' Dylan agreed as he once again walked to the front of the room. This time, instead of standing, he sat in the lotus position, floating several feet off the floor, the way that Thea had done that morning. Once he was settled, the questions began. They wanted to know everything about the human world. Dylan found himself laughing at some of their inquiries, but he supposed that his questions about the immortal world would sound just as ignorant.

Dylan quickly determined that showing his classmates the answers was far more effective and entertaining than just answering them with words. Dylan was relieved when his magic worked and he successfully created a large screen, similar to a movie theatre at the front of the room. When kids asked him a question, he was able to create a 3D answer and project it onto the screen so that they could better experience his responses. Dylan found his magic being tested as he also tried to incorporate feelings into his answers. He wanted his classmates to feel the cold of the snow, and the warmth of the sun. The stickiness of cotton candy sweet on their tongues and the sour, bitterness of bile after you throw up (Dylan couldn't believe that in the immortal world, nobody ever got sick!). Dylan showed them the four seasons, sunrise and sunsets, twilight and dawn. He showed them the human version of school, and mundane tasks like going to the grocery store. He let them see what it was like to go skateboarding, bike riding and waterskiing. Through his memories, Dylan showed them movies and television and radio, computers and tablets and cell phones. And then he was asked this:

'Do humans believe that immortals are real?'

Dylan paused for a moment, to collect his thoughts before he responded. 'I think most humans want to believe that immortals are real. Magic, eternal life, super powers… all that stuff. But there isn't any real proof in the human world that those things exist. There are people who believe it is true and people who will say that they have encountered supernatural beings, but most humans won't admit that they believe immortals are real. But they sure do fantasize a lot about it. You should see how many books and movies and TV shows are made about immortals.'

'Show us,' his classmates clamored. 'Show us!'

And so Dylan did. The students and Ms. Vamdercamp were mesmerized by the images that Dylan put up on the screen. The human version of wizards, witches, warlocks, vampires, werewolves, elves and fairies, Yetis, the Loch Ness Monster, giants and ogres. They watched at first in silence before laughter erupted from all corners of the room.

'They think witches are only girls,' called out one male witch. 'And warlocks are only boys!' responded another.

'They think vampires must have blood in their bodies to stay strong,' said a vampire girl with eyes as clear as glass, indicating that she hadn't consumed any blood for a long period of time.

Ms. Vamdercamp allowed students to continue to critique what they had seen for a few more minutes before she finally interrupted.

'What you are witnessing students, is that humans have strong misconceptions about immortals. What Dylan hasn't shown you are the ways in which humans often fear and despise those they think have special powers. Immortals have been hunted and killed by humans. Even though we have powers far beyond theirs, humans can be cunning and we are not totally indestructible. Innocent people who were believed to be immortal were tortured and murdered. Humans, for the most part, are not able to understand us, nor would they accept us. We must therefore ensure that our secrets are protected. That is the only way to guarantee our safety and survival. Living in the immortal world lets us be ourselves. And those who serve in the human world place their own safety at risk, to perform the services that they do. The human world is full of wonderful things, and as Dylan has shown us, things that I never could have imagined when I was a mortal. But it is also fraught with danger.'

At that moment, the bell rang, signaling the end of the school day. 'Class dismissed,' called Ms. Vamdercamp.

As the students filed out of the room, many approached Dylan with welcoming sentiments, clearly interested in hearing more about his life in the human world. Dylan beamed happily at his new- found popularity and wondered if they would all still be interested in him once the novelty wore off.

When the majority of students had dispersed, Dylan and Remy saw that Thea was still waiting for them. *Let's find somewhere private to talk* Remy said to Dylan in his mind. Dylan nodded his head and motioned for Thea to follow them. Dylan and Remy both wondered what insights Thea might have and how their new- found knowledge could be put to good use, specifically whether they could somehow uncover the mystery of their forced separation.

CHAPTER NINETEEN

Remy, Dylan and Thea lingered outside the classroom as the hallways rapidly emptied of students, rushing to get out. When the noisy chaos of the students' mass exodus from the building had finished, the three decided to head to the Brooding Forest, since there would unlikely be anyone else there to overhear their impending conversation. They didn't notice the small figure hiding behind a semi-closed doorway who overheard their plans.

'Why is it called the Brooding Forest?' asked Dylan.

'Well…' drawled Thea. 'Let's just say it isn't the most cheerful place to hang out.'

'It's actually kind of creepy,' interjected Remy. 'It's always so dark under all the trees, and so quiet. Not many creatures live there, except for a handful of ogres, and they won't be interested in us. They inhabit the deepest part of that forest, and we won't be going so far in. It will give us lots of privacy. We have to fly to get there, you okay with that, Dylan?'

'Yup, I'm feeling good after today's magic class. Flying should be a breeze. Oh – a breeze – that's funny! Get it?' he laughed.

'We might be identical, but we clearly don't share the same sense of humor,' Remy replied with a grin to take the sting out of his words.

'Let's go already!' said Thea impatiently. 'I'll lead the way.' Thea pulled her wand from out of her back pocket, muttered a few words that Dylan couldn't understand and waved the wand with a twist of her hand. The result was that Thea produced what looked like a comfortable, although somewhat battered up armchair. It was dark green in color, made of what looked like crushed velvet although the material looked faded and thread bare in small places. It reminded Dylan of the furniture that his human grandparents had in their house back home. Dylan looked at Thea quizzically and she returned his look with a sheepish grin. She then took off her school uniform and tossed it up into the sky. The sweater flew on its own accord back towards the main school building, to find its resting place until she returned to school again.

'It's my favorite way to travel,' she said biting her lip. 'It's the same chair that I conjured up when I first learned to use my powers to fly. I know it's not the most flashy way to get around, but I like it.'

With that, Thea settled into her chair and then took off at lightning speed. Dylan felt an urgent tugging on his arms, and when he looked down, he realized that his own sweater was desperately trying to pry itself off of his body.

'Oops, sorry sweater,' he muttered as he quickly tore it off and like Thea, tossed it high in the air. Dylan took a quick glance over his shoulder to watch his and Remy's uniforms soaring back to school without them.

Dylan and Remy raced to catch up with Thea. Dylan had never flown at such great speed before, and he had to concentrate hard to avoid the obstacles which floated in the air. Remy could see that Dylan was struggling a bit, trying hard not to crash, and knew exactly what to do.

Let's fly higher, Remy telecommunicated to his brother. *We can go above all the houses where it's clear. You up for that?*

Up for that – ha – you just made a pun too! Looks like we do have a similar sense of humor! Replied Dylan in his mind.

Okay, okay... are you ready?

'Ready.'

'Then up we go!'

Remy turned his body so that he was practically standing upright in the air and shot his body upwards. Dylan followed his brother, without any hesitation and watched the houses disappear beneath him as he flew higher than he ever had before. Once they were well above the tops of the highest structures, Dylan was able to relax since there weren't any more obstacles in his way. He was able to look down as he flew, and he marveled at the world beneath him.

The sky here is always so blue, without any clouds, he thought. *But already, I am missing the changing weather we have at home.*

That's just the way it is here, responded Remy in his mind. *The Ministry has forbidden anyone to manipulate the weather, except for themselves. Same with day and night. You will get used to it.*

After a short time, Remy indicated that they would soon be making their descent as they approached the Brooding Forest. They could see Thea streaking by below them in her chair and knew that they would be arriving at the same time.

Dylan prepared himself for landing and concentrated hard as the ground came closer and closer. He saw Remy land perfectly a split second before him, and then Dylan flexed his knees and hit the ground hard. He stumbled a bit but regained his balance, thankfully before Thea noticed. Thea beckoned the two boys over to where she stood, and they found a fallen log to comfortably sit on.

Dylan looked around. This forest looked exactly like ones

found in the human world with hundreds of trees in various sizes surrounding them. Even though they were at the outer edges of the forest, it was still very dark, and Dylan could only imagine how much worse the lighting would be at the core of the forest. *It must be almost pitch black in there,* he thought and shuddered just a little. The air was chilly, and he shivered but maybe not just from the cold. Unlike a human forest, there weren't any sounds. The place was as silent as a tomb. Thea and Remy didn't look at all worried, so Dylan decided that there was nothing to fear. No question, the place was creepy like Remy had told him, but he trusted his brother and knew that he had nothing to be afraid of. After all, they wouldn't have come here if there was any danger, right???

Thea pulled her wand out of her back pocket and waved it in a small circle over her head. Instantly they were bathed in a small pool of dim light, just enough that they could see each other clearly. Dylan realized yet again how clever Thea was, and he heard Remy's mental groan in his mind. Remy was not enjoying Dylan's romantic interest in the wizard who had always remained so aloof before his brother's arrival.

'Okay,' said Thea getting down to business. 'Tell me everything you know about your birth and we will see if we can figure things out.'

Together, Dylan and Remy told Thea everything they knew about the circumstances of their birth. They also shared what their father had told them about the prophecy and the Ministry's requirement of recording all births, which led them to believe that maybe the prophecy was not just a rumor. After all, why would the Ministry require multiple births be reported if they weren't specifically watching out for these four siblings to be born?

Thea paid close attention and listened without interrupting. When Dylan and Remy finished talking, she sat in quiet contemplation for a few minutes.

'Well,' she finally replied, 'you can't be the siblings in the prophecy. There were only three of you, and the prophecy said there would be four. Unless... are you sure you don't have another sibling somewhere?'

Remy rolled his eyes. 'You think I wouldn't know if I had another brother or sister?' he asked with sarcasm dripping from his voice.

'Well, until the other day, you didn't know about Dylan or the other brother who is still missing. It's possible that there is another one out there, right?' she answered in an equally snarky tone.

'My father would have mentioned it. He told us everything else, so I can't imagine he would hold back information about a fourth child. That doesn't make sense.'

'No, I guess not,' Thea conceded. 'Unless your parents didn't know.'

'You're saying that they had a fourth child and didn't know? Are you out of your mind?' retorted Remy.

'They were told that two sons died, which was clearly a lie. So maybe they were lied to about having another kid as well,' she shot back.

Remy and Dylan looked at each other in wonderment. *Could that be possible? No, we must somehow just be connected to it,* they determined at the same time. *There is no way that we are the children of the prophecy.*

With their uncanny ability as twins to read each other's minds, the two boys at the same moment lifted their right arms to run their hands through their hair. Thea was watching them closely and noticed something unusual.

'Hey,' she said. 'Did you realize that you even seem to have the same birth marks on your inner arm?'

'Yeah, bizarre isn't it?' replied Remy. 'I know we are practically identical, except for our eye color, but you have to admit that it seems impossible for any two beings to have the exact same placement of freckles! That's a little extreme, don't you think?'

'Well, let me get a better look. I'm sure I saw the similar marks on both of you, but maybe they aren't actually identical,' she replied.

The three kids huddled closer on the log. Dylan and Remy each turned their right hand over to reveal the skin on their inner wrists. Sure enough, both boys had the identical markings – three dots in a straight, diagonal line in the exact same place. Thea grabbed Dylan's arm, and pulled it closer to her face to scrutinize.

'Hmmm… those freckles look like Orion's Belt,' Thea stated matter of factly.

'What's Orion's Belt?' asked Remy. 'I've never heard of it.'

'That's because you don't pay enough attention in HCS class. Don't you remember when Vamdercamp gave the lecture on human astronomy and how mortals use star constellations to navigate in the human world?'

'Uh no…' Remy replied a little embarrassed for having been caught not paying attention by this know-it-all wizard.

'You don't remember her talking about the North Star? The Big Dipper?'

Remy gave her a blank look. Thea sighed heavily.

'Okay, what about when she showed us pictures of Egyptian pyramids and Mayan ruins? And how they lined up perfectly with the stars? Don't you remember that at least?'

Recognition dawned on Remy's face. 'Yeah, I remember the pyramids. Those were cool to learn about.'

'Do you also remember that we learned humans use stars to navigate their way when they are travelling and that some people even use stars as a way of predicting the future? What did Vamdercamp call that again? Horror scopes? No, that's not right, hour scopes? Shoot, that's not right either…' Thea racked her brain for the correct term.

'Horoscopes?' interjected Dylan, trying to be helpful.

'Yes, that's the right word!' exclaimed Thea.

'There are definitely people who believe in horoscopes,' Dylan replied. 'My human mother used to read hers every day, but I don't know if she actually put much faith into it. But I do know that some people genuinely believe that stars could predict the future. I have heard that people would pay big money for an astrologer, which is a person who claims that they can read the meanings in the stars, to map out their life based on the position of the stars at the moment they were born. It always sounded kind of silly to me. I never believed that horoscopes were true.'

'Dylan, you seem to know a lot about star constellations. Do you know anything else about Orion's Belt?' asked Thea.

'I know a little about Orion's Belt,' replied Dylan. 'My dad, my human dad, bought me a telescope at home. We used to look at the stars sometimes. He liked to tell me the stories behind the constellations.'

'I don't know any stories about the stars,' Thea exclaimed.

'Tell us!'

'I don't know too much, just what my dad told me. He said Orion was a character from Greek mythology. That's like an ancient human civilization where there were lots of myths about gods with supernatural powers and other immortal creatures, like flying horses and birds that can be resurrected when they die. Anyways, Orion was a half god, his father was Poseidon, the god of water. Orion was the greatest hunter on earth but he was killed by a giant scorpion and then when he died, Zeus who was the most powerful of the gods, placed Orion in the stars. Orion's belt is made up of three stars and since they are easy to spot, it lets people find the other stars that make up his body and sword. Sometimes Orion's Belt is called the Three Kings. That's all I know.'

As Thea and Remy were contemplating this information, they heard a low, menacing growl coming from somewhere close by. Their heads shot up in unison, their eyes all trying to scan their surroundings for the source of the rumbling snarl. The darkness outside of their intimate circle made it impossible to see much more than a foot in front of them. The grumbling noise became louder and in a flash before they had time to react, a large, hideous looking beast stood before them. It looked like an impossibly giant man with razor sharp teeth and wild looking black hair covering its head and much of its body. Its shoulders were hunched but even then, the creature towered over them.

'An ogre,' breathed Thea in fright. 'They aren't too smart, but they are strong and have nasty tempers.'

'What should we do?' whispered Dylan terrified that they were about to become the ogre's next meal.

'We have to get out of here,' retorted Remy with desperation in his voice. 'Now!'

Thea grabbed for her wand, at the same time that Remy shot up into the sky. But before Dylan had a chance to use his powers to escape, the ogre reached out a massive hand and clamped it around his neck. Dylan felt himself being lifted off the ground as the hold around his throat tightened.

Remy stared in horror, hovering in the sky out of the ogre's reach while Thea looked helplessly on from her perch in her flying chair. Dylan tried to struggle to escape, but he was no match for the ogre who maintained an iron clad grip on his prey. Dylan's hands were free and he tried to pry the ogre's fingers off of his throat, but to no avail. Dylan wanted to use his powers to escape but he didn't know what magic he could use. His mind whirled as he desperately tried to come up with a plan.

We have to tele transport through the portal! Dylan heard his brother screaming in his mind.

We don't know how! Dylan's thoughts raged in response.

Yes we do. We did it in class today. It's our only hope, Remy concluded. *I'm coming in close. When I reach you, grab my hands and concentrate on creating a portal to get us home. Ready?*

No, I can't do this!

You can't do this alone, but we can do this together. It's your only chance! Ready?

Ready...

Remy eyed the exact position of his brother in the ogre's grasp, took a deep breath, and swooped downward like a bullet, straight towards Dylan. When he reached him, he grabbed his hands in his own, and silently screamed *NOW!*

To their intense relief and amazement, the portal appeared, twisting and turning in the air right between the brothers. The portal entry was not large but would be big enough for the boys to fit through, if they could just get Dylan out of the ogre's paws!

'Hey, you big, stupid oaf,' taunted Remy to the ogre. 'Get your hands off my brother!'

The ogre didn't respond. He didn't see Remy as any real threat.

Then Remy used his magic to flash beams of bright light into the ogre's eyes. But even that didn't work. The ogre was stupid, but he knew his orders not to let the child free. So the ogre maintained his grip on the boy even though the light was hurting his eyes and making his head feel funny. Remy was desperate. He knew their powers weren't strong enough to maintain the portal for much longer.

But just then, Thea barreled down and landed on the ogre's head. The ogre instinctively used his hands to swat away the girl, and the instant he did, Remy tugged Dylan hard and the two boys shot through the portal and disappeared. Dylan felt a sharp pang of fear and regret that Thea had been left behind. He worried about his new friend and wished that she was with them. Remy's thoughts were contrite as he realized what he had done by forcing Dylan into the transport portal, but he mentally assured his brother that Thea would be fine. And Remy was certain that she would be, for he knew that a dumb ogre was no match for the brilliant wizard. Fortunately for Thea, the ogre wasn't smart enough to realize that when he pushed Thea off his head, he used such great force that it propelled her far enough away that it gave her time to escape before he could catch up with her. Thea clambered onto her chair and took off faster than she had ever travelled before.

The ogre watched her retreat with puzzlement in his eyes. He looked down at his empty hand where just moments ago, the boy had been ensnared. The ogre was afraid. He had not carried out the orders that had been given to him, and he stomped his massive feet in frustration. He lumbered back into the depths of the forest and hoped that he could hide in his cave. But he had no such luck, for when he arrived at his destination, there sat the mean, little elf waiting for him.

The elf heard him approaching and stood up expectantly. When he saw the ogre was alone, the elf rushed over and elevated himself to face the ogre eye-to-eye.

'Where is he?' demanded Reus. 'Where is the boy?' 'Did you eat him? You better not have caused him any harm you moronic idiot! Where is he?'

The ogre looked into the angry, raging eyes of Reus and crumpled to the ground in a huge thud. Reus sighed with impatience and decided he needed to change tactics.

Reus too lowered himself to the ground and placed a gentle hand on the beast's head. 'Now, now. I'm not angry, just anxious to take the boy back where he belongs. If you ate him, I'm sure we can get him out of you… it's not like you would have chewed him…' Reus knew that to get the boy out of the beast's stomach, only one of them would survive, and it would not be the ogre.

'No eat,' rumbled the ogre. 'No eat. Not allowed.'

'Good, good,' replied Reus somewhat relieved that he would not have to slice open the dumb creature to get what he needed. 'So, where is the boy? I showed you which one. You saw what

175

he was wearing. You understood your orders. Where did you put him?'

'Gone,' the ogre stated, his booming voice quivering with uncertainty as to what would happen to him.

'Gone?' Reus questioned. 'How could he be gone? Gone where?'

'Hurt eyes. Hurt head. Then…' the ogre lacked the words to explain what had happened next, so he used his hands instead to try to convey to Reus how the boy had escaped. He waved his hands in the twisting motion of the transport portal, and then hit himself on the top of the head to signify Thea's brave actions. Finally, he opened his hands wide to show that they were empty. And simply said again 'Gone.'

Reus was astonished. He couldn't believe that the boy had managed to escape the ogre. And he couldn't believe that Remy and Dylan had successfully created a transport portal. Almost nobody in the realm could accomplish that. The feat required such great powers that it was almost impossible to achieve. He hoped desperately that they had survived it…

Reus stared at the ogre, his temper flaring, his blood boiling but taking his anger out on the ogre would be useless. Reus shook his head in frustration and briefly contemplated what Baltazar was going to say. He knew that he had to report this immediately and after the last failed attempt with the sleeper serpent, Reus realized that he was going to have to face Baltazar's wrath. He had failed yet again. But even more important than his own survival, Reus worried about the fate of the boys. It seemed impossible that they would come out of a transport portal that they created by themselves unscathed. Just coming out of it in one piece, even if those pieces were not in the right place, seemed highly unlikely.

Reus took a deep breath, snapped his fingers and to the great relief of the ogre, disappeared.

Remy and Dylan did not successfully make it home in the transport portal, but they were close! After disappearing into the portal in the Brooding Forest, the boys felt themselves spinning and twisting as they hurtled through space. It was the strangest sensation – it felt as if their bodies had come apart into tiny, little pieces and yet still remained connected. It was almost like a magnetic force held the components of their body together rather than sinew and muscle.

When the journey ended, instead of landing at their home, as they had planned, the portal spit them out only a hundred feet away from their front door. They could see their house hovering in the sky, offering them the safe haven that they desperately craved after their close call with the ogre. The boys whooped with joy having successfully transported pretty close to their desired destination. And even if they didn't come out exactly where they had intended, at least they came out with their bodies intact and perfectly formed.

Dylan's thoughts immediately returned to Thea. He wished he knew that she was safe and had escaped the ogre unharmed. Remy heard Dylan's mental distress and reassured his brother that Thea was more than capable of outsmarting an ogre. The beast would never be able to capture her, Remy soothed his brother through his own thoughts. Dylan's mind could not stop thinking about the worst despite his brother's calming influence and just as Dylan was about to turn around and head back to the Brooding Forest, a note magically appeared in his hand.

I'm fine, in case you're wondering. See you tomorrow.

We have lots to talk about.

Thea

Dylan sighed loudly in relief and the boys flew home, but they didn't feel like themselves. Their bodies felt really strange. Their joints felt looser than usual as if they were rag dolls, floppy all over. It took them longer to get home than it should have because they were so uncoordinated. They wanted to get home and lie down to recover. But interestingly enough, in the time it took to get home, and float upstairs into their now shared bedroom, the boys felt almost back to normal. The effects of the portal were clearly short lived, to their great satisfaction.

Remy and Dylan sat on Dylan's bed having an internal conversation. They were mulling over what they had discovered with Thea about their birth marks and wondering whether that had any significance at all. And they once again celebrated their great escape from the ugly ogre through the use of their combined magic.

Together we are really special, thought Dylan.

I wonder how much more power we would have if we found our missing brother, responded Remy.

Starting tomorrow, I think we have to look for him.

Agreed. But where do we start?

We need to see our delivery records. Where would those be, do you think?

Only the Ministry will have them.

Is D3W3 part of the Ministry?

Could be. Let's start there. But no mention of this to mom or dad!

As the boys were working out their next move, Via floated over and perched lightly on Dylan's shoulder. She was happy to have him back home. She nuzzled sweetly under his chin and Dylan smiled in delight.

'She is definitely attached to you,' said Remy out loud.

'She sure is,' interjected a voice from the doorway. 'You certainly have a way with animals, Dylan,' the voice crooned.

Dylan looked over to see who was speaking to him. Two individuals stood side by side. Dylan had never seen them before but something about their eyes, their unusual color, looked so familiar to him. He gazed into their faces, straining to recall where he had seen these two before.

'Why Dylan, don't you recognize us?' she asked.

When Dylan shook his head no, she gave a small laugh. 'What about now?' she said.

And to Dylan's amazement, their bodies tremored for a moment, and then, standing before him were his beloved dogs, Halle and Oliver. Their clothes lay in heap on the floor. Dylan rushed over to hug them close, he had missed them so much. Dylan crouched down to be on the same level as his beloved pets. His shapeshifting canines gazed into his eyes with adoration and wagged their tails excitedly. Oliver tried to scamper into Dylan's lap and knocked him over in the process. Remy laughed to see his brother splayed on the floor with the dogs straddled on top of him.

'I wonder why they're here,' mused Remy. In response, Halle barked several times and a low growl escaped from her throat.

'I don't know, but it doesn't sound good,' responded Dylan.

And Halle nodded her head in agreement.

In the blink of an eye, the dogs' bodies again began to shake and once more the animals shifted back to human form. The two, without any embarrassment, casually started to dress themselves in front of the boys.

'We are here to protect you, like we have done for your entire life,' Oliver said.

'Protect me from what?' asked Dylan.

'Sleeper serpents, ogres, what's next?' Remy reminded him. 'Having extra protection is something I wouldn't turn down. I don't know why exactly, but I feel like something's not right. Like something is out to get us.'

'I know what you mean,' concurred Dylan.

'We sense it too,' piped in Halle. 'But don't worry we will be staying close by. We will protect both of you.'

Dylan grinned. 'Just like it was at home…our other home. You were always there watching over me, except at school. You couldn't go to school with me there and you can't come to school with me here.'

'Why not?' demanded Halle. 'Who says we can't go with you to school?'

'Oh Halle,' soothed Dylan. 'It's not necessary. Nothing will ever happen to us at school. We are surrounded by teachers and other students and the administrators. You worry too much. Besides, it's hard enough being the new kid. I don't want to be there with babysitters, no offence you understand.'

Halle bristled at the insult. 'We are not babysitters. We are protectors and we cannot fulfill our purpose if we are apart from you.'

'I promise you, we are perfectly safe at school. Please Halle, try to understand…'

Oliver sidled up to Dylan and pushed himself as close as he could into Dylan's side. 'I get it, Dylan,' he said. 'We will be here waiting for you both when you get home.'

'You really can be so stupid, Oliver. This is not a good plan,' Halle snapped. 'We should be with the boys at all times.' Halle was angry that Oliver wasn't following her lead, the way he always had in the past.

Oliver just gave Halle a goofy grin. 'They will be fine. Have a little faith, sister,' he replied.

'Fine,' Halle muttered. 'If that's the way you all want it, but I don't have to like it and I sure hope that I never have to say I told you so!'

Dylan laughed at the antics of his former dogs. Their personalities as talking shapeshifters were exactly the same as they had been when they were unspeaking canines. Dylan gazed at the two for moment, debating whether to ask the question that was burning in his mind. He finally made his decision and inquired softly, 'Can I ask, how's my mom and dad?'

Oliver looked downcast and Halle shook her head sadly. 'They won't ever give up looking for you. They love you too much. They aren't doing so well, but they are leaning on each other for support, so I think they will manage. But they won't ever be the same,' she said with tears welling in her turquoise eyes.

'I just wish I could let them know that I'm doing alright. I wish I could send them a message or something…'

'Don't worry, sweetheart,' said Maggie who had suddenly appeared in the doorway. 'I already have. And I promise, whenever I can, I will send them updates just to let them know that you are safe and loved.' She came over to hug her son and held him tightly in her embrace. When she pulled away, she scrutinized Dylan's face and was relieved to see that he looked pleased with her response. 'Are you happy to see your faithful companions again?' she asked gesturing to Halle and Oliver.

'I'm so happy, I can't even tell you how much. Halle and Oliver have been with my family… my human family since I was a newborn. Someone left them in a basket on our front porch when I was just a few days old. I was told that they had little ribbons around their necks with their names. I grew up with them. They were my best friends,' Dylan explained. *Remy,* Dylan called out frantically in his mind. *How much of our conversation do you think that mom heard?*

Remy scrutinized his mother's face carefully and responded in his thoughts. *I don't think she heard anything except for you asking about your human parents. She doesn't look worried and she would have said something if she thought we were in any danger.* The boys both felt relief and Dylan exhaled loudly.

Maggie smiled at Dylan, completely misunderstanding the reason behind his sigh. 'And now they're back and they can stay with us for as long as they want,' she reassured her son.

'That might be a while,' replied Halle warily. Everyone, except for Maggie knew why, but nobody said a word.

CHAPTER TWENTY

Reus stood in the main entryway of Baltazar's underground castle and waited to be summoned by his master. He was even more nervous than the last time he had been here. This was his second failure to bring the boy to Baltazar, and Baltazar's reactions could be so unpredictable that Reus didn't know what to expect. He knew that his death was a possibility and he desperately hoped that his centuries of loyalty would save him from extinction at Baltazar's command, for it wasn't just his own life that was in peril!

A large mirror in a golden frame hung on the wall to Reus' left. That mirror had been there for over two hundred human years. As Reus stood waiting for Baltazar, the mirror silently slid upwards on the wall to reveal a small doorway. Reus knew what to do. He walked over slowly, prolonging the dreaded conversation that he knew was about to take place. Then he grasped the small knob and pulled. A long, dark tunnel lay before him. Reus pulled himself up and into the entrance, and then began to crawl along the cold, stone floor. The passageway had many twists and turns through the underground lair and dim lighting showed Reus which tunnels he should take. He couldn't see much, so he just carefully followed the small illuminations that guided his way. Finally, Reus hit a dead end. A stone wall blocked his ability to move forward and when he twisted around to retrace his steps, Reus found that another barrier made of rock was now preventing him from going back.

Reus waited. And waited. Nothing happened. Reus snapped his fingers futilely to use his magic to get him out of the stony cell but as he knew, his magic was useless here. He was completely trapped within the underground tunnel. Reus began to panic. Maybe this was Baltazar's way of punishing him. He would be left here forever. And then after what seemed like an eternity, a glimmer of light could be seen coming through one of the walls that encased him. Reus turned his head to get a better look. The hole was far too small for him to climb through, but it gave him some hope that perhaps this ordeal was coming to an end. Although he didn't know if what awaited him would be even worse. Over the course of several hours, the hole slowly widened. At last, Reus could poke his head through to the other side. There sat Baltazar behind his massive desk, staring at Reus.

'M-m-master…' stuttered Reus with fear trembling in his voice.

'You have failed me yet again, Reus,' replied Baltazar coldly, the voice in his mind fueling his anger as the stone glimmered hidden beneath his clothing.

'Yes, I know. The ogre let him escape.'

'So, you blame the ogre for your failure, Reus? You gave the ogre his orders. You were in charge of the creature. Using that logic, then am I to blame myself for your incompetence? Are you suggesting that I am at fault?'

'No, of course not! Baltazar please…let me explain,' Reus begged.

'What is there to explain? Your second attempt to bring me the boy was as abysmal as your first. Perhaps I am at fault. I don't think you understand what is at stake, Reus. Our entire world, every being who lives here and even those who inhabit the world of humans is at risk. Without the boy under my control, I fear for the continued existence of all immortals.'

'Yes, master. I understand.'

'Do you indeed? Reus, I have already told you more than any other immortal knows. You are aware of the prophecy and its contents, and yet you do not demonstrate an understanding of the magnitude of the situation. Reus, I am once again going to reveal to you something that only the Ministers have been privy to. I am going to impart upon you one more time the urgency and necessity of your orders. And if you fail me again, then you will die. I am entrusting you with this secret in the sincere hope that it will motivate you, since nothing else I have done seems to have had the proper influence. You have been faithful to me for many centuries and it pains me to think of your demise and yet...' Baltazar's words trailed off, leaving Reus with no doubt that this would be his final chance.

Baltazar stood up and walked over to the hole in the wall that had Reus' head protruding. He placed an ice-cold hand on Reus' cheek in a fatherly gesture and sighed. Then Baltazar put both his hands inside the hole, one on either side of Reus' head and pushed in an outward motion. The stone was no match for the vampire's strength and it crumbled away, leaving sufficient room for Reus to crawl out of the confining space and stand on shaky legs next to his master.

'Come and you shall see for yourself,' commanded Baltazar. Wordlessly, Reus followed him out of the library into a hallway that Reus had never been in before. They walked in silence with Reus trailing slightly behind his master until they reached a large, imposing door that was guarded by three ogres. Each beast was uglier than the next and drool dripped out of their mouths, pooling in a puddle on the floor. Baltazar looked in distaste at the mess and stepped carefully to avoid the sour smelling liquid.

The ogres let their master pass between them to approach the massive door. Baltazar withdrew an old- fashioned looking key from his pants pocket and placed it in the lock. A loud click echoed through the hallway as the heavy door swung open. Baltazar motioned for Reus to follow him. In his rush to keep up, Reus did not pay careful attention to the placement of his feet and it was only when he heard the loud squishy sound that he realized his left foot was standing squarely in a pool of ogre drool. He raised his foot and grimaced as the sticky, foul smelling liquid stuck to his shoe. But he could see that Baltazar was impatient, so Reus ignored the mess and continued to walk.

When they passed through the ogre guarded doorway, Reus found himself in a confusing underground maze. Passages led off from the trail they were on in all different directions. Lanterns hung in random places that cast strange shadows on the narrow walkways. The walls were old looking and marked with the passage of time. Reus hurried to stay close to Baltazar. He was terrified that he would get lost in this place, where his magic would not work, and be left there forever. Baltazar walked with confidence and deftly maneuvered them through the jutting pathways. Suddenly, Baltazar stopped and Reus crashed into the back of his master. Baltazar glared at Reus who took a step backwards, but still they did not speak.

Baltazar stared at the wall directly in front of them. He spread his fingers wide and placed each digit on a specific crack in the wall. Once all ten fingers were in place, he pushed his fingers gently against the stone. A gentle rumbling could be heard which quickly escalated to an ear shattering roar. The ground beneath their feet trembled as the wall slid upwards, revealing yet another imposing trail to follow.

This time, Reus and Baltazar took only a few steps before they could hear the sounds of rushing water. The cobbled stone was wet and slippery beneath their feet and while Baltazar was easily able to maintain his assertive stride, Reus had to slow his pace and tread carefully as he moved forward. After walking for only a few minutes, the source of the water became clear. To their right, a turbulent river splashed water droplets at their feet and crashed over the rocky path that was only two feet above the fast - moving current. Reus kept his head down to navigate the treacherous path and did not see the eight headed beast until he was literally right in front of it.

This creature was unlike anything that Reus had ever encountered. Each head had the eyes of an insect, with hundreds of visual receptors that glinted eerily in the dim light. Fangs protruded from the mouths that gaped open in threatening grins. The eight necks were elongated and able to stretch for many feet in any direction. The creature had claws like a lobster with sharp, pointed edges that could rip any intruder apart with very little effort. If that wasn't intimidating enough for any individual who tried to get past, the beast had both legs and fins on its bottom. Four pairs of legs would allow the creature to give chase on land, and four sets of fins would make it fearsome in the water.

'A creature of my own making. Well, with some help from Atticus, of course,' stated Baltazar.

The eight headed monster hissed at Reus, but Baltazar soothed the beast to allow them both to pass unscathed. Reus walked directly behind his master to keep himself within Baltazar's protection. They continued to walk until Baltazar abruptly came to a halt. He gestured to his right and Reus could see a small boat tied to the ledge of the rocky shore. At the stern of the boat, sat a figure, his ancient eyes watchful and knowing. He greeted Baltazar with a slight inclination of his head, and it was clear that the two were well acquainted.

Baltazar beckoned Reus on to the boat and when both were settled, the immortal in the back of the boat pulled a wand from his waistband. Then the venerable wizard pointed the wand straight ahead and muttered a spell that Reus could not understand. A bolt of light came pouring out of the wand and the boat took off down the river at an impossible speed. The current was fast and turbulent. The boat was small and did not appear strong enough to withstand the forces pushing it forward. Yet the paltry craft remained steady on its course as it crashed through the waves. Reus hung onto the sides of the boat desperately trying not to become dislodged and go flying out, but Baltazar and the wizard sat calmly as they bounded forward towards their final destination.

Finally, when Reus thought he would not be able to hold on for much longer as his arms were weak with effort, the river slowed. The boat drifted forward on the wizard's magic until it came to a complete rest against the rocky banks.

'Thank you, my old friend,' said Baltazar to the wizard.

'I shall wait here for you, as always,' came the quiet reply.

A question suddenly popped into Reus' head. He had to know the answer, even if it meant irritating Baltazar and the words poured out.

'How can the wizard use magic here?' Reus asked deeply

puzzled since he knew of only one immortal whose powers were not rendered useless in Baltazar's underground lair.

Baltazar replied to the question without hesitation and seemed unperturbed by Reus' inquiry. 'When Atticus created my residence, he left my wizard friend here with his powers. The wizard is my most trusted confidant and advisor. *He* has never failed me in all his centuries of service.' Reus' second-rate status in comparison to the wizard was made abundantly clear, and Reus winced as he contemplated what this meant for him.

Baltazar deftly hopped out of the boat. Reus was not so graceful on his still unsteady legs. They walked only a few feet and then a final doorway stood before them and their destination. Directly adjacent to the doorway, a small blinking light flashed red in the darkness. Baltazar stepped up to the light and pressed his right eye against it. The door began to open.

Reus stretched his neck to see what was behind the doorway, but to his surprise, he didn't see anything spectacular, as he had been expecting. It looked like just another wing of the castle, but much smaller and less ornate than Baltazar's quarters. They stepped through the door and into a hallway. There were several rooms that ran off the main hall and Baltazar walked confidently, knowing exactly where he was going. At the end of the hall was a large open space, and it was there that Baltazar found what he was looking for.

Reus stepped forward and at first, he just saw several immortals relaxing together. He noticed a couple of fairies, an elf or two and a few either wizards, witches, or warlocks – he couldn't tell at this point. And then as his gaze wandered around the room, his mouth dropped open in shock. Playing some sort of board game with a companion was Dylan Dover. Or maybe it was Remy Warston, Reus couldn't tell since they were identical. *How did he get here,* wondered Reus in astonishment?

'Seth,' called out Baltazar, 'can you come here please, for a moment if you don't mind.'

The boy who looked just like Dylan and Remy but answered to the name of Seth immediately stood up and walked over to Baltazar at a fast pace, as if not to keep him waiting.

'Hello, Baltazar,' he said with extreme politeness although Reus was able to detect a slight quiver in the child's voice. 'I wasn't expecting to see you again so soon.'

'I want to introduce you to someone,' replied Baltazar. 'Seth, this is Reus, he has served me well for hundreds of years, and I am hopeful that he will continue to serve me for many more centuries. Isn't that correct, Reus?'

Reus was in such shock that it took him a moment to find his voice. 'Yes, of course Baltazar.' Reus continued to stare at the boy, and from up close, Reus was instantly able to see the one difference between this child and the others. Seth had eyes of intense blue that looked warily at Baltazar.

'Good. I'm glad that's settled then,' stated Baltazar. 'You may go now, Seth. Thank you.'

Seth nodded at Baltazar and quickly returned to his game. Baltazar turned to Reus and fire burned in his eyes. 'Do you understand what is going on here, Reus? Do you now see the importance of bringing Dylan to me?'

Reus looked at Baltazar with uncomprehending eyes and Baltazar growled with impatience.

'Reus, don't you see? I must keep the siblings apart. They cannot find each other, and yet Remy and Dylan have already been reunited. I must have Dylan under my control so that I can sequester him away, the way that I have done with Seth. It is our only hope for preventing catastrophe. They cannot be together.'

'May I ask why, Baltazar? Why for all these years have you been so insistent on keeping the siblings apart? When I delivered them as infants to you, I did not know your reasons or your plan for them. I now understand that you placed Dylan in the human world and kept Seth here in your own castle. I don't know what you did with the fourth child. But I still cannot understand the urgency of keeping them apart.'

Baltazar gripped Reus' upper arm in a vise-like hold, and propelled him back down the hallway, out of ear shot of the others.

Baltazar hissed at Reus. 'We have been warned of these four siblings, who together will be so powerful that they will be unstoppable. They could bring about the complete destruction of our world.'

'So why not just kill them, at least one of them? Wouldn't that solve your problem?' Reus questioned, feeling the need to keep up his ruse more than ever before.

Baltazar stared at Reus as if he were a complete idiot. 'Reus, the realm may one day need their powers. They are too precious to destroy, but they must be controlled. The fourth child is still in place and only I know where that is. I must be the one to determine if and when they shall meet, and I shall be the one to train them to use their powers to serve the Ministry. This cannot be left to chance. It is too risky to continue to let the boy exist freely. Leave Remy with his parents but you must bring me the other one. You must bring me Dylan, and this time, I will accept no excuses. Am I making myself clear to you?'

Reus nodded in assent. He understood all too well. One more failure and that would be the end of him, with his own objective being destroyed in the process.

'Then let us go now,' Baltazar commanded as they began their way back through the heavily guarded trail.

As they walked, Reus searched his mind for a fail proof plan. This time, there could be no errors. He would have to take care of the matter himself.

CHAPTER TWENTY-ONE

The next day, Dylan found himself back in the classroom, alone with Thea as they waited for Reus to arrive.

'I've been thinking,' Thea stated.

'That could be dangerous' joked Dylan in reply. He smiled at Thea to ensure that she realized he was only teasing.

'I've been thinking about you,' she responded seriously.

Dylan felt himself blush. *How can this girl have such an insane impact on me?* Dylan wondered as he consciously tried to restrain his physical reactions to her. *Breathe,* he commanded himself and looked away to try to gain control again.

'So like I was saying. I've been thinking a lot about you, and Remy of course. Specifically, about the birth marks that you and Remy share.'

Dylan felt his breathing slow to a more normal rate and yet at the same time, he was gripped with intense disappointment that Thea had been thinking about both him and Remy. That wasn't quite the way he wanted her thinking of him! Dylan waited for her to continue.

'I believe that it is literally, absolutely and completely impossible for two individuals, even if they are identical twin warlocks, to have the exact same markings on their bodies like you two have. That's just not possible. And yet we all saw it and there is no doubt at all that the placement of your freckles is one hundred percent identical. So, I have concluded that your birth marks cannot be random. There's no way it just happened like that. So that means…'

'So that means that there is reason behind it. The birth marks must have some special significance. We must have them for a specific reason.'

'Exactly,' concurred Thea. 'So, what are *we* going to do about it?'

'We?' questioned Dylan.

'You aren't planning on excluding me, are you? Of course, we! And aren't you lucky to have me volunteer to help you. You can hold your thanks until after we figure this out, but don't worry, I know that you're grateful!'

Dylan was thrilled that Thea wanted to help. Not only because he wanted to spend all the time with her that he could, but because he genuinely believed that with her brains, she could be of great benefit. *Remy and I need her,* decided Dylan conclusively.

'So, what's the plan? Did you and brother talk about what you are going to do next?' she inquired.

'We think we should start by seeing if we can get a hold of our delivery records. Maybe that will give us something to go on.'

'Okay, great. That's at least a starting point. When?'

'Today after school? No time like the present!' Dylan responded. Thea nodded in assent. She lived on her own and therefore had nobody that she had to check in with or who would be wondering where she was after school. Their conversation was cut short when Reus suddenly appeared before them.

Reus gave them a curt nod before he launched right into the first lesson of the day. Dylan was initially irritated that Reus had so abruptly interrupted his discussion with Thea, but within

194

minutes, Dylan found himself engrossed in Reus' lecture as he discussed what he referred to as 'Cross-Faction Perspectives'. Dylan's attention was riveted as he began to learn more and more details about the varying powers and magical abilities of the different immortals that inhabited this world. Thea too was mesmerized, and Reus went into far more details than any of her other teachers had ever done before. Both students were amazed at the depth of Reus' knowledge. He seemed to know all the inner workings of the various factions, their strengths and their limitations.

Dylan was primarily fascinated by vampires, since his new-found knowledge was nothing like the portrayal of fictional vampires that he had grown up with. Dylan learned that vampires had supernatural abilities when it came to strength and speed. They didn't actually need any blood in their bodies at all, since they were technically not alive. But as Reus explained, the only times that a vampire could feel any physical sensation was when they did have blood inside their bodies. Without blood, vampires were totally numb all over. The more blood inside of them, the stronger the physical sensations they could experience. *How bizarre!* Dylan thought. *I never in a million years would have guessed that. Well, if I would ever have even believed in a million years that vampires are real!*

Dylan was also astounded to discover that vampires didn't have to bite a human and suck their blood, although Reus told him that it was an option. Vampires could use anything sharp, their teeth, a fingernail, another object, to draw blood from anywhere on a human body. And they could then create a small puncture in their own skin in order to let the human blood penetrate their body. Only the tiniest amount of human blood was needed to bring sensation back for the vampires. But the more blood in their bodies, the more intense the feelings and the longer it would last. Dylan learned that it was easy to tell how much blood vampires had inside their bodies at any given time simply by looking at their eyes. Without any blood inside of them, their irises would be completely colorless but the more blood they had, the darker their eye color would become. Reus further explained that vampires were extraordinarily hard to injure or kill. Without blood in their bodies, they would feel no pain at all. And their physical strength made them almost impossible to destroy.

'Reus,' asked Dylan. 'Has there ever been a time that you know of when a vampire was killed?'

Reus paused for a moment and pursed his lips, thinking about whether he wanted to share this information with his students or not. Having made his decision, Reus responded in grave tones. 'Once and only once has a vampire been killed in the immortal world.'

'Tell us, please Reus,' begged Thea. She was floating on the air in the lotus position and leaned so far forward stretching towards Reus that she almost lost her balance and toppled over. But she quickly regained her equilibrium and stared intently at Reus, waiting in anticipation for him to share this story with them.

Once again Reus contemplated how to proceed. He decided that in order to gain Dylan's complete trust, which would be needed for whatever plan he came up with to capture the boy, that he would tell them at least the partial truth of what had happened. Some of these details were not well known to anyone outside of the Ministry, but Reus hoped that Baltazar would see the release of this information as a necessary part of the cause, and of course, he would not reveal more than was necessary. He would stick to the Ministry's version of the events that transpired.

'There was a vampire who lived amongst us, when our world was in its infancy, whose name was Cius Vamnodstrom. Cius was of the belief that the immortals should rule the human world. He was very vocal about his dissatisfaction with the truce that was created. He did not want to live here. He wanted to stay with the mortals and continue his existence on the other side of the vortex.

Atticus and Callista considered his request to remain in the human world, but they decided that he posed too much of a risk. Cius was too out of control, too much of a rogue to be trusted, and so his application was denied. Cius did not take this rejection well. When other vampires were permitted to cross back and forth through the vortex to bring blood to those vampires who resided here without humans, he saw this as a great insult. He began to cause great problems for our leaders, who remember, were still very new in their power as rulers of the realm. He was seen as a threat to the peace and harmony that the Ministers and their Deputies were trying so hard to establish.

Cius was warned repeatedly but to no avail. The final incident which condemned Cius to his death was when he stormed the border guards and tried to forcibly enter the vortex to the human world. The border guards had magic but Cius was cunning. His intelligence combined with his incredible speed and strength enabled him to kill one of the guards. Cius was captured before he managed to escape into the vortex and was brought before the Ministers for justice. The leaders had no choice. They could not risk the potential of Cius escaping from any sort of confinement that they could construct, and they had to set an example for everyone else. Cius had to be punished and he had to be stopped.'

'So how did they do it?' asked Dylan softly.

'The Ministers meted out justice as they saw fit. They had two options for his destruction. Death by fire, in which case Cius would not feel a thing. His body would be numb, and he would simply be consumed in flame. Or...'

'Or what?' Thea and Dylan demanded in unison.

'Human burning,' whispered Reus. 'The most dreaded of all possible outcomes for vampires. Human burning requires that the vampire's body be saturated with blood so that their physical sensation is at its peak. Their skin would be so sensitive that the simple touch of a feather would resonate sharply within the vampire's body, causing pain from something so slight. So imagine what the vampire would feel in this physical state if their body was lit on fire.'

'Oh,' gasped Thea, her black eyes wide with shock.

Reus nodded gravely. 'And that is how Cius was sentenced to die. Atticus and Callista decided that only they and their two Deputies, Alexia and Baltazar would be present to witness his destruction. When he was given his last opportunity to speak, Cius apparently revealed something that shocked those four who were present. A curse or perhaps a blessing...a prophecy...' Reus' voice trailed off.

'What did the prophecy say, Reus? Please, you must tell us!' begged Dylan.

Reus shrugged his shoulders. 'There was allegedly something

said about four siblings who would have the power to either save or destroy our world. That is all I know. Only the leaders who were present with Cius know for certain what was said if anything at all, and they harbor this secret amongst themselves. Perhaps it was nothing more than the rantings of a condemned vampire. If there was any truth in what Cius said, then it is not something that I am aware of. This happened so long ago, and it is almost never spoken about by anyone. Cius' name does come up from time to time, usually as an example for those who may be inclined to defy the rulings of the Ministry for his destruction is a well- known fact but his final words... well, those are never spoken of and whatever he said remains only with our leaders, who in their wisdom, deny any sort of prophecy at all.'

Thea and Dylan were silent, lost in their own thoughts. Finally, it was Thea who broke the silence. 'Reus, do you believe in the prophecy?' she inquired.

Reus thought for a moment, not willing to let these children know the full extent of what he knew to be true. 'Yes, Thea. I suppose I do.' And he let it go at that.

The bell rang signaling the start of the lunch break. Reus looked directly at Dylan and said, 'Just remember, Mr. Dover that prophecies, if they do even exist, are nothing more than predictions. It is how we use our powers and the decisions we make that determine our future.' Then Reus snapped his fingers and in an instant, he vanished.

Thea and Dylan were animatedly dissecting the information that Reus had given them. As they walked to the cafeteria, they leaned in close together so that others could not hear what they were discussing. Their gait was slow, their feet shuffling along at a speed that would be more suitable for humans than immortals with great powers. And their presence did not go unnoticed.

'Hey! Dover or Warston, whatever your name is, and you, Thea who doesn't even have a last name, what's the big secret? What's going on with you two?' shouted a familiar and yet very unwanted voice from above.

Dylan and Thea looked up and saw Traysik hovering over them, staring down with a menacing glare.

'We would tell you, but I doubt you would be capable of understanding, Traysik. You need a modicum of intelligence to follow this conversation,' retorted Thea with disdain dripping from every word.

Traysik swooped down and planted himself directly in their path. 'Is that so?' he demanded.

'Yeah, that is so,' Thea stated firmly, her voice steady. 'Whatcha gonna do about it, Traysik?'

'I'll show you what, you stupid, insignificant nothing of a wizard,' he hissed.

Thea took a step back and pulled her wand out from her waistband. Traysik raised his right hand and pointed his middle finger directly at Thea. Instinctively, without any thought whatsoever, Dylan jumped between them, desperately hoping to prevent a fight from breaking out.

Unfortunately for Dylan, this was no playground fight, like he was used to in the human world. As Dylan launched himself between the girl that he had such strong feelings for, who happened to be a wizard, and the boy who seemed to hate him, who was already a well-trained warlock, he was hit with full magical power from both sides. Waves of pain coursed through his body, sending him into convulsions. Dylan crashed to the ground unconscious, and the back of his head struck the walkway – hard. As his limbs continued to shudder, Traysik took off, flying away at full speed, as if that would keep him out of trouble.

The ground beneath Dylan started to turn red with the blood that was seeping out of a massive gash in the back of his skull. The left sleeve of his sweater had been pushed up from when he fell and his arm could be seen lying at an awkward angle. One of the bones in his arm could be seen almost protruding through the exposed skin.

Thea dropped down to her knees next to her friend, not knowing how to help him. She kept shouting for help as she took a visual inventory of Dylan's injuries. Thankfully his tremors had stopped but he was still out cold. Thea used her wand to create a small pillow to absorb the blood that was still pooling underneath Dylan's head. She gently placed one hand underneath his skull to lift it off the ground and place the cushion beneath him. As she did, Thea felt the sticky wetness of the blood flowing over her fingers as her hand touched his gaping wound. Once the pillow was in place, she softly ran one finger over Dylan's broken arm, and was able to confirm without any doubt that there was a bone out of place. With a feather-like touch, she covered the traumatized area with her palm, hoping to keep the bone from being displaced even more.

In only a few moments, a huge crowd had gathered. Remy was practically in hysterics seeing his brother lying in his own blood, still unconscious. The Warlock Magic teacher, Ms. Warmaster materialized right next to Dylan. She crouched down to further assess his injuries. Her face was fraught with concern and her forehead was wrinkled with concentration. She could see he was breathing and knew that his life wasn't in any danger, but she could also tell that the damage was significant. She didn't want to touch his head for fear of worsening the injury. Ms. Warmaster knew that Dylan would need a lot of powerful magic to heal him and that he would have to be bedridden for many days before he would be up and about again.

'Move your hand, Thea,' the teacher instructed in order to get a better look at Dylan's arm. Thea did and placed her hand on Dylan's forehead instead. At that moment, Dylan opened his eyes. It was clearly apparent that his pupils were dilated, and his irises were so dark that they appeared almost black.

'Thank goodness, you're coming around,' sighed Ms. Warmaster in relief. 'Just stay lying down, Dylan. You've suffered quite extensive wounds, but we will get you taken care of. Don't you worry about a thing. The school has already called for medical assistance. They should be here any minute now.'

Dylan looked up into the kind eyes of his teacher and took a mental inventory of his body. Remy, hearing his thoughts looked on in disbelief. Dylan sat up and with a small, apologetic smile said, 'I'm fine. Really. I'm sorry for worrying you and causing so much commotion.'

'You're not fine, Dylan,' snapped Thea. 'Lie down. Your head is bleeding profusely, your arm is shattered, and you were unconscious for several minutes. So stop being a hero!'

'My head is bleeding?' questioned Dylan. 'That's strange. My head doesn't hurt at all.' Dylan gingerly touched the back of his head with his fingertips. When he pulled his fingers away to examine them, he could see some dried blood stuck to his skin, but there wasn't any fresh blood. The wound wasn't bleeding anymore. He displayed his fingers to Thea to demonstrate to her that she was over-reacting. There wasn't any blood pouring out from his head, and he wasn't feeling any pain.

'Well, what about your arm? It's broken. I could feel the bone out of place,' Thea replied somewhat confused. The blood that lay puddled on the ground was clear evidence that she wasn't crazy, so how did the gash on his head close up so quickly?

Dylan looked down at his right arm and then waved it in the air. 'No problem, see?' he crowed triumphantly.

'Your other arm,' Thea replied drily.

Dylan lifted his left arm and began to twist it in all directions, flexing the muscles, and moving it around. Clearly, there was no break.

'Hmmm…' Ms. Warmaster grunted. 'Well, we should all be grateful that you are not as seriously injured as we first suspected, Dylan. But I still want you checked out by the medical team when they arrive, and Thea, I assume you will be able to tell me what caused Dylan's mishap to begin with?'

'Yes, Ms. Warmaster. I know what happened, but can we talk about it later? I would like to stay with Dylan, if that's okay. You might want to speak to Traysik. If you can find him, that is. He took off pretty fast.'

'Thank you, Thea. You may accompany Dylan when he is taken by the medical responders. You can tell us your version of events later. I will have the principal locate Traysik.'

'I'm going too,' demanded Remy.

'Yes, of course dear. And your parents will meet you at the healing center,' Ms. Warmaster responded.

At that moment, the principal of the school, Mr. Fairshelf arrived with the medical responders in tow. Mr. Fairshelf's wings were still beating fast as he landed softly next to Dylan on one side, with the medical attendants on the other. Relief washed over his face as he could see that Dylan was doing fine.

'Well, this is not as bad as I was expecting,' he said.

'No, luckily Dylan appears to be fine,' Ms. Warmaster gushed happily.

The two medical responders bent down to be closer to Dylan. One looked into Dylan's eyes. 'Well, your pupils look fine. No dilation, same size, that's good,' she stated.

No dilation thought Thea. How is that possible? Can his pupils go back to normal so quickly after that much of a head trauma? 'But he was unconscious for several minutes,' Thea informed the medical attendants. 'And I saw his eyes when he first opened them. His pupils were huge!' Thea looked into Dylan's eyes again and saw that they were in fact normal, and the dark color that had been there only minutes before had softened to a light grey.

'Well, they look fine now, and that's what is important,' was the official medical response. 'There is a lot of blood on the ground though.'

'Well duh… his head was gushing blood,' Thea snapped at the stupidity of the comment.

'It's not gushing blood any more, that's for sure,' was the confident response.

'This doesn't make any sense,' Thea muttered under her breath.

'Well, Dylan we are going to take you in for observation. Just to be sure that you are okay.'

'No problem,' Dylan replied as he started to stand up.

'Oh no you don't,' the attendant said as she gently pushed Dylan back down. With a wave of her arms, a stretcher appeared magically underneath Dylan's body. 'Now lie back and enjoy the ride. Who is coming with you?'

'I am,' Remy asserted, as he pushed his way forward through the crowd. 'Me too,' interjected Thea. The two hastily pulled their school uniforms off and threw them into the air. Dylan's sweater began to vibrate uncontrollably and Dylan, realizing what was happening, easily sat up to remove it from his body. He didn't even wince when he had to move his arm that had seemed to be so badly fractured just a few moments before. Then before he could be chastised, he lay back down as he had been told. The medical staff looked at Dylan with disbelief and confusion. The one closest to him shook her head.

'I've never seen anything like this before,' she muttered. 'Come stand closer,' the attendant instructed Thea and Remy. The two medical responders, Thea, and Remy all stood shoulder to shoulder with Dylan's stretcher floating in front of them at the height of their mid-sections. Another wave of her hands and the five of them were tightly ensconced in a transparent bubble. The bubble floated upwards and away from the school, moving at a rapid pace to the healing center.

Back on the ground, the students began to scatter – all except for the vampires. With Dylan now gone they were free to indulge. A vampire knows that the legends which exist in the human world about blood sucking undead demons, such as themselves, are comical. Myths that vampires need human blood to survive are ridiculed by the vampires who know the truth. As immortals, they need nothing to survive, at least physically. They have no need of nutrition or water or even air to continue their existence. They will exist for eternity unless something obliterates their bodies, which is why vampires, who fear almost nothing, are so afraid of fire. Fire can easily incinerate their bodies, and that will bring about their destruction.

The only reason that vampires truly crave blood is because as a vampire, they have none of their own. To become an immortal, all of their bodily fluids would have first been drained completely from their human carcass, and then the eternity sustaining venom would be injected by their creator which allows the transformation to take place. In their new immortal state, without blood feeding their nerve endings, vampires have no physical sensations at all. Only the ingestion of human blood will temporarily restore their sense of touch. Devoid of blood, vampires feel no physical pain, but also they cannot experience tactile pleasures. Vampires, who were all at one time human beings, still hunger for physical sensations even as immortals. Just as a human requires physical tenderness and affection for their mental well-being, vampires do not lose this desire upon becoming immortal. In fact, this emotional need is intensified in the vampire psyche since they do not have the ability to feel anything in their normal state of existence.

Equally laughable to vampires is the human notion that vampires must bite their victims, usually on the throat, to obtain their blood. While this would certainly be a very efficient method of blood acquisition, it would also be messy and very conspicuous. While in the human world, vampires know that their continued existence and that of all immortals, depends upon their ability to hide their secrets from humans. And unlike other immortals who can exist forever without the need for human contact, vampires depend upon interactions with humans to obtain blood.

While immortal blood could be substituted for that of

humans to satisfy the vampire cravings, it is well known by vampires that immortal blood is less potent than that of humans. Immortal blood does not have the same effects in the vampire's body. Immortal blood brings less intense sensations that last for a much shorter period of time. So if a well - intentioned immortal offered blood to a vampire, it would be accepted for to refuse it would be seen as a breach of etiquette, however, the gift would not be received with the same enthusiasm as that of human blood. Knowing this, vampires require interactions with humans in order for their blood to be obtained, which can then be shared with other vampires. And this means that vampires cannot leave visible signs that can be detected by humans. A bite to a mortal's jugular vein would quickly fill a vampire with human blood, but would also leave behind a dead human cadaver, which would surely bring human scrutiny and possible detection. Therefore, vampires have perfected ways of obtaining human blood without having to kill, or maim or even alert their victims. Blood can enter the vampire's body through any opening in their marble hard skin. Yes, they can suck blood, which perpetuates the human myths of vampires, but the preferred method of blood acquisition is not through the mouth at all, but rather through strategically placed piercings that open the vampire's skin just prior to coming into contact with blood. The vampire then just needs to create a small wound on the human which would cause blood to flow, unless the human already has started bleeding from a different cause. When the blood comes in contact with the opening on the vampire's skin, the blood will be instantly transferred from its human host to the vampire. This method is definitely less efficient and more time consuming for the vampire, but it is easy to conceal these interactions with humans, who usually don't even feel the exchange of blood at all. Vampires might explain it as similar to receiving a mosquito bite where a person will often not realize that it is happening until later.

The vampires were now all surrounding the massive pool of blood which Dylan had left behind. While the vampires anticipated that the blood of a warlock would not be as inviting to them as that of a human, it was still better than nothing, and they didn't have to work to obtain it. Each vampire pricked a small hole somewhere on their body – most chose a finger or two, but some made a larger incision on an arm or a leg. In a very organized and coordinated way, the vampire students formed a circle around the puddle of blood that remained on the ground. When the circle was complete, one by one, each vampire took a step forward to dip their exposed incision into the blood and let it seep into their skin. Once their turn was fulfilled, the vampires stepped politely out of the way to make room for the next.

As each vampire came into contact with Dylan's blood, they each reached the same surprising and joyous revelation. This blood was more potent than that of not only any immortal, but any human blood that they had ever ingested. There was something special and unique about Dylan's blood that sent immediate intense feelings through their limbs. And while the vampires were sorry that Dylan had been hurt, they each silently thanked him for giving them this precious gift. Without knowing it, Dylan had just made himself a whole lot of new friends and allies. Traysik had yet to be found.

CHAPTER TWENTY-TWO

The bubble carried its occupants high over the buildings that floated in the bright blue sky. From his position lying on the stretcher, Dylan could only see above him, and he couldn't help but compare the brilliance of this world to that of humans. The color of the sky here was so blue that it seemed unreal, which clearly it was. There was simply no equivalent for this particular shade of blue on earth. There were no clouds, just vast emptiness that seemed to stretch endlessly and forever. It was very beautiful but also daunting and eerie.

Soon Dylan felt the bubble start to descend and he twisted his position to get a better look at what was coming. Beneath them, the structures were getting closer and Dylan momentarily panicked as he envisioned this fragile capsule bursting if it hit something, but his fears were unfounded. The bubble was well under control and drifted purposefully towards its destination. One building, significantly smaller than the others, came into view. It was in the shape of a half moon, and its pale green exterior reminded Dylan of the color of hospitals in the human world. This building was so small that it was dwarfed in height by the others, and its perimeter was less than a quarter of the size of any other that Dylan had seen in this world before. Even his own house was bigger than this!

The bubble drifted downwards, its speed decelerating as it got closer to this tiny structure. As they approached, the roof of the building split down the middle and opened wide to accept them. Dylan gasped in horror. When the roof opened, its insides were revealed to be a bright scarlet color, with a yellow border around the periphery. As they got closer, Dylan could see that there appeared to be thin, hair-like projections surrounding its edges. *This reminds me of a Venus flytrap,* thought Dylan, once again apprehensive. *You will have to explain to me later what that is,* replied Remy in his mind. *I have never heard of that.* The bubble continued to lower itself, drifting downwards into the open roof, or as Dylan thought, the large carnivorous mouth waiting to devour them!

Nobody else seemed to be the least bit concerned, so Dylan tried to control his fear. Once the bubble had entered the building, the jaw-like roof snapped shut and threw them all into complete darkness. Dylan screamed, he couldn't help it. *This is like a bad horror movie. We are going to die being eaten by a hospital that devours its patients! Hashtag: come for treatment, stay to die.* Dylan couldn't see his brother's face in the darkness, but he clearly heard his thoughts. *Maybe you hit your head harder than you realize. I think you are over-reacting just a tiny bit, Little Bro. Just relax. And what the heck is a hashtag?* The bubble continued to slowly drift down. Dylan's thoughts were racing... *How can we keep going lower? This place is so tiny we should have hit the floor by now!* At that moment, he felt all movement stop. Then an ear-splitting POP shattered the silence and the bubble disintegrated.

'Now what?' whispered Dylan expecting one of the medical responders to reply. But there was only silence.

'Remy? Thea?' called Dylan. Nothing. He was alone in the dark in a strange place and all the people he had travelled with to get here were gone. He couldn't even hear Remy's thoughts anymore.

'What is happening here?' he cried out in anguish. This couldn't be the end. He wasn't old enough to die, especially like this – devoured by a hospital that was clearly not a hospital at all! Dylan's survival instinct kicked in. He couldn't just lie on the stretcher and wait to be the next course! He didn't know how far above the floor he was, since he couldn't see but then he remembered…he was a warlock! He could use his magic to help him. In his mind he envisioned a flashlight, but not just any flashlight. The biggest, strongest, flashlight that could ever exist. Bright enough to penetrate the darkness of outer space, like astronauts would use to explore Jupiter, he thought. Dylan concentrated on all the details, like he had been taught – the size, the shape, the texture of the handle…and was rewarded when the object suddenly appeared in his hand. Dylan clicked the button and immediately, the space was illuminated with bright, white light. As Dylan had suspected, he was completely alone in a tight, confined space. He shone the light around the room and saw three white washed walls, completely barren. But where there should have been a fourth wall, Dylan saw empty space. Below the stretcher, there was a floor, but it was transparent, as if it was made of glass and yet he couldn't see anything below the clear barrier. He could only see the reflection of the stretcher glimmering eerily in the beam of light as it bounced off the floor.

He needed to get off the stretcher and see what was going on but remembering his years of water safety training in swim class, he wasn't about to just jump off the stretcher! In his mind, he conjured up a pebble. He held the rock in his hand and rubbed his thumb along its smooth edge. Then he whipped it with all his might at the floor. He didn't hear a sound when the rock made contact with the floor and the barrier held firm. Just to be extra safe, Dylan used his magic again to create a larger rock, much heavier than the first. It was so heavy that Dylan could not throw it to the ground; he was not even able to lift it up off the stretcher. *Use your magic,* he instructed himself. He focused on the task and using his powers, the massive boulder rose into the air and floated weightlessly to the middle of the tiny room. And then the huge rock fell straight down to the floor but even its heavy mass did not make a sound when it made contact with the ground. Dylan shone his light to investigate and found that the floor held. Not even a dent!

Knowing it was safe to stand on, Dylan slipped off the stretcher and placed his feet firmly on the floor. Then he walked slowly towards the space where the fourth wall should have been. He was grateful for the flashlight that illuminated his way. Dylan took one step and then another. Slowly and cautiously working his way forward until he could not walk a single step more. An invisible obstruction blocked his progress. He couldn't see it, but he could feel it. He tried to puncture it with his hands, but it was like punching an impenetrable wall which he couldn't break through. Dylan was frustrated and scared. He didn't know what else to do. He crumpled to the floor and put his head down between his knees to think.

Just then, when Dylan's despair was at its peak, he heard a whooshing noise and looked up, not sure what he would find. Had help finally come or was he about to be dessert? The room suddenly was bathed in light and the darkness disappeared. Dylan blinked several times, trying to get his bearings. A man who looked like he must be hundreds of years old stood before him. He had kindly eyes, a gentle smile and more wrinkles than anyone Dylan had ever seen before in his life! The man wore a white robe, tied at the waist with a red sash. His head was bald with creased skin that looked soft and papery. Despite the man's ancient appearance, he stood up straight and had a regal bearing.

'Hello Dylan. I am Chai. How are you feeling?' he inquired in a soft voice, as if not to scare Dylan any more than he already was.

'I'm fine,' Dylan sputtered looking around, completely disoriented. 'Where are Remy and Thea? What have you done with them?' he demanded, coming to his senses.

'Not to worry, Dylan. They are in the waiting lounge. I'm told that your parents are there as well. I needed to have you in isolated observation. It was critical that I be able to observe your response to certain stimuli to assess the extent of your injuries. From what has been described to me, you should be a lot worse off than you appear to be.'

'I just told you, I'm perfectly fine.'

'Hhmmm…let me ask you some questions then.'

Dylan nodded in assent.

'How were you feeling when you realized that you were alone in the darkness?'

'Truthfully, I was terrified.'

'Yes, yes a perfectly reasonable response. And you wanted to be able to see, correct?'

'Of course.'

'And so you wanted light.'

'Yes, that's why I created an extremely powerful flashlight, so that I could see.'

'Hmmm...'

'What does that mean, hmmm? I needed light; I used my powers to make a flashlight. That makes perfect sense. See, I told you, I am 100% fine. Please, I want to go home now.'

'Dylan, why would you create a flashlight which only provides beams of illumination where you aim the light. Why did you not use your powers to light up the entire room?'

Dylan bit his lip and thought for a moment. 'I guess I didn't think about that,' he responded sheepishly. Dylan laughed nervously. 'That would have been a better option,' he conceded.

Chai nodded his head and came over to where Dylan was sitting. Chai put his wrinkled hand on Dylan's shoulder. 'I think it's best if I admit you overnight for continued observation. Just to be sure that you are in fact, completely healed. You took a hard hit to your head and I don't want to release you prematurely. Let's get you admitted and then you can have your visitors come see you. Okay?'

Dylan couldn't help it. Tears welled up in his eyes. He didn't want to stay in this strange, scary place. Especially not alone!

Chai could see that Dylan was visibly upset. 'Please Dylan, you don't need to be frightened. I just want to keep you under observation. Just a few tests to see how you respond and when I am confident that you are fully recovered, you can go home.'

'I don't like it here,' pleaded Dylan. 'The building looks like a Venus flytrap – like it wants to eat anyone who comes inside.'

'You knew that? I'm amazed, Dylan. I don't think anyone has ever before commented on the design of the building. I don't even think anyone realizes that it is meant to mimic the plant from the human world. For that matter, I don't think that most immortals even know what a Venus flytrap is, not unless they have had contact in mortal societies. How do you know about the Venus flytrap?'

'It's a long story,' Dylan muttered. 'But why would you construct your hospital to look like a carnivorous plant? That's just creepy!'

'Ah, but she serves a function, young man. This place is not a building. She is in fact, alive. But not to worry, she is very well trained. She safely lets in those who are supposed to be here. If someone tries to enter without the proper authority... well, let's just say that escaping her trap would be quite impossible. Fortunately, she doesn't need to feed often, and we have never had a problem with intruders. You don't need to worry, Dylan. You and the people who accompanied you here have the Ministry's permission. You are all safe and well protected while you are in my care.'

'Can I please see my family now?' Despite Chai's reassurances, being held in a flesh-eating plant for medical observation did not rank at the top of Dylan's bucket list! He was frightened and desperately wanted his family.

'I'm going to send someone in to get you settled. I will go get your family and fill them in while you are being admitted. I promise they will be with you shortly.' With a few words uttered softly under his breath, Chai disappeared from the room. His ability to teleport was confined solely within the confines of the medical center, courtesy of Atticus who provided Chai with this ability to make his job performance more efficient. *How did this child know about the Venus flytrap?* Chai wondered.

Chai rematerialized in the waiting lounge where he was met by the worried gazes of Dylan's family. Maggie immediately jumped to her feet and rushed over to where Chai stood.

'Where is Dylan? Is he okay? Can we see him now?' the words came tumbling out of Maggie at rapid speed. Ben stood beside his wife, holding her hand and waiting for Chai's response.

Chai looked intently into their faces and was instantly overwhelmed with a distant memory from years before. He recognized them. Chai's eyes scanned the room to see who else was present, and quietly sucked in his breath when he saw the exact duplicate of Dylan perched on the edge of a chair next to a young girl. *This cannot be,* he thought in a panic. *I will have to report this to Baltazar. What is he going to do?* Chai had thankfully not had any contact with Baltazar since that dreaded day when the infant warlocks were born, and he had to participate in the most evil deception that he could have ever imagined. But Baltazar had been true to his word and left him alone since.

Chai had not thought about that day since it happened, but now his emotions flared up, wracking him with guilt, regret and fear. Chai's mind churned, his thoughts tumbling on top of each other as the siblings' delivery came rushing back in vivid detail. Just as he felt an overwhelming urge to blurt out everything that he knew, along with a profuse apology for his role in the subterfuge, a warming sensation against his hip instantly quieted his emotions. A melodic voice crooned softly in his head, erasing all doubts. In the front pocket of his robe, the small, round stone glowed, radiating its heat outwards penetrating Chai's body. His mind immediately calmed, he no longer felt the urge to divulge what he knew, and in fact, he sensed the importance of keeping his knowledge hidden. Chai realized that he would have to re-establish contact and advise Baltazar that two of the males had been reunited. *Maybe this is part of Baltazar's plan? I am so relieved to see that at least two of the infants have grown and thrived. I wonder what became of the other two.* Chai fully regained his composure. He knew exactly what he had to do.

'Dylan appears to be recovering well, from what seems to be a blunt force trauma to the back of his skull. He clearly lost a significant amount of blood, based on the witness accounts but I am happy to report that there is no longer any sign of an open wound. He is however showing some minor impairment in cognitive thinking, so I want to keep him here overnight for continued observation.'

Maggie cocked her head to the side and stared intently at Chai. 'What did you say your name was?' she inquired.

'I am known simply as Chai,' he replied softly with recognition in his kind eyes. There was a moment of silence and tension crackled in the air.

'I remember you,' she whispered in response. 'You were there when the boys were born. You were the Master Deliverer.'

'Yes. I no longer am involved in deliveries. After your…situation, I asked to be removed from those duties and reassigned. I have been working here ever since.'

'You told us they were dead. You showed us their lifeless bodies. You held our boys in your arms and they disappeared. But that was a lie. Clearly, that was a lie! Where is my other baby? Where is he? What did you do with him?' Maggie was raving and becoming hysterical. Ben was enraged as understanding dawned on him. He clenched his fists in anger. It was Remy who intervened to calm everyone down.

Remy jumped off the chair and placed himself between his parents and Chai. 'Hey, you don't know that Chai lied to you,' Remy said in a soothing voice. 'You wouldn't have done something so awful, right? There must be some explanation.' Remy raised his arms up with his hands spread before him in a gesture of peace. Chai instantly noticed the distinctive markings on Remy's inner right wrist. Chai clearly remembered the identical pattern on the second and third born male warlocks that he had delivered and whom Reus had taken immediately after their birth.

Chai stood there, not knowing how to respond. He certainly couldn't tell them the truth. Baltazar's orders were very clear and despite the passage of time, his commands still carried the same threat as they had when they were first issued. The inner voice in his mind reinforced Baltazar's orders, softly whispering instructions that overtook all of Chai's independent thoughts. Clearly, the parents still had no idea about the fourth child, the female, who he had allowed to be taken as well. Chai's regrets were quieted by the words he heard so clearly in his mind and he repeated the explanation out loud for the benefit of the parents.

'I don't know how to explain what happened to your children,' he said sadly. 'I remember so clearly handing the first child over to you, and then holding your other babies. I remember them disappearing. I don't have any idea what happened after that,' replied Chai. Technically, what he said was accurate. 'There must be some very powerful magic that saved your other son,' he continued. 'I wish I could tell you more.' Chai was satisfied with his response, and he wasn't the only one.

Chai cleared his throat and decided to try to steer the conversation back into safe territory. But he had a sinking feeling that the parents were not going to relent and would not give up in their pursuit of the truth.

'Shall we talk about Dylan's condition?' Chai queried in a hopeful voice.

'Dylan is very special to us. We just got him back and if anything happens to him...' Maggie's voice broke off as tears overwhelmed her. Concern for her son combined with the recognition of the Master Deliverer threatened to push her over the edge. Her body trembled with emotion and Ben gently guided her to a chair.

Ben looked directly into Chai's eyes, trying to assess whether he could be trusted. Chai gazed back, his face clearly demonstrating his remorse for what had transpired when the boys were delivered. Ben's shoulders slumped. Chai was in charge of his son's care. What choice did he have but to trust him?

'Dylan was raised by mortals,' Ben informed Chai. 'We don't know how, but he stumbled into the vortex from the human world. He knows nothing of how he was placed there, he only knows that he was raised with this family from infancy. He was adopted by them when he was only a few days old. We have not been able to learn anything of the circumstances that led him there or back to us.'

Chai nodded his head slowly in contemplation. *Clearly Baltazar placed him in the human world, but I wonder why...* 'Perhaps that better explains Dylan's reaction when I had him under isolated observation.' Chai quickly described Dylan's reaction to the darkness.

'Magic is still really new to him. He's still learning,' piped up Remy in response. 'But you should see how good he is. He picks things up so fast, you wouldn't believe it! And, you should see what we can do together!' Remy quickly realized that he had revealed more than he should have. He clamped his mouth shut and groaned inwardly at his mistake.

'What can you do together?' Maggie asked with trepidation. She did not want her sons to be anything more than regular warlocks. Those with extraordinary powers in the immortal world did not go unnoticed by the Ministry. They would be under intense scrutiny if they did in fact have unusual powers, and Maggie did not want to risk her sons being taken from her again.

Just then, a fairy flew into the room. Her long blond hair streamed out behind her, and her dimples flashed as she gave them all a warm smile. 'Dylan is ready for company now,' she announced in a tinkling voice. 'Come with me!'

Maggie, Ben, Remy and Thea all followed the fairy out of the waiting lounge. A short corridor with only one door was visible. The fairy ushered them through the doorway and to their great relief, there sat Dylan, hovering in the air in the lotus position. Maggie rushed forward to embrace her son and pulled him into her arms. Dylan was so relieved to see her that he gripped her as hard as he could and buried his face into her shoulder. 'There, there,' she soothed repeatedly as she stroked his hair.

One by one, each of the others were able to hug him. Dylan was a little embarrassed when Thea had her turn, but he definitely did not push her away! This might not be the way he had fantasized about but knowing that she cared so much about him made Dylan flush with pleasure.

'So what's going on?' Dylan asked. 'Did Chai tell you anything?'

'Just that he wants to keep you for observation, sweetheart.

Nothing to worry about. And I am going to stay with you, so you won't be alone,' Maggie replied.

'Are you allowed to stay with me?' asked Dylan somewhat skeptical but hopeful that his mother could remain with him.

'Let them try to stop me,' she said fiercely before they all broke into laughter.

'Okay then, it's getting late. Why don't I take Remy and Thea home now? Maggie, you will let me know how it's going here later, right?' said Ben.

'Of course, darling. I'll be in touch.' Maggie got up and enveloped Remy in her arms. Then she turned unexpectedly to Thea and pulled her into a hug as well. 'Thank you for helping my son,' she whispered. Thea had never known a mother's embrace before and was overwhelmed with emotion. She simply nodded her head in acknowledgement, unable to find words to respond to the affection that Maggie had shown her.

Chai stood in the doorway of Dylan's room and cleared his throat to make his presence known. Maggie promptly informed him of her intention to stay and Chai did not contradict her. But he did ask that the others leave so that he could continue the testing and observation that he felt was necessary. Ben, Remy and Thea all gave Dylan one more hug and then Chai began to chant some words so quietly that it just sounded like murmurs to everyone else. In an instant, the ceiling split open and the bright pink and yellow mouth opened once again, but this time, to let them out.

Thea pulled her wand out of her waistband and used her magic to summon her flying chair. As the three emerged from the hospital, Ben asked Thea where she lived so that they could accompany her home.

'I live anywhere I want to. It's just me, so I kind of move around a lot,' she replied.

'Where are your parents, Thea?' Ben asked sympathetically. Thea looked to be the same age as his boys and he couldn't imagine someone so young living by themselves. Although in the immortal world, you never could tell someone's age for certain. *Maybe she's older than she looks,* Ben thought.

'I'm an orphan. I never knew my parents. I was placed by D3W3 with some other families for a while, but that never worked out. They finally gave me permission to live on my own, as long as I graduate from school.' Thea could see the distress in Ben's face, so she continued. 'It's not so bad really,' she explained. 'I have my independence, and nobody bothers me.' She paused. 'And now I have Remy and Dylan as friends, so things are definitely looking up!'

'You must have had friends before now, surely?' asked Ben.

Thea shook her head in disagreement. 'No, I never wanted friends before. Until now that is.' She smiled shyly at Remy, hoping that she wasn't saying too much. After all, she and Remy had not gotten along before Dylan came into the picture.

'Thea, would you like to stay with us? At least for tonight. We have lots of space and I hate to think about you all alone. What do you say?'

'Is that okay with you, Remy?' she asked.

'Sure, Thea. It's okay with me,' Remy agreed.

'Great. Then it's settled. Let's go home and get something to eat. I'm starving!' replied Ben. Thea and Remy smiled tentatively at each other before they flew off in great haste.

CHAPTER TWENTY-THREE

Dinner that night in the Warston home was somewhat subdued with Maggie and Dylan's absence, but Thea had never felt so comfortable as she did sitting at the large table with Ben and Remy. The conversation was light. Nobody asked her any questions that were too personal, and Ben went out of his way to make Thea feel welcome in their home. When Ben discovered Thea's interest in the human world, he described for her some of the experiences he had had there when he was serving the Ministry OTV, out of the vortex. Thea was enraptured by his stories and she sat transfixed, twisting a long strand of her straight, black hair around her finger as he spoke. Every so often, she would interject with a question, and to his delight, Ben found her to be of quick intelligence. He certainly approved of this girl as a friend to his two sons!

After they had finished their meal, Ben excused himself to prepare a bedroom for Thea. Once Ben left the room, Remy leaned in close to Thea and asked her what exactly had happened that afternoon. Thea explained how Dylan had courageously come between her and Traysik during their argument and took the brunt of both their powers at the same time.

Remy exhaled loudly and let out a long whistle. 'How did he survive it? I mean, seriously? How is it possible that Dylan walked away from that with so little injuries? That doesn't make any sense!'

'But he was severely hurt! You were there. Don't you

223

remember the huge amount of blood that he lost? He was lying on the ground, unconscious and he lost so much blood from his head wound that he was literally lying in a pool of red liquid. You saw it too, didn't you? I mean, it wasn't just me, right?'

Remy nodded his head in agreement. He remembered all too clearly the extensive injuries and blood loss that he had seen with his own eyes. 'But I also remember that Dylan woke up soon after I got there. He sat up. And his head had stopped bleeding.'

Thea was lost, deep in thought as she remembered everything she had witnessed that afternoon. Remy did not disturb her and waited patiently for Thea to respond. Finally, she blinked in rapid succession as an idea dawned on her.

'We need to find somewhere more private to talk,' she whispered. 'I don't want your dad to overhear this. He might think I'm crazy,' she said softly to Remy.

'Okay. We can go to my room, well our room actually. Dylan and I share a room now. We can close the door. My dad won't bother us. He's big on respecting privacy.'

Remy and Thea flew upstairs, and Remy peaked his head into his parents' bedroom. 'Dad, Thea and I are just going to hang out in my room for a while before bed. Is that okay? Did you need me for anything?'

'Nope, all good here. I just spoke to your mom. Dylan is feeling fine and will hopefully be released in the morning. Don't stay up too late though. It's a school day tomorrow and you and Thea have had enough excitement for one day.'

'No problem, dad. We won't stay up long. Thanks.'

'Sure. Close my door when you leave, would you? I'm going to bed. I feel like I haven't slept for a week!'

'Okay! Have a good sleep, dad. See you in the morning.' Remy left the room and pulled the door shut soundly behind him. Then he motioned to Thea to follow him into his shared bedroom.

Once inside the room, Remy closed the door and checked just to be sure that it was firmly shut. He sat down on his bed and watched as Thea surveilled the room. She wandered around, picking up things and touching objects as she moved. She did not notice but another set of eyes was watching her intently from its position, hidden under the blankets of Dylan's bed.

'It must be so nice to have a family,' Thea said wistfully as she examined another knick knack that sat on Dylan's desk. 'And a permanent home, with people waiting for you to come back.' She sighed heavily. 'I don't really have any things to decorate where I live. I guess I never thought about how empty my place is. I don't even know what this is,' she continued as she carefully picked up a foreign looking object. 'What is it?' Thea asked.

Remy glanced over to see what Thea held in her hand. 'Oh, my dad gave that to me years ago, and then I gave it to Dylan. I thought it might make him feel closer to home, since it came from the human world. My dad brought it back from one of his trips out of the vortex.'

'Oh… it's beautiful, but I still don't know what it is,' replied Thea. She reverently ran her fingers over the shiny white object that felt smooth and cool in her hand.

'It's a sea shell. From the ocean,' Remy informed her. 'I wish I could see the ocean for real. My dad showed me images though. It looks so cool!'

Thea nodded her head. 'I've seen what oceans look like in HCS class. Vamdercamp even arranged for me to taste the ocean.'

'How did she do that?' wondered Remy.

'She was able to get someone to conjure up a few drops for me to try. She said she remembered from the time before she was changed, how the ocean was full of so many different tastes and smells and since she knew that I was so interested... well, it was just really nice of her to go out of her way like that for me. It tasted salty, like teardrops.'

Thea's black eyes glistened, and Remy was afraid that she was going to cry. He wouldn't know what to do if she did, so he quickly changed the subject. 'Let's get back to what we were talking about downstairs. We have full privacy now. My dad is asleep. The door is closed. Let's hear it.'

'I was thinking about Dylan's injuries. I know for certain that he had a massive gash on the back of his head that was bleeding profusely. I also know that his left arm was broken – I felt the bone practically coming through his skin. He was unconscious. Completely out cold. And then...' she paused, not sure that Remy was going to believe what she was going to say.

'And then...' he prompted her.

'And then, I touched his arm right where it was broken, and then it wasn't broken anymore. And I touched the back of his head where he was bleeding, and then the wound closed up and the bleeding stopped. When I touched his forehead, he woke up. And his eyes were so dilated and dark when he first opened them, but within minutes, they were totally back to normal.'

'What are you saying?' demanded Remy.

'I – I – I think that I healed him,' Thea muttered

226

incredulously. Even to her own ears, her theory sounded completely ridiculous.

'You think that you are responsible for fixing Dylan's injuries?'

'I can't explain it, but yes, I think… no, I am almost positive that it was me. It must have been me!' Thea's mind was whirling with her new discovery but the more she thought about it, the more she realized that it must be true.

Remy stared at her for a moment. His green eyes lit up with an idea. 'We need to test this. Let's do an experiment.'

'What kind of experiment?' Thea asked confidently warming to his idea.

'We both know what kind of experiment we need to do. The only question is what kind of injury am I going to have to endure?'

'You're willing to inflict pain on yourself to find out if I'm right?'

'You bet I am,' laughed Remy nervously. 'Okay, maybe we should start small. Nothing too serious at first. If this doesn't work…'

'It will work. I know it. But okay, let's start small.' Thea pulled her wand out from the waistband of her pants and pointed it directly at Remy. With a quick flick of the wrist, the magic was unleashed. Remy instantly felt a burning sensation in his right palm and held up his hand. They could both see the three -inch gash that ran down from the base of his middle finger to his wrist. Blood bubbled up from the incision and started to dribble down his skin. Remy bit his lower lip to hold in the pain and held his hand perfectly still for Thea's inspection.

Thea walked over to Remy and sat down next to him on the bed. She placed her palm directly over his. Thea could feel the blood sticking her hand to his, but she didn't move her position for several seconds. When she finally took her hand away, Remy and Thea both peered down at Remy's outstretched palm. A tiny pink line marked where the cut had been, but aside from dried blood, the wound was perfectly healed. Remy sucked in his breath in amazement. Thea grinned.

'Should we try something more substantial?' she asked.

'NO!' shouted Remy, and then quickly lowered his voice. 'No, I think we can safely say that you have some incredible healing power.'

The two sat side by side on the bed, contemplating what this could mean when they were interrupted by a small visitor, who nudged herself between them. Thea looked down in surprise as the little fireball nestled closer into the wedge between her arm and her elbow.

'Who is this?' Thea giggled with delight as she felt the tickling sensation in the crook of her arm. Thea stroked the tiny projections radiating from the creature's body and felt a slight buzzing sensation as the low voltage electricity coursed through her fingers.

'That's Via. She's kind of Dylan's pet. I think she likes you.'

Soft clicking sounds emanated from Via, as she expressed her happiness at the attention she was receiving. Just then, she darted up and hovered right in front of Remy. Via looked deeply into Remy's eyes, an unspoken question clearly visible to him as she showed him Dylan's face.

'I know, Via. You want to know where Dylan is. He's okay, girl. He will be home tomorrow. Maybe you want to sleep with

Thea tonight?' Remy reached out to stroke the affectionate fireball and she gravitated to his touch. Then Via spun around and flew over to Thea. She settled comfortably in Thea's lap and closed her eyes in contentment.

'So what's the deal with your healing power, Thea? Did you have any idea before today that you could do this?'

'Absolutely not. This is a complete revelation for me. I wonder how this happened. How can we find out?'

The two were silent for a moment, trying to figure out where they could go for answers. Just then there was a knock at the bedroom door. Remy looked quizzically at Thea and shrugged his shoulders. 'Come in,' he called.

The door opened to reveal the dark hallway, now that night had fallen. There, standing side by side, their blond, almost white hair glimmering stood Halle and Oliver.

'We couldn't help but overhear,' Halle started to say in her lilting voice.

'And we have an idea for you,' continued Oliver, his voice almost an octave lower than his sister's.

'In the human world, there are stories,' Oliver stated.

'More than just stories, legends,' interrupted Halle.

'What kind of legends?' asked Thea, not even caring that she didn't have a clue to whom she was speaking.

'Legends about immortals with special powers. Immortals who lived amongst humans centuries ago. Immortals who could heal with just their touch. Immortals like you, Thea. Just like you,' Halle whispered.

'I need to learn more,' Thea cried. Remy shushed her before she woke up Ben.

'Sorry, I got carried away,' Thea apologized. 'I know, why

don't we speak to Vamdercamp tomorrow before school. She lived in the human world, maybe she will know about these legends.'

'Sure, that's a great idea. We can go to school early tomorrow and catch her before classes start,' replied Remy.

'Thanks…you two,' Thea said towards the unknown guests. 'Might I ask who you are exactly?'

Halle's laugh sounded like a tinkling bell. 'I am Halle and this is my brother Oliver,' she said as she gestured towards her brother. 'We are shapeshifters and were Dylan's protectors in the human world.'

'Now we are his protectors in this world,' interjected Oliver. Halle nodded in agreement.

Thea smiled in thanks, and scooped Via up from her lap. 'Well,' she said. 'I'm going to bed. We are going to have an early start tomorrow! No need to show me the way, I can see the room your dad made up for me. Goodnight everyone.' Then Thea was gone.

After Thea left the room, Oliver and Halle settled down on Dylan's bed. 'I'm so glad he is going to be okay,' Halle said.

'Yeah, but I sure miss him,' Oliver replied sadly sniffing Dylan's pillow.

Remy changed into pajamas and used his magic to turn off the lights. Remy lay down on his bed and thought about his brother. *Can you hear me, Dylan?* He asked inside his head. Nothing. He concentrated harder. *Dylan?* Still nothing. Remy squeezed his eyes shut as hard as he could and pictured his brother's face, so similar to his own except for the color of their eyes. *DYLAN!* He screamed inside his head. And then, the faintest reply came through: *I can hear you, Remy. Am I imagining this?* wondered Remy. *Maybe I am just making up this conversation in my head.*

No, Remy. You aren't making this up. I really can hear you.

How do I know that I'm not imagining this conversation too?

Okay, I can prove this to you, but you won't believe me until I see you tomorrow.

How?

Code word. Ask me tomorrow when I see you for the code word and when I know it that will prove that this really happened.

Sounds like a good plan. What's the code word?

Legend.

Remy gasped. *Out of all the words in existence, why would you choose that one?*

I don't know. It just came to me. Like it was sitting on the tip of my tongue waiting.

Okay then. Legend it is. When I see you tomorrow, if this was real then the first thing you need to say to me is 'legend'.

Got it. Remy…?

Yeah?

I miss you.

I miss you too.

See you tomorrow.

Goodnight, Little Bro!

For you maybe. This Chai guy keeps watching me. It's freaking me out a bit.

You've got mom watching over you.

Yeah, but she fell asleep a while ago.

Don't worry, Dylan. She is right there. Nothing bad will happen while she is with you.

I know. But I still wish that I was home with you, and Dad and Via and Oliver and Halle…

Not to worry. They are all taken care of. Get some sleep. We have lots to talk about tomorrow.

I'll try.

Remy heard a sound in his head that kind of resembled the click of a lock when it was being shut. And then the only sound in his mind was that of his own voice. *This mental telepathy thing is really cool. If it's real, that is. I can't believe that we can hear each other's thoughts from so far away! It seems that we can let each other into our thoughts or end the conversation and keep the other one out. We will have to play with this more to figure it out.* And with that, Remy fell into a deep sleep.

Remy dreamed that night of a giant green plant with scarlet and yellow leaves that opened and shut. First he was flying over it, then the next thing he knew, the plant stretched out one of its leaves and plucked him from the sky, pulling him into its depths. Remy woke up abruptly, sweating and his heart racing. *What a nightmare* he thought!

When he looked out the window, he could see that it was still dark. The Ministry had not yet switched on the outside light. But he couldn't go back to sleep. He was just too wired up. He glanced over to the other bed and could see Halle and Oliver lying head to toe on top of Dylan's blankets. He turned his mind to Thea's healing powers. He had never heard of someone having that kind of magic before. Even what he knew about immortals like Chai, who had extraordinary powers to remedy injuries, didn't (at least to his knowledge) have abilities as strong as Thea's. Remy sat up and waited impatiently for the morning to begin. Once there was light outside, he could wake up Thea and they could get going. He was anxious to hear what

Vamdercamp might know.

Finally, after what seemed like forever, but was really less than an hour later, Remy saw the last of the night disappear as the Ministry turned on the daytime switch. The sky outside his window was the bright, brilliant blue as always. Remy was in too much of a hurry to get dressed the standard way so today he used his magic to get himself ready for school. Then he pounded on Thea's door to get her up as well.

'Thea, up and at 'em! Let's go, let's go! Can you hear me? Are you up? Thea?'

'I hear you, Remy. Gee… give me a few minutes to get ready, okay?'

'Two. I am giving you two minutes. That's it. Hurry, okay?'

At that moment, Thea opened the door. Her jet-black hair was not lying flat against her back as it usually did. Instead, pieces of it were sticking up and she looked disheveled. Remy laughed.

'What?' she asked.

'Your hair,' he replied with giggle.

Thea self-consciously patted her hair for a minute before she gave up. She pulled out her wand, waved it over her head, and within an instant, she looked like her usual glamourous self again.

'Great, now you're ready. Let's go,' Remy urged her impatiently.

'Bye Dad,' Remy called out.

'Bye Mr. Warston! Thanks for everything,' Thea shouted. Then the two took off. They didn't even use the front door, but rather flew out of a window. Ben saw only the back of Thea's flying chair as they darted out into the morning light.

'I wonder where they were going in such a hurry,' Ben muttered under his breath, before turning around to go back into his room. 'Well, I sure hope that Thea comes around again. I really like that girl!'

Remy had never made it to school so fast in his entire life! He flew at a speed that he didn't even know he could manage. Unfortunately for him, he wasn't used to going so fast, so he didn't start to slow down until it was too late. Remy came crashing down to the ground and landed awkwardly on his ankle.

'Ouch,' he cried out just as Thea landed gently and gracefully next to him.

'Next time, give yourself more time to decrease your speed, genius,' Thea scolded but with a smile to take the sting out of her words.

Remy tried to take a few steps, but the pain was too great. He winced in agony if even the slightest amount of pressure was put on his ankle. Thea watched him hobble about for a few seconds before he sank down to the ground in defeat. Remy pulled up his pant leg to examine his injury. They could both clearly see that it was already swollen, and the skin was turning an ugly shade of purple. Remy was fighting back tears, but a few trickled down his cheeks. The pain was unbearable.

Thea crouched down beside her friend and gently cupped her hands around Remy's inflamed ankle. The area was so swollen that her fingers couldn't touch each other even though she stretched them as wide as she could. Thea kept her hands in place and felt Remy's body shudder at her touch. As gentle as she tried to be, Remy was clearly suffering from even the softest contact.

In less than a minute, Thea was able to grasp her fingers together. The swelling was decreasing! After another minute, Remy's body visibly relaxed as all the pain had disappeared. Thea took her hands away and together they peered closely at Remy's ankle. It looked perfectly normal. The horrendous purple color was gone and in its place was a healthy shade of pink. The stretched shiny skin that was there only moments ago now appeared exactly as it should. Thea tested the area by gently prodding it with her finger. Remy didn't react at all. So she tried again but this time, she slapped him really hard, right where the injury had been.

'Hey!' cried Remy.

'Did that hurt?' asked Thea concerned.

'Not really, but you hit me,' he complained.

Thea grinned. 'Okay Remy. Up you get. Let's see if you can walk on it.'

Remy jumped up without any hesitation. There was no pain at all.

'Thea, you are definitely good to have around,' joked Remy. 'Now, let's find Vamdercamp and see what she knows.'

Thea and Remy's school sweaters had been hovering over them anxiously waiting to be put on by their owners. As soon as the crises had passed, the sweaters swooped down and launched themselves at Remy and Thea who immediately obliged and put on their uniforms. The school was still deserted. It was far too early for any students to show up.

'Let's try the faculty lounge,' suggested Thea.

The two sprinted off in the hopes of finding their HCS teacher this early in the morning. Luckily, Ms. Vamdercamp was just about to walk into the building when Thea and Remy spotted her.

'Ms. Vamdercamp,' they called out in unison. Their teacher turned around and smiled at her students. She waited patiently for them to reach her to see what they could possibly want so early.

'Hello Remy, Thea,' she greeted them warmly when they reached her side. 'How is Dylan doing, Remy? Any news?'

'He was totally fine yesterday. They just kept him for observation last night. Hopefully he will be released today.'

'That's great news! I'm so glad that he is okay. From what I heard, he was seriously hurt. I know that there was a lot of blood loss. I guess the reports exaggerated the extent of his injuries.'

Thea and Remy exchanged a pointed look. They both hoped that the other was thinking the same thing – not to tell what they knew about Thea to Ms. Vamdercamp. At least not yet.

'So, what can I do for you this morning?' asked Ms. Vamdercamp curiously.

'We wondered if you could give us some information about some things we are interested in from the human world.'

'Oh!' she exclaimed delightedly. 'I love when students demonstrate interest in my subject of expertise. Let's go to the classroom where we can talk more comfortably.'

The three chatted about nothing of consequence while they made the short walk to the HCS classroom. Inside the room, the lights were off, and Ms. Vamdercamp made no move to turn them on. Instead, she sat down at the large teacher's desk at the front of the room and indicated that Remy and Thea should sit close to her. Remy perched on the side of the desk while Thea assumed her favorite position of floating, lotus style in the air.

'Ms. Vamdercamp, what can you tell us about immortals who have healing powers in the human world?' inquired Thea.

'That's quite an interesting question, Thea. What made you think of this?'

'Oh, I don't know. Remy and I were just talking about things that Dylan told us about living with mortals. It seems to us that immortals have interacted with humans for hundreds of years and we were just curious about some of the things that immortals would do for humans.'

'Mmmm, yes I can see how Dylan would have many interesting ideas to share with you. Well, as you know from class, immortals have formed relationships with humans throughout history. Some even had children together. The Ministry assigns some of our kind to live in the mortal world to watch for these half-bloods.

There are some immortals who did indeed possess unusual and special powers, including the ability to heal, which they would sometimes share with humans. Of course, humans did not always realize that the individual who cured them of illness or repaired injuries were immortals per se, but they were given recognition as having divine powers in many instances.

Humans are so easily fooled of course, which allowed our kinds to continue to inhabit the human world without fear of being discovered for what we truly are. Yes, humans would latch on to an explanation that suited their own purposes, but it was to our benefit as well you understand. That being said the power to heal is one that is very unique and quite extraordinary, even among our kind. Not many immortals possess that kind of power. In the human world, there have been a few immortals that have been given credit as healers, though not recognized as immortal as we know them to be. And there are some who were believed to be gods with those powers. One such story from Greek mythology tells the tale of Althaea, who was the goddess of healing and compassion. Oh my, Thea, what a coincidence – I believe your full name is Althaea, if I'm not mistaken?'

Thea blinked in surprise. She shared the same name as a goddess of healing? Was that actually a coincidence like Ms. Vamdercamp assumed, she wondered.

'Are there other stories from the human world about immortals who had special powers?' asked Remy.

'Why of course,' replied Ms. Vamdercamp.

Remy suddenly had a thought. 'Was Orion one of them?' Thea looked at Remy with immediate understanding as to why he had asked this question.

'Certainly, Orion was known as a master hunter. Orion was believed to be the son of the sea god, Poseidon. When he died, the myth says by the sting of a scorpion, he was turned into a constellation by Zeus, the most powerful of the Greek gods, and placed in the heavens in the form of stars.'

'You're talking about Orion's Belt, right?' asked Remy.

Ms. Vamdercamp clapped her hands. 'Remy, you have been paying attention in class. I'm overjoyed. Orion's Belt is composed of three stars that make up part of the Orion constellation in the human universe. It is sometimes referred to as the Three Kings. Do you remember when I showed it to you in class?'

Ms. Vamdercamp pressed a button inside her desk drawer and spoke the words: 'Orion constellation.' A holograph of the star formation that made up Orion, including Orion's Belt, appeared before Remy and Thea. Thea reached out to trace Orion' Belt with her index finger. Her thoughts were flying in so many different directions as she started to piece together bits and pieces of ideas that she had considered over the past few days.

'Ms. Vamdercamp,' she finally said, 'Do you know of any stories about prophecies in the human world?'

'Yes, Thea. It's interesting that you should ask that. The idea of prophecies has long been linked to the stars, by humans that is. Many mortals have associated significant historical events with the placement of the stars. One of the most well -known mortals to use the stars to predict future events was named Nostradamus.' Ms. Vamdercamp's voice triggered a new vision to appear – that of Michel de Nostradame, later known as Nostradamus. 'He would make predictions, or prophecies if you will, based on the movement of the planets and stars. Aside from Nostradamus, there have been many other mortals who have claimed to possess such abilities, but none as well known or as well documented as he. And then of course there is the vampire who, as the story is told, had the power of foresight as well. But that is the only immortal that I have ever heard of with this talent.'

'A vampire that could predict the future, Ms. Vamdercamp? Wow! Can you tell us more?' asked Thea with her eyes opened wide to appear innocent and not betray the fact that she already knew about this. Thea hoped that Vamdercamp might reveal some new information.

'Well, Thea there is not much known about this vampire. After I heard about him for the first time, I tried to do a little personal research since I was so interested. You may not know this but as a human, I used to dabble a little with astrology – that means the study of celestial bodies like the stars and planets, that are visible in the mortal world, to predict the future and explain human behaviors. I have always had an interest in this so when I heard about a vampire with prophetic abilities, I was intrigued and started digging for information. My human birth date makes me a Taurus and we are known to be naturally curious, to the point of reckless in our pursuit of knowledge.' Ms. Vamdercamp paused, not sure if she was rambling and had lost the attention of Thea and Remy, but they appeared as eager as when they started, so she continued.

'So I didn't give up, we Tauruses can be stubborn and relentless in our actions you see, and so I did manage to find out some small tidbits of information that was not part of the original story that I was told.' Ms. Vamdercamp paused for dramatic effect and smiled at the two young immortals who listened so intently. 'Let me backtrack for you to the beginning of how I initially heard about this vampire. I met an elf at a conference for new immortals. Vampires when they are first transformed must attend these meetings to learn about the laws of the immortals, and this elf was there as one of the keynote speakers to inform us about the realm and the expectations upon us. That is where I first learned about the rebellious vampire.'

Thea and Remy listened intently, not wanting to interrupt. Seeing her pupils so enraptured with her impromptu lesson, Ms. Vamdercamp was encouraged to continue. 'The elf in his speech told us that when the immortal world was first created after the civil war, there was apparently a vampire who rebelled against the new regime, and ultimately was executed after he killed a border guard. Apparently, the vampire was known to have the ability to foresee the future, but that did not save him from his execution. That was all we were told, until I uncovered something more. I believe that this story was shared with us at the conference as a warning to let new immortals know what will happen if we do not fulfill our responsibilities to the realm.

Anyways, I found this elf to be an extremely engaging and knowledgeable speaker so after the conference, I approached him to ask some questions. Initially he didn't tell me anything more than what he had said in his speech but when he learned that I would be starting my position here at the school teaching the Human Culture and Societies class, he agreed to meet me the following week to talk further. Before I met up with him again, I searched all the written documents I could find and asked almost every immortal that I met what they knew about this vampire. Interestingly, despite all my research I couldn't find any additional information. There is very little in the immortal public record, and nothing more than we were told at the conference, which I thought was strange since this vampire seemed in my mind to be so important to the historical narrative of the creation of the immortal world. But when I met with Reus the following week-'

'Reus!' cried out Thea and Remy in unison. 'The elf was Reus? My teacher?' exclaimed Thea in disbelief.

'Oh yes, my dear. Imagine my surprise when I saw Reus here at school to teach Dylan, and now you. But Reus is certainly well known to the Ministry as Deputy Baltazar's closest adviser, and he is so old that he existed before the civil war occurred and therefore has first- hand knowledge about both the human and immortal worlds and their histories. So I do think that he is a logical choice to be placed here as an educator, although, I wonder why he was specifically assigned to Dylan, and now you too Thea, rather than to a regular class. It seems odd for him to be teaching a class of only two students when there are so many more that could benefit from his wisdom. Perhaps the plan is to start him where he is and then assign him larger classes later... well, in any event, I digress.

When I met up with Reus following the conference, I inquired about the rebellious vampire. He confirmed that this vampire had unusual powers. As you know, vampires do not have magical abilities. We have speed, strength and immortality but nothing more than that. This particular vampire, however, was revealed to me by Reus to have the gift of foresight when he was human, and apparently, this ability stayed with him as a vampire. I was also told that as a human, this vampire made many significant predictions that all came true, and that as a vampire, he foretold of the potential destruction of the immortal world in a final prophecy that he made just before he was executed. The prophecy said that four immortal siblings, born at the same time would be the catalyst to the end of our world.

The elf cautioned me about sharing this information since the leaders did not want to panic immortals, and he also told me that he, himself, would not put too much credence in this prophecy since hundreds of human years had since passed and the realm was stronger than ever. No signs of impending doom. I don't normally share this information with students because I don't want to worry them unnecessarily, but since you two are so interested and intelligent, I feel comfortable telling you. I know that you won't make more of this than it is – an interesting story that is not supported by any real evidence. So please don't worry about the prophecy. If it hasn't come true yet, and there are still no signs of it coming true, then I don't think it is likely to happen.'

'But do you believe that prophecies can be real, Ms. Vamdercamp?' asked Remy solemnly.

Ms. Vamdercamp paused to consider the question. 'Well, I will tell you this, Remy. When I was human, I did believe in the power of astrology and I still believe that there are those who do have a genuine gift of seeing the future. And then there are those who pretend that they have that ability, but are frauds. I also thought that stories about Greek gods and mythical creatures were nothing more than fictional stories. I didn't believe any of that kind of stuff to be true. I loved reading about myths and legends – who wouldn't, after all, those stories are always exciting and fun to imagine, but I didn't believe any of it was real. But then again, I also didn't believe that vampires really existed either. Or witches, warlocks, wizards, fairies, none of it. And we all know how wrong I was on that account!'

'So are you saying you do believe in prophecies? Do you think that there really may be predictions about the future that could come true?' Thea asked, her voice trembling just a little bit with trepidation.

'Yes. I do believe it's possible. This new life has shown me that anything is possible. But possible does not equate to probable or even likely to be true. I do believe that the rebellious vampire had the gift of foresight, but that doesn't mean that all of his predictions will come true. Sometimes I think we also have to look beyond the literal meaning of messages that we receive. Sometimes, it is more the symbolic aspect that we should be paying attention to in these situations and I do not know exactly what the prophecy said. They may be other valid interpretations rather than just the destruction of the immortal world. Reus told me that he didn't know the precise details of the vampire's prophecy. So I sincerely do not believe that this is anything that should cause you any concern. In the human world, there have been thousands of apocalyptic visions reported that have predicted the end of humankind, including Nostradamus, but clearly those have all been false prophecies. You can't let your existence be ruled by fear, children.'

She paused and looked directly into Remy's green eyes. She could tell that he was nervous, something was clearly bothering this student who was usually so happy and laid back. 'It seems like you may be worried about something, Remy. You too, Thea. Is there anything you want to tell me? Perhaps I could help?' asked Ms. Vamdercamp, gently prodding her students to open up to her.

Thea and Remy once again exchanged a meaningful look. 'No, Ms. Vamdercamp. We have nothing to tell you. We were just interested, that's all. Nothing more to it than that. Just Dylan telling us about some Greek mythology and stars and stuff...' Remy's voice trailed off.

'Okay kids, but remember, you can always come to me if you ever want to talk about anything at all,' Ms. Vamdercamp replied sincerely.

Thea smiled. 'Thanks. We will keep that in mind, if anything comes up that is.'

Loud noises could now be heard coming from outside the classroom. It was getting close to the start of the school day. Thea and Remy couldn't wait to talk to Dylan later that day and made plans to see him right after school. If he wasn't at home yet, they would go back to the hospital. 'We'll talk,' Thea promised as they took off in opposite directions, both of them hoping that together they would be able to figure out the answers they needed.

CHAPTER TWENTY-FOUR

Dylan had a strange and unsettling dream that night in the hospital. He dreamt that he was flying carefree and happy, high above the ground. He was thinking about how easily flight came to him, like he had been doing it his entire existence and not just for a few short days. He was soaring between the floating houses, swooping higher and then lower, glorying in the freedom that being airborne gave him. Then all of a sudden, he looked down and right below his feet was the pale green, crescent shaped building that had long, skinny protrusions that waved gently in the breeze. When he was directly over its middle, one of the tentacles reached out and grabbed his leg, wrapping itself around his ankle so that he couldn't escape no matter how hard he struggled to free himself. The cavernous mouth opened revealing the bright scarlet inside with the yellow perimeter. Sharp teeth glistened menacingly as he was pulled deeper and deeper into its body. In his dream, Dylan saw his eyes open wide with fear, but then he realized, those weren't his eyes. What he saw was the clear green eyes of his brother. *I'll save you, Remy* he called out in his dream. Abruptly Dylan woke up with a shudder and sat up to get his bearings. As his head cleared, he was able to remember where he was… in the Venus flytrap of a hospital! No wonder he had that dream! He saw his mother, still sound asleep on a cot next to his bed. And staring at him from several feet away with an unblinking, penetrating look was Chai.

Chai softly called out to him. 'Do you feel strong enough to fly?'

Without hesitation, Dylan nodded his assent. He hoped that if he could prove that he was feeling fine, Chai would release him from this creepy place.

'Okay, then. Follow me,' Chai instructed. Chai muttered a few words that Dylan could not make out and then levitated off the floor and out the door. Dylan found to his immense relief, that he was easily able to fly after him, without having to use much concentration at all. Flying was becoming second nature to him!

Chai turned around once to ensure that Dylan was behind him, and then led Dylan down a short corridor and into a different room. Chai beckoned Dylan with his wrinkled hands to sit down on another stretcher which hovered over the floor. The stretcher was identical to the one that had carried him into the hospital when he was admitted. There were no windows, so Dylan had no idea if it was day or night. He reflected on the fact that the immortal world didn't seem to use clocks or time telling devices of any kind. The only way to have any idea of the time was from the Ministry's use of light and darkness and even that was very imprecise. The amount of light did not strengthen or fade, nor did the darkness increase or decrease the way that it would in the human world as the day progressed.

'Now,' Chai said in a kindly voice. 'Tell me how you are feeling today.'

'I feel totally fine, but I told you that yesterday. Please believe me. I want to go home now,' responded Dylan.

'A few questions first, Dylan. I ran some tests on you while you were asleep, and your results indicate some unusual findings.'

'What do you mean by unusual findings? Is something wrong with me?' Dylan was frightened. 'Should my mom be here for this?' At that moment, Dylan wished to have his mother's comforting hand holding his before he heard what he assumed would be terrible news.

'No, Dylan. Your mother does not need to be here. I didn't mean to alarm you. Nothing is wrong, just ... well let's just say that I haven't come across results quite like yours before.'

'I don't know about how these things work in the immortal world, but where I come from, the last thing you want to hear from a doctor is that they have never before encountered something like you have. That can't be good,' sighed Dylan.

'Where do you come from? Perhaps you need to provide me with a little more information about your background. That might help with my clinical evaluation of your condition,' coaxed Chai who was desperate to know more about this young immortal who he had ripped away from his family the equivalent of twelve human years ago.

'I grew up in the human world, until now that is. I was adopted by mortals and I had no idea that I was not human until I somehow ended up here. Apparently, I fell into the vortex. I didn't even know that there was such a thing. Then through pure luck, someone at D3W3 sort of recognized me – she thought I was my twin brother, Remy who you met yesterday. I was reunited with my immortal parents only a few days ago. But it seems like so much longer. Time passes strangely in this world compared to humans…' Dylan's voice trailed off. He didn't know what else to say and he wasn't sure that he fully trusted Chai, despite his kindly mannerisms and concerned face.

'Hmmm,' Chai pondered. 'Let me ask you this, when you were being raised by humans, did you ever notice any unusual powers or skills? Things that happened which you couldn't explain.'

Dylan thought hard. There were certainly experiences that he had living as a mortal which were sort of strange but that he didn't give much thought to at the time. Once he remembered when he was about eight years old, his parents had taken him to the park. There, he saw another child holding a bright red helium balloon and Dylan recalled how he desperately wanted one just like it. But there was no balloon seller to be found. Dylan remembered being so disappointed and he thought about that balloon for the rest of the day. That night, before he went to bed, a scratching noise at his bedroom window caught his attention. When he got to the window, to his great surprise and delight, an exact duplicate of that very balloon sat wedged between his window panes. But the one experience that seemed to be of the greatest significance occurred right before he fell into the vortex. Dylan closed his eyes and could picture himself running away from the bullies in the forest and how he leapt over the running water that seemed like an impossible feat. It was almost like he was... flying? Dylan's eyes popped open and Chai could see that Dylan had recalled an important memory.

'You need to tell me, Dylan. I must know if I am going to be able to decipher these strange test results.' Chai leaned closer and put his weathered hand on Dylan's shoulder. 'I promise, Dylan. You can trust me.'

Dylan thought for a moment. He desperately wanted to trust Chai. He needed to find out what Chai knew, and yet, he hesitated.

'You were present at my delivery,' Dylan stated matter-of -factly. Chai nodded sadly. 'You told my parents that I had died. And another brother as well.' Chai nodded again. 'So how can you explain that? You want me to trust you? Why do you think I should after everything that happened?'

Chai steepled his fingers together under his chin and gathered his thoughts. What could he say to this child that would not compromise his relationship with Baltazar? Chai felt the warmth against his leg before he heard the whispers in his head. And then he knew just what to say. 'Dylan, I cannot explain to you what happened at your birth. I can only tell you that I am so grateful to know that you are safe and well, and that you have been reunited with your warlock family. I wish I had more information for you...' *That is the truth,* Chai consoled himself. *And yet I have still maintained my promise to Baltazar. He should not have any reason to be angry with me...* The voice in his mind reaffirmed for Chai that the words he had spoken were the right ones.

Dylan looked into the clear, guileless eyes of Chai, this immortal who seemed sincere in his desire to help him. And yet, Dylan had a gut feeling that this person was not to be trusted. He knew more than he was saying, of this Dylan was positive. And if Chai would not be honest with him, well there was no way that he was going to reveal anything in return. But Dylan also knew that he had better fake it or else Chai would know that something was amiss.

'Sorry Chai,' Dylan said apologetically. 'I know that you are just trying to help me. I was just thinking about skills that I had in the human world. I was really good at math. Top of my class actually! And I hate to brag, but I was also a great singer.

I always got the leads in school musicals and people loved me in the talent shows that I performed in. Oh, and I was a pretty decent tennis player. I had a wicked backhand, you know!'

Chai cocked his head to the side and stared deeply into Dylan's grey eyes. 'Is that all you want to tell me?' Chai asked.

Dylan shrugged his shoulders and pretended to be clueless. Now, things that he never really understood or questioned in the human world were suddenly starting to make sense. Dylan thought back to his incredible ability to slam dunk a basketball. His skills were mediocre at best when it came to dribbling and passing, but he remembered with great pleasure how he was able to lift his small frame off the court floor to make baskets that were worthy of NBA status. And of course, there were his final moments in the human world when he jumped over the water to escape the boys who were pursing him. Dylan mentally calculated his best move and decided to continue to play dumb.

'Why? Were you expecting something more?' Dylan questioned.

'No, perhaps it was just wistful thinking on my part. I had hoped that something from your past might give me some clues about how to interpret your results.'

'Can you please tell me what specifically you are talking about?' begged Dylan. *What does he know about me,* Dylan wondered frantically.

'Nothing to be alarmed about. I assure you. It is just that a few of your test results showed some unusually high readings for powers that are not commonly so well developed in an immortal as young as yourself.'

'Please, Chai. Can you tell me something more concrete? I don't understand what you are saying,' cried Dylan in frustration.

'Well Dylan, let me ask you this. Since arriving in this world, have you noticed any unusual powers or skills here? Obviously, there is nothing for you to tell of your time being raised by mortals, but perhaps there is something of significance you can share with me since you came through the vortex?'

Dylan quickly assessed how much he could share with Chai and decided that some things were a matter of public knowledge. Surely, he could tell him about those incidents since Chai could easily find out if he asked around. Dylan told Chai about his accomplishments with Remy in magic class and how they created a successful, although small transport portal together. Dylan deliberately withheld the story about how they escaped from the ogre in the same way!

'Fascinating,' exclaimed Chai. 'Creating a transport portal is something that most immortals never achieve. And yet you did so with so little magical training and so young…' Chai considered this for a moment. 'But you say you did this with your brother, not on your own?'

'That's right. Remy and I were able to achieve this together. I don't think either of us could do it by ourselves.

'Also fascinating,' Chai enthused again. 'Any other special powers that you can think of?' he prodded.

Dylan grinned unable to contain his pleasure and pride. 'Well, I have been able to pick up the ability to fly pretty quickly. I was told that it usually takes a while to perfect that skill, but it seems to come sort of naturally to me.'

'Hmm, well that does seem to accord with the test results. I think Dylan that perhaps you have some very special gifts and if I may offer some advice, I would suggest that you work diligently at discovering your talents and then doing whatever you can to develop them. Your skills may be of great benefit to all immortals. Just one more thing, if I may?' asked Chai as he stretched out his hand, remembering from all those years ago one more key component of the child's birth. Chai did not wait for Dylan's consent, but instead reached for Dylan's right arm and turned it over. There on the delicate skin of his inner wrist were the telltale markings that Chai vividly remembered from when Reus had examined the infant warlocks immediately after their delivery. The three dots in a diagonal line.

Dylan looked quizzically at Chai. *How would he know to look there?* 'Chai, why did you do that?' Dylan politely inquired, not wanting to seem rude to the one individual who would determine whether to release him or not.

'Oh, I thought I noticed something there yesterday when you were admitted. I just wanted to see what it was to make sure that you didn't have another injury, you see.'

'Okay,' Dylan said, seemingly accepting of the explanation but knowing that Chai was holding back information. 'So, can I go home now?'

'Yes, indeed. You seem to be fully recovered from yesterday's events. Perhaps your injuries were exaggerated by your teacher who reported it. I suppose she was just being overly cautious. Based on her account, you should have been suffering from much more extensive damage. But I am very pleased that I can release you today. Let's go find your mother, shall we?'

Dylan was not entirely sure how much he was remembering accurately from the time when he was knocked unconscious by being a direct target for both Thea and Traysik's powers. But knowing that something was not right, he again decided not to share any further details about what he thought he remembered of Thea's healing powers. *I can't wait to talk to Remy and Thea!*

The release process was very fast. Chai woke up Maggie and had her press her left index finger to his right temple. 'Do you understand the findings and my recommendations for release?' Chai asked her after a moment had passed.

'Yes, absolutely. Thank you, Chai. We will be on our way now. Dylan, are you ready to go?' she asked her son.

'Absolutely, get me out of here!' Dylan shouted in glee.

'Take it slowly, Dylan. Chai doesn't want you to over-exert yourself. Do you want me to help you get home?' she inquired. Maggie came to stand next to Dylan and placed her hand softly on the top of his head. She lovingly pushed the hair that had flopped over his eyes away and stroked the funny cowlick with her middle finger.

'I'm perfectly fine, mom. I can fly on my own. We can go slowly if it makes you feel better.'

'It will make me feel better,' she responded with a smile. 'Let's go then.'

Chai murmured some words which sounded completely foreign to Dylan and the bright scarlet ceiling over their head began to pull away. The giant mouth of the plant opened up exposing its inhabitants to the sky. Maggie grabbed Dylan's hand and together, at a reasonably controlled pace, the two of them disappeared from Chai's view. As the mouth of the hospital closed up again, Chai knew that he could not put off his responsibility any longer. It was time to contact Baltazar.

Back at school, Thea waited in the classroom, getting more and more bored by the minute. She knew that Dylan would not likely be at school today, but where was Reus? Without a teacher, Thea was aware that she should report to the administrative office but then they would just place her in another class, which she knew from experience that she would hate. So instead, Thea decided to do some independent research in the school library. She left a note for Reus, telling him where she would be, floating on the air right in the middle of the room. She used thick, red writing with flashing lights surrounding it. He could not miss her message, if he ever decided to show up.

Chai slowly walked backed to his office. He was in no hurry to get there, and this method of movement would delay his arrival by a couple of minutes. Not really anything significant, but he was so wary about what he had to do, that extending the time by even a few seconds seemed to be the most preferable option. When he arrived, he was surprised to see the door was already ajar. As Chai stepped into the room, he immediately noticed that his chair was facing backwards, towards the far wall. Chai cleared his throat and the chair swiveled around. There, with his head quite a few inches below the top of the chair, sat Reus. Chai tried to hide his fear and instead gave Reus a tepid smile.

'Reus, it's been a long time,' he said in a calm voice, thankful that his agitation was not betrayed.

'Yes, indeed it has been Chai. Twelve human years, wouldn't you agree?'

'The boy was just released a few moments ago. I was coming here to contact Baltazar immediately. I have not forgotten my obligations.'

'Really? Well, Baltazar will be most pleased to hear that. When I informed him that the child was admitted to your care yesterday, he expected to hear from you long before now.'

'I had nothing to report then. I had to wait for the test results and the ability to interpret their meanings before contacting him,' Chai's voice quivered slightly as he tried to regain his composure. He mopped his hand over his brow in a nervous gesture. He knew that Reus was Baltazar's direct servant and clearly, Reus was displeased. That could only mean that Baltazar too was not happy with him.

Reus leaned forward over the desk, practically his entire body, small as it was, coming out of the chair. Reus' sharp eyes glared at Chai. 'You didn't think that reporting the boy's admission was important? You didn't think that Baltazar would want to be immediately informed that he was here?'

'I'm sorry, Reus, but no. I didn't realize that Dylan's mere presence would be of any interest to Baltazar. Not without specific details, that is.'

'For your sake, I hope you're right. You have been summoned to him. Immediately. I will escort you.'

Reus climbed down off the desk and stood side by side with Chai. The top of Reus' head barely reached Chai's torso. And yet the elf, so small in stature clearly intimidated the much larger immortal, who was known by Reus to be a witch with extraordinary healing powers. Reus snapped his fingers, and they were gone.

CHAPTER TWENTY-FIVE

Reus and Chai stood together in the grand foyer of Baltazar's underground castle. Chai had never been here before and prayed that he never would be again. He fervently hoped that this encounter would extinguish his obligations to Baltazar and that he would be free to continue his existence without owing any more debt to this powerful and vengeful leader of the realm. Chai looked around the hallway, taking in all the ornate fixtures and trying to relax. He knew he had done nothing wrong and that he had followed exactly Baltazar's orders from so many years ago.

Just then, the huge crystal chandelier that hung over their heads began to rattle. The noise became deafening as the object lowered itself down, closer and closer to where they stood. Chai's knees trembled in fear and yet Reus appeared to be quite unaffected. When the fixture hovered directly over Chai's head with only an inch separating him from the dangling crystal elements, he felt a vacuuming sensation, like suction, coming from above him. In an instant, he was sucked into the center of the chandelier, surrounded by crystals and metal and lit candles. He tried to hold still, wary of the small fires that burned in such close proximity all around him.

Reus remained on the ground and gave a wave which Chai could not see. Then Chai felt himself raising rapidly upwards, the noise of clanking crystals shattering inside his ears. He pressed his eyes shut and tried not to move but rather to let the motion carry him along. Soon the upwards motion stopped. Chai looked up and could see the ceiling above him. It was a cupola, a domed roof with intricate carvings that depicted scenes so artfully sculpted that they looked alive. Chai saw visions of immortals of all types performing acts to demonstrate their loyalty to the Ministry. Some were bowing down to the two Ministers and their deputies. Chai easily recognized Baltazar's profile. Others were dancing in celebration for the new world which gave them their freedom and offered peace and harmony to all immortals.

Chai blinked in amazement as he realized that the carving was actually moving. Little figurines were alive on the ceiling. One of the tiny dancers lowered herself down on a string no wider than a spider's thread and extended her hand to Chai. When he didn't move, she beckoned to him impatiently and he tentatively reached out towards her. As soon as their fingers touched, Chai was instantly sucked up again, until his head hit the ceiling with a thud. The miniature carvings surrounded him and together, they gave him a huge push upwards. Chai's head burst through the ceiling and he found himself in a dark tunnel. He was disoriented and confused as he continued to feel himself being shoved upwards against his will. Once he was fully in the tunnel, a lit pathway showed him the way forward. Knowing that he had no other options, Chai carefully stepped forward one foot at a time, slowly and gingerly. Until he reached a heavy wooden door. He tentatively tried the doorknob and the barrier swung open.

Standing before him, wearing his official Ministry robes, stood Baltazar. The deep purple color of Baltazar's attire indicated his mighty status within the realm. The Ministry's emblem emblazed in gold stood out in the dimly lit room. Baltazar's eyes were devoid of all color except for the silver ring that surrounded the otherwise invisible iris, and the penetrating stare of the vampire instilled great fear in Chai. The master healer stood unmoving under the Deputy's gaze and waited in silence.

When he finally spoke, Baltazar's voice was mellow and smooth. 'Chai, my old friend. It's been many years since we have had to make each other's acquaintance. I trust that time has been good to you? That you have enjoyed my protection to your benefit, am I correct?'

Chai fell to his knees before the great leader. 'I am most grateful, Baltazar. I assure you that I have followed all of your commands fully and completely. I have done exactly as you asked of me.'

'Have you now? As I recall, one of your orders was to report to me immediately if you ever came in contact with any of those warlocks from the exceptional birth, was it not? As I understand it, yesterday you came in contact with not one, but two of those boys. Or am I mistaken?' Baltazar's tone remained quiet but Chai could hear the implied threat beneath the words.

Chai dropped his head in obeisance and desperately tried to think of something that he could say to appease his master. 'I was on my way to contact you when I found Reus in my office. I swear. I am so sorry if you think that I delayed too much. I was waiting to have specific information for you. I didn't want to contact you prematurely.'

'So then old friend, tell me what information did you find after having the child in your custody for so long? I assume you found something of significance to report, since you waited for so long?'

Chai knew that his only hope for survival was to convince Baltazar of his sincerity and his usefulness since clearly Baltazar's interest in these young warlocks had not waned over the passage of time.

'The boy named Dylan lived in the world of humans until just recently,' began Chai. Baltazar showed no visible response. *Clearly he knew that,* realized Chai. 'He fell through the vortex without having any knowledge of his immortal status. Dylan revealed to me that he had no awareness of any special powers while he was being raised by the humans, but I did also find some very unusual information after my examination, that I think you will be interested in,' continued Chai hoping that this would appease Baltazar.

'I'm listening,' replied Baltazar nonchalantly, betraying nothing of his true emotions.

'Dylan's test results showed extraordinarily high readings for air borne powers. This was corroborated by the boy when he told me of the ease in which he has learned to fly.'

'And why is this of any concern to me?' asked Baltazar sounding bored.

'Well master, perhaps the Ministry can make use of this power. Anything to do with air, including flight and portal transport, seem to be something that he will excel at. In fact,' Chai's voice sped up with excitement, 'He also told me that together with his brother, the one who was raised by the warlock parents, they have actually created a successful transport portal together.'

That got Baltazar's attention. 'The boys constructed a

transport portal?' he repeated. 'Yes, I believe I had heard of that already from a different source. Anything else?'

'He still has the markings on his inner arm. And I observed the same markings on the first brother to be born when he was in the waiting lounge yesterday. I don't know if there is any significance to that or not.'

'Well,' Baltazar responded with a twinkle in his translucent eyes, 'Would you be interested to know that the third boy has the identical symbols on him as well?'

'That is certainly of interest, Master. That cannot be a coincidence. There is evidently something of importance with regards to the markings. Would you like me to conduct further examinations?'

Baltazar sighed. 'No Chai. Sadly, your participation is no longer required for this matter. Our time together has come to an end.'

Chai looked up delightedly. 'It's been a sincere honor to serve you, Baltazar. I am always at your command, should you ever decide that you require my services again. I thank you for your ongoing protection...'

Baltazar laughed. 'Oh, dear friend, did you believe that I was releasing you from your duties? My apologies if I misled you. No, Chai you are not being released ... you are being, shall we say, disposed of? You know too much and yet you know so little. Too much to let you go, too little to be of any further use to me. I promise it shall be painless.'

Baltazar strode over to Chai in just a few steps and stood directly in front of the master healer, staring intently into his eyes. Baltazar placed a hand on Chai's left shoulder and the other, he held outstretched before him with his palm facing up. A slight warming sensation heated Chai's skin on his upper thigh and the breathy whisper of a voice in his mind told Chai what to do. Chai reached into the pocket of his robe which lay directly above his thigh and extracted the small stone. The amulet was deposited into Baltazar's waiting hand, and immediately the heat and the voice disappeared from Chai's consciousness. For Baltazar, the inner voice in his head became stronger.

'Goodbye, Chai. May you rest for eternity in peace,' stated Baltazar softly but with menace laced in every word.

Chai watched in disbelief as Baltazar strolled casually from the room and the heavy door shut with a loud thud behind him. Chai heard the lock turn, preventing any hope of escape from this room and remained motionless on the floor. He knew his powers would be useless here – Baltazar would have seen to that. But just out of caution and with the tiniest ounce of hope, Chai uttered the magical words that would usually enable him to become invisible. If he couldn't be seen, perhaps he could sneak out of this prison and save himself. Where he would go after, he did not know but he had to try. Chai said the words once. Twice. Three times, but nothing happened. He knew he was powerless here under Baltazar's control. He was defeated. Chai closed his eyes and waited for what he did not know, but he knew that his life was now to be measured in minutes.

Every sound echoed within his head and made him jump with fear. Time passed slowly and yet nothing happened. Chai's shoulders finally slumped in exhaustion and he lowered his head to the floor. It was at that moment that he heard a slight whisper in his right ear. The voice was sweet and melodic, singing him a lullaby. He could not see the creature that hovered behind him, but he could feel its presence. And then, a similar sounding voice was now crooning to him in his left ear. Together the two voices weaved together an intricate harmony of sounds that were not composed of any words. He felt soothed and so very tired. His body relaxed. Soon the beautiful song that was singing him to sleep quieted as the humming moved away from his ears.

Chai opened his heavy eyelids and saw before him the two headed sleeper serpent. Its eyes flashed brightly in the dim light of the room. He was transfixed by their unblinking stare as he fell deeper and deeper under the creature's hypnotic trance. Chai braced himself for what his mind, even in its altered state, registered was about to come. To his immense relief, Baltazar was true to his word. Chai felt no pain when the sleeper serpent lunged forward and wrapped both of its bodies tightly around his torso. Chai felt the increasing force as the serpent squeezed harder and harder, and Chai's breath became more labored as the pressure mounted. As the last vestiges of air escaped from Chai's lungs, his eyes drifted shut and the blackness enveloped him.

CHAPTER TWENTY-SIX

After arriving at home, Maggie fretted about, unable to sit still. She wanted to ensure that Dylan was comfortable, and she felt anxious about her ability to care for her newly found son. This was after all, the first time in his life that she would be taking care of him and Maggie wanted to be certain that she did everything absolutely right.

'Dylan honey, can I get you anything? Food? You must be hungry. Let me whip you up something. Anything you want. You just have to tell me, what can I get for you?' the words poured out of her mouth in a rush.

Dylan walked over to his mother and gave her a comforting hug. He could see that she was nervous, and he wanted to put her at ease.

'Mom, really you don't have to worry. I feel fine and I'm not hungry now. I think I would just like to rest, if you don't mind. I didn't sleep too well last night...' Dylan looked up at his mother, hoping that he did not upset her and wondering if he should let her baby him for a little bit. He really did want to sleep, but he also wanted to make her happy.

Maggie stared into the clear grey eyes of her son and felt reassured that he was not in any pain. 'I'm sorry, sweetheart. I know I'm being over-protective. Of course, you go to your room and take a nap. When you wake up, if you're hungry, just let me know. And if you need anything, all you have to do is call me. I will be home with you all day, just in case.'

'Thanks, mom,' Dylan replied softly and reached up to give her another hug. Maggie pulled him in close and rested her chin on the top of his head. Dylan's eyes welled up with tears. His other mother, his human mother, used to do the same thing. He blinked hard and fought back the wave of home-sickness that suddenly flooded through his body. Maybe it was because of his injury that these feelings were coming on so strong. He had never been hurt or sick before without the warmth of Olivia and Mike, his human mom and dad, to make him feel better. He didn't want Maggie to guess that he missed his other parents because he knew it would hurt her. Dylan bit his bottom lip and concentrated on keeping his emotions in check. After another minute, he felt Maggie's arms loosen their grip, and by then, Dylan had everything back under control. He smiled at his warlock mother, and then flew upstairs to his room.

When Dylan opened the door, Via came lunging at him and rammed into his chest.

'It's a good thing you don't weigh very much,' he laughed as he stroked his pet softly. 'I missed you too, Via. It's good to be home.'

Via nuzzled in closer and scurried up his torso. She parked herself firmly in the crevice between Dylan's shoulder and neck and made contented purring sounds as she nestled there.

Waiting on his bed were two more friends. Halle and Oliver sat perched on the edge of the bed in their human looking form. Their unusual turquoise eyes were filled with concern as they scrutinized Dylan from head to toe.

'You look okay to me,' grunted Oliver. 'I don't see anything wrong with you.'

'Ollie, don't be so rude. Just because he is fine now, doesn't mean that he was in the same condition yesterday. They wouldn't have kept him overnight if they didn't think it was necessary. We're just so glad that you're back, Dylan,' chimed in Halle. 'We were worried about you.'

'And we missed you,' stated Oliver.

'I'm just saying though,' said Halle in her typical no-nonsense voice, 'I told you so. I didn't want to say it, but I feel that I must. I told you before that we should have been with you at school. We can't protect you when you are so far away from us. I feel like we failed you, Dylan…even though it was your fault.'

Dylan couldn't help but laugh at Halle's haughty tone. 'Oh Halle, there was nothing you could have done, even if you had been there. It was just a freak accident. There was no evil plot to take me down.'

Dylan sat down on the bed between them. He felt the urge to hug them close, the way he would have done if they were in their canine form, but it just felt too weird to embrace them looking like people. 'I missed you too,' he said.

Oliver nudged his head under Dylan's hand and looked up at him with sad eyes. Dylan could read the unspoken message there, and gently patted Oliver's soft, silvery hair. Underneath his fingers, Dylan could feel Oliver's body begin to tremor and in an instant Dylan found his beloved husky sitting on his lap. Dylan laughed at his protector's antics and feeling much more comfortable, leaned over to rub Oliver's belly. Oliver closed his eyes in contentment while Halle looked on impatiently.

'Really, Oliver. Is this necessary? Couldn't you refrain from becoming an animal for a little longer? We were dogs for twelve years straight – isn't that enough for you?'

Oliver barked but what that meant, Dylan didn't have a clue. Halle seemed to understand her brother and she leapt off the bed. Her little foot tapped impatiently on the floor as she stood with her hands on her hips and a scowl across her pixie-like face. Then Halle looked at Dylan, the boy she loved with all her heart and who she was determined to protect from all harm. Dylan was lovingly patting Oliver and had a forlorn, wistful look in his eyes.

'Is something wrong, Dylan?' she asked perceptively.

'Seeing Ollie like this and being hurt yesterday without my mom and dad around, well, you know who I mean... it just makes me think of home. My other home, that is.' Dylan sighed. 'I miss them,' he whispered. 'I wish I could talk to them.'

Oliver barked again, more loudly this time. 'What is it boy?' Dylan asked. Oliver whined. 'I think maybe you will have to change back for me to understand you,' Dylan said.

Oliver's body trembled again as he transformed back to his human-like stature. 'We can deliver a message for you,' Oliver declared. 'Like what Maggie did, but this time, it can be from you.'

'No, Ollie,' interjected Halle. 'We'll get in trouble, and so will Dylan. You know we aren't supposed to do that. And Olivia and Mike would recognize us. Then what would we do? It's impossible.'

'First, nobody has ever *directly* told us that we can't deliver messages. Second, sometimes you have to take risks. Maybe this is one of those times that it is worth doing something you might know you shouldn't do, but that is really the right thing. And, who says we have to show up as huskies? We can become anything. They would never know it was us.' Oliver smiled triumphantly. Usually it was Halle who did all the thinking and he just went along with her plans. Oliver was very pleased with himself. Halle, however, sniffed in derision, clearly unimpressed with her brother's plan. But Dylan latched on to Oliver's suggestion with full enthusiasm.

'You would do that for me, Oliver?' Dylan asked, his grey eyes shining with hope. 'I could create a message really quickly. It would be short and sweet. Just something to let them know that I'm okay and that I love them and I'm thinking of them. Then you could deliver it for me today, like right away, couldn't you?'

'Sure, Dylan. I would do anything for you,' replied Oliver.

'Oh fine. If you're intent on doing this, I'm not going to let you go at it alone. We will do it together. But it's going to be fast, Oliver. I'm warning you. We are going in disguise and we are not sticking around. We will deliver Dylan's message, watch for their response and then come right back here. Before anyone realizes we are missing, agreed?'

'Whatever you say, Halle. I agree,' Oliver said without any hesitation.

'That's great! Let me create the message,' Dylan responded happily. Using his magic, Dylan conjured up an ordinary piece of paper and a marker. Using his neatest, most legible printing he wrote:

Dear Mom and Dad,
I miss you both very much. I'm fine but I

can't come home, at least not now. I think about you every day and I love you both so much. I promise that I will see you again one day. Please try not to worry about me. Love, Dylan

As he finished writing, a single tear drop fell onto the paper. Dylan kissed the tip of his finger and gently touched the drop of wetness. 'I love you,' he whispered again softly. Then he folded up the paper into a small square and held it out Halle.

'One second, Dylan. Let us make the change, and then you can attach your note under my collar. But make sure it's hidden. We don't want the border guards to catch us when we pass through the vortex. They know us now so I don't think that they will bother to stop us. I'm not too concerned, but we should make sure that they can't see it.' She turned to look at her brother. 'Cats this time, Ollie?' she asked. Oliver nodded enthusiastically. Their bodies began to shake and their limbs to contract. In the blink of an eye, two Siamese cats with beautiful turquoise eyes blinked up at Dylan. Halle deftly leapt up onto the bed and stretched out her neck so that Dylan could clearly see her sparkling pink collar studded with rhinestones... or were those real diamonds, Dylan wondered?

'Always fashionable, aren't you Halle?' Dylan joked. He placed his note firmly beneath the collar and kissed the top of Halle's smooth head. 'Thanks guys,' he said. 'Come back soon and be careful!' Oliver jumped into Dylan's arms and started to purr. Halle, business-like as usual, hissed at her brother to hurry him up. The two disappeared out of the bedroom and began their journey back to the vortex which would return them to the mortal world.

Dylan lay down on the bed with Via and closed his eyes. In an instant, he was fast asleep.

Back at school, Thea was alone in the library with the exception of the librarian, a friendly little fairy named Ms. Fairstone. After fluttering around her for a few minutes, Thea finally convinced Ms. Fairstone that she really didn't need any help and that she was just looking around while she waited for Reus. Ms. Fairstone went back to her desk, which gave Thea a little bit of freedom to roam the shelves of books which lined the walls from the ceiling to the floor of the well-appointed library. After all, Thea couldn't tell the librarian what she was really looking for!

'I don't even know what it is exactly that I'm hoping to find,' Thea muttered to herself. She finally decided that what she really wanted to learn more about was prophecies. But would there be something in the school library about the specific prediction she was seeking? Probably not, she thought but figured it was worth a try.

Thea pulled her wand out of her waistband and decided to forgo her usual flying chair. It was too cumbersome for searching the library. She would just have to get around the more common way of levitating. Thea flew over to the section of the library that housed the books on magic. Maybe there would be something of interest there. Thea scanned the titles of dozens of books on magic. She even opened them up to take a closer look inside. Nothing.

Okay then, Thea thought to herself. *Maybe I need to look at books about humans. Maybe there will be something about prophecies in the human world.* She darted across the library to where the books on human culture were stored. She scanned many books looking for a title that seemed relevant to her research. She even read a few pages in one book where she learned about biblical prophecies. *These are extremely interesting,* she mused, *but not quite what I'm looking for.* If she wasn't on a specific quest for information, she would have lingered over this one. *This stuff might be useful when I am serving in the human world.* Thea decided that one day soon, she would have to come back to this section.

Now where should I look? Then it came to her – an epiphany! *I should look in the History section! Maybe there will be something about the specific prophecy there!* So once again, Thea flew at breakneck speed back across the library again to the History section. Ms. Fairstone called out a warning to slow down, which Thea instantly obeyed. She did not want Ms. Fairstone coming back over to check on her. Too many questions would not be good!

Thea ran her hand over the spines of books, searching for a title that might be useful. Until finally she spotted it: The Immortal World: A Complete Century of History Starting From The End Of The Civil War. Usually, this was the type of book that would have Thea bolting in the other direction. What could possibly be more boring than this? But maybe, if she was very lucky, there would be some reference, even the tiniest little bit of information, that would be useful to help figure out the prophecy that nobody seemed to know about.

She quickly pulled the book off the shelf and blew away the dust that heavily coated its cover. *Clearly this book has not been read in a very long time,* Thea thought. The library was still empty but who knew if it would stay that way, so Thea found herself a comfortable, worn armchair in a secluded corner, hidden by stacks of books. She settled in to read. The first few chapters she was able to skim through quickly. There was nothing there except excruciating details about the factors that led up to the immortal civil war. The next several chapters discussed the war itself – specific battles that were fought, the casualties, and the human response. *Okay, that was actually sort of interesting,* Thea conceded. *It's amazing how humans found plausible explanations for things that happened which were really supernatural. I guess that either they are very gullible or perhaps, they just don't want to believe in the existence of immortals.* Thea squirreled away the information to think about later, when she would have the luxury of time. Right now, they needed this information fast!

Thea continued to flip rapidly through the pages until she found a reference that was of some use. She read the passage several times, contemplating how this new information fit in with what they already knew. The author wrote:

The Ministry was finally created, and its leaders in place. It was essential to establish rules to govern the new realm and to create a society of immortals who would acquiesce to the current order. Rebellious acts, no matter how small, could not be tolerated as such behavior could compromise the effectiveness of the leaders entrusted with constructing this new society. The first such instance of rebellion occurred almost immediately after the leaders came to power. This vampire was strongly opposed to the terms of peace that lead to the creation of the immortal world. The leaders acted swiftly, and mightily. Their first unified decision was to call for this wayward vampire's destruction in the worst possible manner, in order to send a strong message to all immortals in both the new and old worlds. This misguided vampire was given an opportunity to express his final thoughts, but the Ministry wisely paid no heed to the rantings of a condemned immortal and the statements made by this errant vampire died with him in flames.

Thea mulled over this paragraph. *Okay, nothing specific about a prophecy. But it validates the story we have been told about a vampire being put to death by the leaders, and clearly he said something before he died, which could have been the prediction that we are looking for. If only there was something more concrete. A single clue about the prophecy...*

Thea repositioned herself and crossed her legs, with the book splayed across her lap thinking. She flipped to the next page and as she did, a tiny piece of old parchment paper, yellowed and brittle with age floated up off the page and swayed gently in front of her eyes. 'What's this?' Thea whispered softly as she reached out to capture it in her hands. Three sides of the paper were perfectly straight, but the bottom edge was ripped and jagged. It seemed as if someone had impulsively torn a strip off. A single line was scrawled in old fashioned writing. The ink was slightly smudged, as if it had been written in haste and not given time to dry before being inserted into the book, where it had clearly lain for hundreds of years, never having been read or viewed from the looks of it. The sentence said this:

You must heed the utterings of the one condemned — A blessing or a curse, our fate rests in the hands of four.

A small black mark lay below the words, and it seemed to Thea that there had once been something else written there. Thea cradled the thin piece of paper in her palm, but despite her attempts to handle it with great care, the tiny square of writing disintegrated in her hand. She was left holding nothing more than tiny bits of ashes which poured out through her fingers and disappeared in a wisp of smoke.

Finally, a breakthrough, Thea rejoiced. Not that she had any proof of it anymore, but at least she had found a small reference to the prophecy. Thea's mind raced. She realized that anything published would have been approved by the Ministry and clearly the leaders would never have allowed something about the prophecy to be printed and available for distribution. *So then who had written it? Who would be willing to risk the wrath of the Ministry if this was ever discovered? And why would they want someone to find out about the prophecy if the Ministry went to such great lengths to hide it?* How *did that tiny square of writing get sandwiched between the pages of the book? And what had been written there which had been discarded so that nobody would be able to see it?* Questions were flying through her mind, but she couldn't think of a single answer that made any sense.

Thea turned back to the title page of the book to see who the author was in the hopes that perhaps that would give her some insight. When she saw the listed author, her eyes widened with astonishment. The writer's name was listed simply as Reus. *Could it be the same Reus?* Suddenly, she heard voices at the front of the library. Ms. Fairstone was talking to someone. It didn't take more than a minute before Thea was able to see who it was. At the end of the row of books from where she sat, stood Reus, staring right at her.

'Thea,' he intoned in a low voice.

Thea quietly closed the book and discreetly tried to hide it behind her back. 'Hi Reus,' she answered casually, hoping that she sounded calm and collected. 'I guess you saw my note. I hope you don't mind that I came here. I thought it would be more productive to work in the library since you weren't in the classroom.'

'Certainly. Not a problem, Thea. Now tell me, what is it that you were working on?'

'Oh, you know. Nothing in particular. Just homework from some other classes. This and that... '

'This and that?' Reus prodded, instinctively understanding that this child wizard was withholding something.

Thea laughed nervously as Reus walked closer to where she sat. 'Let me see what reading material you selected this morning,' he demanded as he held out his hand waiting for Thea to comply with his instructions.

Knowing that she had no choice, Thea reached behind her and gingerly placed the book in Reus' outstretched palm. He glanced at the cover and his eyes opened wide in surprise. 'This is what you were reading?' he asked incredulously.

Thea nodded. 'The author's name is Reus. Any relation?' she joked.

Reus nodded solemnly. 'Yes, it is I. I was commissioned by the one of the deputies to write this as a tribute to the Ministry's victory after the first century of peace in our new world had been achieved. I have also authored sequels every century thereafter, to commemorate the accomplishments of our leaders.' Reus gestured with his head towards the shelves where Thea could see the complete series. 'I was unaware that any student was particularly interested in this topic. I don't think that anyone in the school has ever read my book before. I'm impressed, Ms. Wiz. Now tell me, what precisely were you reading before I interrupted you?'

Thea didn't know what to say. On the one hand, she felt protective of the information that her and the twins had learned so far. Maybe she needed to keep it to herself. On the other hand, Reus seemed to have more knowledge than anyone else she had encountered. Was there a way for her to pry any information out of him without making him suspicious? Thea quickly calculated that the risk was too great. She just couldn't let on what she had actually been reading. So she lied.

'I had just started, so you know the stuff about why the civil war broke out when immortals lived in the human world.'

Reus narrowed his eyes in disbelief. He knew that Thea was very clever, and he guessed that she would not have attempted to conceal the book if she was not hiding something. He tried to remember what he had written all those centuries ago when he authored the book. *What has her so interested and so willing to lie?* he wondered to himself. Reus walked slowly closer to where Thea sat. Due to his small stature, when he stood in front of her chair, his eyes were level with hers. Reus stared intently into Thea's dark eyes and began to chant ancient words in a low, melodic voice. Thea instantly fell into a trance and her eyes drifted shut.

'Now tell me, Thea,' Reus purred, 'what were you reading

about in my book?'

'A vampire rebelled and then he was executed.'

'Was anything else in the book of interest to you?'

'Not the book. The parchment. The prophecy.'

Reus' eyes widened with concern. *How much does this child know beyond the very basic information that I provided? And what parchment is she talking about?* he wondered.

'*What parchment are you referring to, Thea?*'

'Gone...gone...' she waved her fingers gently and sighed.

'Why are you interested in such a prophecy, if indeed there was one?' inquired Reus softly.

Thea's answer was very short. 'Dylan and Remy,' she said tonelessly still deeply entranced by Reus' magic.

Reus was taken aback. *This child knows a lot more than I would ever have given her credit for. But how can she know this? And who else knows?* he thought in a panic.

'Thea,' Reus prodded, 'What about Dylan and Remy? How are they related to this prophecy, do you think?'

'I think they are connected to the prophecy,' she replied. 'But we don't know how.'

'Who is we?' probed Reus.

'Dylan, Remy and myself.'

'Do you have any proof that they are connected to the prophecy?' Reus held his breath as he waited for the answer.

'No,' was her reply.

Before Reus could ask any more questions, he was interrupted by Ms. Fairstone who fluttered over, trying to be helpful. Reus had to break the spell and Thea was released from the trance that he had put her under. Thea had no memory of what had transpired.

Reus' mind raced. It was imperative that Baltazar not discover what these children had found, for if he even suspected that these young immortals had connected the boys to the prophecy, then everything that Reus had worked for over the centuries would be obliterated. Reus knew without a doubt that Baltazar would kill all of them immediately without remorse. While Baltazar wanted to keep the siblings alive for now, Reus was certain that those intentions would change in an instant if Baltazar knew what was happening. Whatever plans Baltazar had envisioned for these children would not be worth the risk if he learned of the children's discovery. And of course, Reus still had not been able to deliver Dylan into Baltazar's custody yet either. This would not do! Reus now realized that the children's lives, including this young wizard, were in greater peril than ever before. The only way to protect them and keep them safe was to deliver Dylan to Baltazar. Reus would be able to ensure their safety so long as Baltazar continued to believe that Reus was serving him. Reus knew he had to act fast. He had to get Dylan out of his house and into Baltazar's underground castle – today! And he would have to find a way to warn these young immortals of the danger they were putting themselves in by their quest for knowledge. He needed to get home immediately and put his plan into action.

'Thea,' Reus instructed, 'You can remain here until lunch. Then go to your regular afternoon classes. I have something to attend to now.' Reus snapped his fingers and was gone.

Thea looked at Ms. Fairstone who stood smiling at Thea. 'Well dear, you won't have long to wait. The lunch bell is going to ring anytime.'

'Can I sign out this book?' Thea asked the librarian.

'Of course! With pleasure,' she replied delightedly. Ms. Fairstone waved her hand over the spine of the book and then over Thea's hand. 'Done.' The bell rang signaling the start of lunch. 'Off you go, dear. Come again soon!' Thea flew off with the book clutched tightly in her hand. She had to find Remy!

CHAPTER TWENTY-SEVEN

Thea flew into the cafeteria so quickly that she almost slammed into a group of students who were hovering near the entrance. 'I'm so sorry,' she mumbled in response to the dirty looks that she received. But Thea had much more important matters on her mind and she darted through the crowd into the large open room. Her black eyes scanned the students searching desperately for Remy. Finally, she found him, in the most unusual of circumstances. Remy was surrounded by a large group of vampires, all of whom were clamoring around him. As Thea approached them, she could hear that the vampires were all asking Remy about Dylan, anxious to know if he was doing okay. Thea could see that all of their eyes, usually so pale that they were practically translucent, had deep color to them, which clearly indicated that their bodies were full of blood. When Thea was standing directly next to one particularly pretty vampire named Jessie, she was finally able to ask the question that was so perplexing.

'Hey Jessie, why the sudden interest in Remy and Dylan?'

Jessie flashed a wide smile showing a perfect row of pearly white teeth. 'Dylan gave us the greatest gift yesterday. He gave us his blood, and there was something very special about his blood compared to others.'

'Really,' questioned Thea somewhat confused. 'Isn't blood the same no matter who it comes from? I mean, blood is blood, right?'

'I would have thought so too, at least based upon the blood that I have consumed,' agreed Jessie. 'But after ingesting Dylan's blood, now I know otherwise. His blood makes us feel... different.'

'Different? How? What do you mean?'

'It's hard to explain to a non-vampire but essentially, we feel stronger, more vibrant. All of our nerve endings are more sensitive than ever before. We can feel sensations differently with his blood running through us – more alive, I guess you could say. His blood is so much more potent than others. I mean, he lost a lot of blood no question, but look how many of us were able to be satisfied from his injury. There were fifteen of us who were all fully nourished from the blood loss that he suffered yesterday. And the way I'm feeling now, I imagine that it will be several weeks before the effects completely wear off. So we are very grateful to him. He had to suffer for us to benefit, and we were worried that he might not survive. He looked terrible yesterday, but Remy says he is doing much better today. Apparently, he is already back home! We wanted Remy to send him our best wishes.'

'You think that Dylan's blood is special. Do you think that Remy's might be as well?' asked Thea, her mind whirling with the implications of what this might mean to their theory.

'Hmm... I don't know. But they are identical, so I would think that Remy's blood would be equally as satisfying for us as Dylan's. Maybe Remy would be willing to donate a little blood in the name of scientific research,' laughed Jessie. 'But not now. Perhaps when Dylan's blood has left our systems we could try it out. Thanks for the suggestion!'

Thea tried to get close to Remy. She really needed to talk to him, but his new vampire admirers wouldn't let up. Every time she pushed herself a little bit closer to him, she got nudged backwards in the shuffle. *Literally one step forward, two steps back* she thought. Finally, she made eye contact with him and she motioned him to come closer to her so that they could talk. Remy mouthed a silent apology to her and shrugged his shoulders to indicate that he was stuck where he was. As Thea took a step back to wait for him, she was able to observe that Remy didn't seem to mind his new-found attention. Especially when it was beautiful Jessie's turn to drape her arm around his shoulder and whisper something into his ear. Finally, the bell rang indicating that the lunch period was over. The vampires left all together in their group, heading off for their vampire class. Thea knew that she had to get to her wizardly magic class too, but she had to speak to Remy first. It was urgent.

'Remy, I found out some things this morning that might be useful. And Jessie said something that I think might also be important to our investigation.'

'Jessie said something to you about me?' Remy asked excitedly.

'It's not what you're thinking, so you can put your tongue back in your mouth now. You seem to be drooling a little bit!'

'Oh come on, Thea. Jessie is the most gorgeous creature in the school. If she was talking about me, I want to know exactly what she said. Word for word!'

'Listen, Remy. I will be happy to fill you in, word for word as you wish, but after school. Can we meet up to talk?'

'Yeah, sure. My mom let me know that Dylan's back home. Why don't you come over again today right after school and then the three of us can talk together?'

'Perfect. We can go right after HCS class. I feel like we are on the verge of a breakthrough, if we can just put all the pieces of the puzzle together. See you then, okay?'

'Yup,' replied Remy. Just then the second bell rang. 'Darn, I'm late for magic class and until Dylan got here, I wasn't doing too well. I don't think that Ms. Warmaster is going to be very happy with me. And I need to go to my locker first. Got to go. See ya!' Remy took off with a whoosh leaving Thea standing alone in the empty cafeteria.

'I guess I better get to magic class as well,' she muttered to herself but unlike Remy, she wasn't in such a hurry. Thea had so many ideas flying around in her head and wished that she could just have a little time to put them together in some sort of order. *I just know that there is something going on. All these bits and pieces of information must connect somehow! If only we could figure it out...*

'Ms. Wiz,' a stern voice rang out behind her. Thea turned and saw the principal, Mr. Fairshelf with his arms crossed over his chest standing in the cafeteria doorway.

'Yes, sir. I know I'm late for class. I'm going right now.'

When Mr. Fairshelf realized that Thea was not being defiant, his demeanor instantly changed from firm to concerned. 'Everything okay, Thea?' he asked.

'Yes, sir. I'm just working through some things.'

'Can I help?' he asked with genuine warmth in his voice.

Thea seriously considered his offer. Maybe this was someone that they could trust. But she just wasn't sure and didn't want to make that decision without talking to Remy and Dylan. 'Thanks, Mr. Fairshelf. Not now, but if something changes, I will let you know.'

'I'm always here if you need me,' he replied. Then he waved his fingers and a late admit slip appeared in Thea's hand. 'Thank you, sir,' she said in response and then she flew out the door to her magic class.

Inside the classroom where the warlock magic course was held, the teacher, Ms. Warmaster was teaching new information to her students. At the front of the room was a large cart that held several pots of flowering plants. Some had small blooms that were yellow and orange. Others had drooping petals in various shades of red and pink. And then there were some that had hundreds of tiny purple buds not quite ready to burst open just yet. Ms. Warmaster was explaining the properties of the various plants.

'Now students, it is imperative that you pay close attention to today's lesson and carefully observe the specimens that I have brought here today to show you. There are some plants that are completely harmless to immortals however, you must be aware that those which are benign very closely resemble plants which have significant effects on supernatural beings. Some of those effects can even be deadly. Immortals are almost impossible to destroy as you know, however, the magical properties of some of the plants we will look at today, can be fatal if our exposure is too great. You need to understand as well that the harmful plants are very rare, and their magic is so strong that they are resistant to intervention by immortals. Our Ministry has tried to eradicate them but without success. Their seeds are practically invisible and the plants which can affect us grow amongst the plants that resemble them but have no impact on us at all. It makes it almost impossible to spot them until it is too late. If you ever see plants such as these, you must take great precautions to ensure that the dangerous plants are not present. Come closer so that you can see the differences and be able to protect yourself should you ever encounter this type of flora. But do not touch anything,' she warned.

Ms. Warmaster beckoned her students forward and they gathered around the cart at the front of the room. First Ms. Warmaster elevated two pots of flowers with red and pink petals.

'One of these plants,' she stated 'will have no effect on any immortal whatsoever. The other, has mind altering powers that will induce feelings of happiness and love. These effects are temporary and will wear off quickly, but these mood enhancing flowers can ease tensions, reduce anger and create feelings of contentment, if only for a short time. While I wouldn't classify these plants as dangerous, it is always concerning when our minds become impaired and our ability to make rational decisions is altered. Now, let me show you the differences between the two.'

Ms. Warmaster had one of the pots float closer towards the students, but still at a respectful distance. She used her magic to have a beam of brilliant white light illuminate the stem of the plant. 'This plant is known by its common name Jubilee, however, its scientific title is non-maganliaphyta julisbee. Notice the stalk of this plant. The diameter is fairly thin, and you will also see that there are flecks of brown that cover its length as well. This plant is completely harmless and will have no impact on any immortal.'

Next, she had the second pot of similar looking flowers also come closer to the students before it stopped directly next to the first. Now the light shone brightly on the stem of this second plant.

'Notice that the stalk of this flower is much hardier. It is thicker, close to the width of your thumb. That allows the magic to flow at great speed and volume from its roots to its blooms. This stem is completely green without any additional markings as you saw on the first plant. You may also notice that the color of the petals is darker, more vibrant, although the difference is subtle and you will not be able to make a distinction based on the color alone. You need both plants side by side to notice such a difference. This mind-altering plant is referred to as Infatualization, but it is scientifically known as maganliaphyta interruptus. Any questions?'

The students all remained silent and waited for their teacher to continue.

The red and pink flowers floated back to the cart and were replaced by two more pots. This time, the petals were various shades of yellow and orange. Ms. Warmaster explained that one of the plants had no magical properties however the other one would burn someone's skin immediately upon contact. Only vampires who did not have any human blood within them would be immune to such pain, but the plant was still strong enough to eat the skin and leave a hole where it had been. If those flowers were ingested, great damage would be caused internally and only a master healer would be able to assist the poor immortal who had consumed it. Once again, Ms. Warmaster used a beam of light to illustrate the differences. This time, the light shone on the leaves of both plants at the same time.

'Students, notice that these two plants are almost identical. The colors of the blooms are the same intensity. The stem diameter and shape of the petals are all the same. The difference is in the leaves. I want you to begin by counting the number of points on the leaves of the plant to the left. How many points are there on each side of the leaves?'

'Five on each side,' called out one student.

'Excellent, Grayson,' responded Ms. Warmaster. 'Remember this rhyme,' stated the teacher. 'Five on a side, remain alive. How many points are on the leaves of the plant to the right?' she asked.

'I count six,' stated another student.

'That's not right,' retorted another. 'I counted four on each side.'

Ms. Warmaster nodded. 'You are both correct. The second plant has leaves that differ from each other on the same plant, but its leaves will never have five points on a side. It may have three, four, six or seven, but never five. So, if you ever come across plants that look like these, be sure to very carefully count the points on the leaves. Five on a side, remain alive. If less or more, it will burn to the core. The plants that will cause no harm have the scientific name of non- maganliaphyta regina. Its common name is Regatta. The plants that will burn you, are called Inferno, but their scientific name is maganliaphyta ignitius. Questions?' Ms. Warmaster paused but the students remained silent. 'Very well, on to the last and most deadly of the plants.'

The orange and yellow plants were replaced by two pots of flowers that each had buds of deep purple. The students instinctively took a step back in fear of being too close. Ms. Warmaster noted their trepidation and acknowledged their wisdom in being respectful of the distance between them and the potentially lethal flowers.

'One of these plants poses no risk of harm. The other, especially when it is in bud form, contains one of the most pungent and dangerous poisons known to immortals,' warned Ms. Warmaster. She went on to explain that just before the buds opened, the magic was at its peak. An immortal who made even the briefest of contact with one bud would immediately be rendered unconscious and fall into a deep sleep for several minutes. The longer the exposure, the longer the sleep. And if someone should ever ingest a bud, the immortal would fall into a coma that could last for weeks on end. If they consumed too much of the plant, then death could easily follow. The plant lost some potency once the buds were in bloom but coming into contact or swallowing part of a single flower, could still have severe consequences, including death if too much was consumed.

'Now students,' Ms. Warmaster said, 'let us observe the differences between non- maganliaphyta polayaris, also known by its common name of Polyaris which cannot harm you, and maganliaphyta mortuarisis, usually just called Mortuarisus. The problem with distinguishing between these two types of flora is that they are completely identical in every way except for one.' She paused. 'And that one way, cannot be seen when the buds are closed. You can only notice the difference when the flowers are in bloom. Watch,' she demanded.

The bright lights shone directly over each pot of flowers and the students waited tensely to see what would happen. After a minute had passed, the tightly closed buds began to unfurl. The plant on the left opened to reveal petals of pale lilac with a pale blue center. The plant on the right also unfolded. While its petals were a similar shade of pale purple, at its core a flaming burst of red indicated to the students that this was the flower to avoid at all costs.

'So, which of these two flowers do you think poses the threat?'

Without exception, every student pointed towards the plant on the right with the bright red warning easily seen by everyone in the room.

'Yes, you would think so, wouldn't you? But in fact, that plant will cause you no harm whatsoever. The one that can kill you is the one that seems harmless. But appearances can be deceiving, and it is the plant on the left that has the potential to end your life. I am trusting all of you to be very careful examining these plants. At this stage in your education it is important for you to be exposed to the real thing, so that you will be able to recognize them and learn how to protect yourself and others should you ever come across their path. While they are rare, they are extremely hardy and can grow under the most extreme conditions. Remember what I told you - the Ministry has tried to get rid of them, but these plants are indestructible, so it is extremely essential for all of you to learn to be respectful of the flora that surrounds us in our world. Please return to your seats and I will call you up one at a time to get a closer look.' Ms. Warmaster had the plants return to their original place on the cart.

Traysik put up his hand. 'Yes?' Ms. Warmaster asked.

'No offence Ms. Warmaster, but my dad has already talked to me about these plants. And what you are saying seems to me to be a huge exaggeration. He said that when he was in school he was also taught that these plants are highly dangerous, but in his experience, he thinks that they are actually pretty harmless.

A little pain, a little sleepy maybe but nothing more.'

Ms. Warmaster gave Traysik an exasperated look. 'Is that so, Traysik? Do you want to come up and demonstrate that for us?'

'Me? Demonstrate?' Traysik's voice betrayed the fear that he was feeling but he didn't want to back down in front of his classmates. 'Yeah, sure. I trust my dad. He wouldn't lie to me.'

'I taught your father, Traysik. I'm sure he wouldn't lie to you, but perhaps he is mistaken? Are you really willing to do this? I assure you that I am telling the truth.'

'Maybe you think it's the truth, but I'm certain that my dad wouldn't tell me something that was false. Yeah, I'm willing to demonstrate whatever you want to prove you are wrong and he is right.'

'Very well, Traysik but remember, you were warned. You can back out at any time, okay? You just have to tell me to stop.'

Traysik nodded.

'Alright Traysik, step forward. Everyone else, go back to your seats and watch carefully. You might never see something like this again. Traysik, we are only going to test out the smallest quantities to demonstrate the power of these plants. Are you still sure you want to do this?' He nodded again.

Ms. Warmaster pursed her lips and paused but decided to proceed. First Ms. Warmaster used her magic to propel the cart holding the plants forward and off to the side, close to the doorway and away from the students. Then she used her powers to ensure that she did not come into contact with the petals herself and had just the tip of a red blossom separate itself from the bloom and float over to where Traysik stood confidently with a defiant glare at the front of the room. The speck of red landed on his bare forearm and everyone in the class leaned forward to see what would happen. Traysik's face immediately relaxed into a goofy looking grin.

'Ms. Warmaster, you're the best, nicest teacher in the whole school. I love your class. In fact, I love you and I love everyone in this room, even the Warston twins,' he declared happily in a slow, somewhat slurred drawl.

'Traysik, Dylan is out of school today and Remy's not in the class right now,' someone shouted out.

'Oh yeah,' Traysik replied. 'Well, someone needs to tell them that I love them too in case I forget later.' Everyone laughed. 'And tell Dylan that I am so sorry about yesterday,' Traysik continued actually looking contrite for what had happened. Traysik's contented mood lasted only for another few minutes before a scowl replaced his lopsided grin.

'Next,' called out Ms. Warmaster. The most minute, tiniest fragment of a bright orange petal separated itself from the rest of the plant. The piece was so small that the students couldn't even see it as the speck floated through the air but when it landed on Traysik's bare hand, they all heard the scream that erupted from his throat. As soon as he began to holler in pain, Ms. Warmaster had the bit of flower instantly remove itself from his skin and it disintegrated in the air in a small fiery poof. Traysik tried blowing on his hand, he licked his hand and he waved his hand frantically in the air to make the burning stop. But the intense pain raged on. Ms. Warmaster again used her magic to create a salve that she smoothed over his hand where the fragment had landed. The hole it left behind was so tiny that it could barely be seen, but a bright red welt marked the precise spot that was causing Traysik so much agony. The lotion seemed to help because Traysik's screams quickly turned to moans and from there, his moans became just loud gasps for air. Traysik was extremely embarrassed, and he blinked hard to stop the tears which were flowing freely down his cheeks. Nobody in the room was laughing though. The point Ms. Warmaster was trying to make had resonated soundly with all of them. These plants were just as potent as she had said.

'Now do you believe me, Traysik? Or do you want to try the purple ones next?'

'I believe you, Ms. Warmaster. I'm done demonstrating for today.' Traysik rapidly took his seat, far away from the flowers.

Just then, Remy came barreling through the door. Since he was rushing because he was so late, he stumbled as he entered. Remy lost his balance and crashed his full body into the cart of flowers. He fell to the floor and petals of all colors rained over his face, his hair, his body. From head to toe, he was covered in blossoms and leaves. When he opened his mouth to apologize, some of the bright purple ones landed in his mouth and he inadvertently swallowed them. He looked up from the ground and saw Ms. Warmaster staring at him in horror with her hand trembling as it hovered over her mouth. Some of his classmates started to scream in terror and even Traysik, his worst enemy, stared at him in pity.

Remy stood up and brushed the flowers off his body. As the remnants of the flowers fell to the ground, he smiled apologetically and offered to clean up the mess he had created. Nobody spoke for the longest time, and Remy was very confused. He wanted to use his magic to sweep up the dirt and plants from the floor but he was worried that he would screw things up, so he just stood there and waited for someone else to do something first. Finally, Ms. Warmaster came to her senses.

'Everybody stay back,' she ordered. 'Remy, are you okay?'

'I'm fine. It was just a little fall. I'm really sorry about your flowers, and the mess.' Remy bit his lip in embarrassment and waited to be chastised by his teacher. Instead, Ms. Warmaster raised her hands and made circular motions in the air. Her hands repeated the movement faster and faster and all the dirt and petals and leaves and broken fragments of pots were soon swirling around, like a tornado over Remy's head. Then with a final whoosh the wind tunnel with all the debris disappeared completely.

Ms. Warmaster rushed over to Remy and grabbed one of his arms. She turned it over this way and that, examining the skin closely trying to find the wounds that should have been left behind. There was nothing there.

Just then Remy started to cough, and he spit the remains of a purple bud into his hand. Remy grinned sheepishly. 'Sorry, 'bout that,' he said. 'I guess I swallowed a few of those.'

Ms. Warmaster gasped. 'You swallowed a *few* of the purple buds?'

Remy shrugged. The class looked on in awe. Ms. Warmaster appeared to be in shock. Her face was pale, her eyes were bulging out and her mouth was agape, just hanging open.

'You okay, Ms. W?' Remy asked worriedly. He looked around the room at his classmates, seeking someone to help him but they all just stared back at him, completely frozen. Remy didn't know what to do. *What's wrong with everyone?* he thought to himself.

Finally, Ms. Warmaster seemed to be returning to normal. She cleared her throat and said, 'Remy, please stay behind for a moment. Everyone else, class is dismissed early. Don't make too much noise in the hallways. Goodbye.' As the students filed out, they all continued to stare at Remy with astonishment on their faces. Nobody said anything to him as they left, and Remy was just as confused as he was before.

'You're sure that you feel okay, Remy?' asked Ms. Warmaster.

'Of course, I'm sure. I feel totally fine. Just a little embarrassed. Sorry again for destroying your flowers.'

Ms. Warmaster shook her head in disbelief. 'I don't understand this. You don't feel any different than earlier today?'

Remy shook his head. 'Well, I am a little hungry. I didn't have a chance to eat lunch today.'

'Go get something to eat before your last class, Remy. I'm so relieved that you aren't hurt or worse.'

'Why would you be so worried, Ms. W? I don't understand.'

'You just came in contact with flowers that should have you writhing in pain, with burn marks all over your body. And the purple buds that you ate, that should have put you into a coma so deep that you may never have recovered from it. But here you are, perfectly fine.'

'I guess that I'm really lucky,' Remy replied.

'Remy, I don't believe in luck like that. There must be something more. You don't have luck. You have a very powerful gift.'

Remy nodded his head solemnly. He would have something to tell Thea and Dylan about this afternoon too. He slowly left the room thinking about what he had just discovered. *What could this mean?* he wondered. He wished that time would speed up so that he could finally go home. He desperately wanted to discuss this with Dylan and Thea, but he still had one more class, unless of course he could convince Thea to ditch last period. Remy decided it was worth a try so he positioned himself directly outside of Thea's magic class so that he could grab her as soon as she came out. *Let's hope she is willing to skip last class,* he thought and counted the final minutes of the period as they slowly passed by.

CHAPTER TWENTY-EIGHT

Remy spotted Thea the second she emerged from her class-room and shouted her name as loudly as he could. Thea heard the impatience in Remy's voice and immediately walked towards him.

'Any opposition to skipping HCS today?' Remy asked, his voice edged with tension.

'Great minds think alike,' Thea replied as she ripped off her school uniform. 'Let's go to your house, now!' She grabbed her wand and in an instant, was sitting in her flying chair and taking off at full speed towards Remy's home. Remy tore off his sweater as well and followed right behind her. They didn't talk at all as they flew since that would have slowed them down. They simply kept their thoughts to themselves and sprinted through the blue sky towards their destination.

It was only a few minutes later before they burst through the front door and literally flew right into Maggie. They skidded to a stop and Maggie laughed, happy to have her first-born son home.

'Hi Remy, hi Thea,' Maggie greeted them warmly. 'You're home early today. What's going on?'

'Oh, we were just anxious to check on Dylan,' fibbed Remy. 'I didn't think you would mind if I missed my last class just for today. I couldn't concentrate too well anyways. And Thea was worried too, so I said she could come. That's okay, isn't it?'

'Of course, honey. I know that Dylan has been wanting to

see you too. He might be asleep though…'

'Don't worry, mom. If he's sleeping, I won't wake him up,' replied Remy, already heading upstairs to their shared room.

'Maybe you won't, but I will,' whispered Thea. 'This is too important to wait any longer. We have to talk!' she hissed between her teeth.

Remy quietly opened the bedroom door, not wanting to startle his brother if he was asleep, but to his relief, Dylan was wide awake and sitting with Via on the bed. Remy dashed towards his brother and enveloped him in a huge hug. Words were not necessary between the two boys. They heard each other's thoughts loud and clear. Thea approached Dylan a little more slowly and sat down next to him on the bed. Thea looked into Dylan's clear grey eyes and felt her insides warm slightly. She also reached out to give Dylan a hug, but it was short and sweet and a little bit awkward.

'I'm so glad that you're okay, Dylan,' Thea said as she pulled back.

'Yeah, me too! Thanks,' replied Dylan lightly, even though his heart was pounding in his chest. Then Dylan stared intently into Remy's green eyes and said a single word, 'legend'. Remy nodded his head solemnly and knew that the conversation in his mind the previous night with Dylan had been real. Thea looked momentarily confused before she broke into the conversation.

'Okay, we need to talk,' demanded Thea, all businesslike and in control. 'Something is going on and I think we all know that it involves the two of you and the secret prophecy. Let's take an inventory of what we have discovered so far,' she suggested.

Dylan held up his index finger. 'For one thing, we know

that our parents were lied to when we were born. They made them think only Remy survived.' He counted on his second finger. 'Second, whoever did it made sure to separate us. They put me in the human world and our other brother is who knows where.'

'Three,' Remy continued, 'When we are together, Dylan and I have these amazing powers that we don't usually have. Like with the transport portals that we can create.'

'But I have also realized that I can do some things on my own that are pretty unusual,' Dylan interjected. 'Like flying. I think that I have some sort of special ability to fly... I know that sounds kind of stupid...' Dylan blushed.

'No, that's totally not stupid. I think I have some special abilities too!' sputtered Remy. 'Remember the sleeper serpent that didn't affect me? Well today, something else really strange happened in magic class.' Remy went on to explain in detail how the magical plants which should have put him into a life -threatening coma didn't affect him at all.

'And Thea,' Dylan added. 'You are a part of this too. You know all about the human world, the constellations and the mythology that seem to be connected to the prophecy. And of course, we can't overlook the fact that you have healing powers.'

'My healing powers? You know about that, Dylan?' Thea asked.

'Of course! Look at the evidence. Think about what happened to me yesterday. You are the one who made the bleeding stop, the bones mend. I was unconscious, and you brought me around. It had to have been you. There is no other explanation,' stated Dylan firmly. Remy nodded in agreement, remembering their little healing experiment that confirmed what Dylan believed as well.

'Is it a coincidence that you are named after the goddess of healing?' wondered Remy out loud.

Thea was rendered speechless. Could it be just a coincidence or was there more to her name than just pure chance? Thea told the boys what she had learned that morning about the prophecy. She told them about the reference in Reus' book to the executed vampire, which corresponded to the stories they had heard. And then she recited the writing from the parchment paper word for word. The three young immortals sat in silence deep in concentration.

'So what do we do now?' asked Remy.

'I think that there is only one thing to do,' responded Dylan, his voice a little shaky with trepidation. 'We have to find our third brother. That is the only way to find the answers we need. If there is a prophecy, and I think we all agree that there is, and if we are somehow connected to it, and I think we all know that we are, then we need to reunite with him. There is no other option. Our original plan to start with our delivery records seems sort of lame, don't you think? More drastic measures are needed now.'

'I agree,' Thea said. 'You two must find him.'

'You have to come with us, Thea,' pleaded Dylan. 'You are just as much a part of this as Remy and I are. Will you help us?'

Without any hesitation, Thea nodded her head. She was in as deeply as the others.

'So how do we find him?' asked Remy. 'We don't have any clue where he might be.'

Remy looked at Dylan, reading his thoughts. 'Of course. You're brilliant, Dyl! That's exactly what we have to do!'

Thea looked at the two brothers questioningly. 'What? What

do we have to do?'

Dylan smiled. 'We are going to create a transport portal but instead of setting a specific destination, we are going to program it to take us to wherever our third brother is.'

'Can you do that?' asked Thea.

Dylan and Remy shrugged their shoulders in unison. 'We have no idea truthfully. But it's the only thing we can think of. If you think it's too dangerous, we understand Thea. You don't have to come with us. But we are going to try,' Remy said.

'I'm not afraid. I'm coming too,' Thea replied with determination. 'So, when do you want to do this?'

'No time like the present,' Dylan stated. 'Let's do this, right now!'

Dylan and Remy stood up facing each other and held hands tightly. They both closed their eyes, and with their minds in synch, they visualized the transport portal that would hopefully take them to their missing third brother and not kill them all in the process. The room was silent as the boys concentrated, their faces still, their eyelids plastered together. An identical furrow ran between their eyebrows as they completely focused on their objective.

A swirling mass soon appeared between their arms. It was not overly large but certainly big enough for three young immortals to pass through one at a time. The boys let go of each other's hands but kept their arms outstretched so that their fingers were almost grazing. The portal widened slightly but still maintained its configuration. Thea stepped forward so that she stood with her shoulders pressed against Dylan's on one side and Remy's on the other. Without speaking, Remy was the first to immerse himself into the portal. Thea jumped in right at his heels. Just as

Dylan was about to enter, Via sprang off the bed with a squeal and leapt into Dylan's hand. He instinctively tightened his grip and so Via too entered the portal. As soon as Dylan stepped through, the churning whirlpool disappeared. They were gone.

CHAPTER TWENTY-NINE

Dylan lay spread eagled, face down on a stone floor. His skin, where it touched the rough surface, was cold and his head ached. His lip was bleeding and he felt that it was already swollen to many times its normal size. He tentatively stretched and found that he could move but he was definitely in rough shape. His shoulder protested in pain as he tried to push himself upright. He managed to gingerly get himself into a sitting position and look around as best he could in the dimly lit room. Via squirmed uncomfortably in his hand, and he loosened his grip on his poor, little friend. He hadn't realized that he was holding her so tightly. At least she seemed okay. Via shimmied out of his hand and found a more comfortable position in his shirt pocket.

Dylan first spotted Remy lying on his back. His left leg was twisted in a funny position and he was groaning and writhing in misery. Dylan tentatively tried to stand up to go to help his brother, but his knees were weak and he was only able to crawl along the floor. *And where was Thea?*

As Dylan was dragging himself forward, his shoulder burned in agony. Dylan closed his eyes as he moved to try to minimize his pain. As he trudged forward, his hand grazed something that felt soft and silky. He opened his eyes, turned his head and saw that it was Thea's hair pooling over the floor. And when Dylan's gaze saw Thea, he cried out. She was also lying on her back. Not moving. *Was she dead???* Dylan leaned over her face and looked at her chest, just like he had been taught in first aid classes. He sighed in relief when he discovered that she was breathing. He lifted one of her hands and kissed her knuckles softly. As soon as he did, he immediately felt his split lip start to feel better. The stinging subsided. The puffiness was no longer there. His mouth felt totally back to normal. Dylan placed Thea's floppy hand on his aching shoulder and held it there for a moment. Thea's healing powers worked miracles again, even while she was unconscious, and within minutes, Dylan was no longer in any pain.

Dylan again checked Thea's vital signs. She was still not awake, but her eyes were beginning to twitch. He placed her hand on each of his knees and immediately felt his strength return. *We are so lucky to have her with us,* he thought. Dylan wondered whether he would be able to lift Thea and take her over to Remy to heal him too, or whether he would have to wait for her to wake up. He didn't have to ponder for very long because before he could even decide the best course of action, Thea's beautiful dark eyes opened, and she instantly sat up. Thea yawned as if she was waking up from a deep sleep and she smiled at Dylan.

'Well, that wasn't so bad,' she murmured quietly.

'Maybe not for you. But I was in pretty rough shape until you fixed me up,' Dylan whispered back, not wanting to be discovered yet. Until they knew where they were exactly, Dylan hoped to remain hidden from others. 'Can you walk, Thea? Remy looks worse off than I was. Can you make it over to him?'

'Of course, I can walk,' Thea muttered. She stood up as if nothing had happened to her at all and quietly tiptoed over to where Remy lay groaning on the floor. Thea crouched down next to her friend and gently placed her hands on his twisted leg. She carefully moved the bones until they were back where they should be and then, just to be sure, she ran her fingers softly over Remy's head, arms, and chest. Just to cover all the bases, she thought. Remy's moans stopped and soon he was smiling his usual lopsided grin. He jumped up as if he had never been injured and looked around.

They weren't in a room like Dylan had originally suspected but in a hallway. Dylan put his finger to his lips to remind the others to be quiet and he gestured that they should follow him. Via seemed to understand and turned off her fire power so that she was almost invisible, buried in Dylan's pocket. They moved forward silently and carefully until they reached a heavy, wooden door. Dylan and Remy's thoughts worked together, and they reached out to touch the lock with their fingers intertwined. The lock clicked open by the force of their magic, and they all stepped forward.

They were in a large room that was completely empty. The room was bathed in soft light which allowed the children to see their surroundings clearly. Tables, chairs, and sofas were organized in different seating arrangements, as if lots of people were often entertained in this room. At the back of the room, they could see another door. So they once again walked forward to see what, if anything was there. It was Remy this time who gingerly pressed his hands against this second, smaller door and pushed gently.

The room wasn't very big and it didn't have any windows. The room was completely dark except for a small lamp that stood on a wooden table which provided a weak glimmer of light. They could make out a small chair, a dresser and a bed. Clearly this was someone's bedroom. The three walked closer to the bed, where all they could initially see was a pile of blankets and pillows. But when they stood directly next to the bed, there was a stirring from beneath the linens and a hand shot out from under the covers. Via, terrified let out a high-pitched yelp and the figure who had been sound asleep until a moment ago, awoke with a start and sat up, his eyes confused and frightened.

'Who's there?' the voice from the bed spluttered, completely disoriented.

'Don't be afraid,' whispered Dylan as he leaned closer to speak to this unknown person. Dylan stared into eyes that were as familiar as his own, except for the color, which even in the dim light, Dylan could see were a deep shade of blue.

Dylan used his magic again to illuminate the room, instantly creating light where before there had been darkness. The boy in the bed had rumpled brown hair, with a cowlick right in the middle of his forehead. Except for the color of his irises, he was identical to Remy and Dylan.

'What's going on?' the boy in the bed asked, clearly bewildered. 'Who are you? And why do you both look like me?' he asked with panic in his voice.

'We are your brothers. Identical triplets actually,' said Remy with a grin.

'That's impossible. I don't have any family,' replied the boy fearfully.

'You're wrong. You were lied to. We all were and now we are trying to figure out this mystery together. Will you help us?' pleaded Dylan.

'This doesn't make any sense,' the third brother exclaimed.

'How did you get in here? Baltazar wouldn't have let you come see me.'

Thea, Remy and Dylan looked at each other, not sure what to say. Dylan took the lead. 'It's a very long story, if you want to hear it?'

Just then, they all heard angry voices approaching. These others were not far away. They were coming down the hallway.

'That's Baltazar,' the third brother whispered in a panic. 'You have to get out of here!'

'Come with us,' pleaded Dylan. 'We'll explain. Just come with us. There isn't any time…'

The boy's eyes were wild with fear. He was afraid of these two individuals who looked exactly like him. How could that be possible? What did they want with him? But he was even more terrified of Baltazar, who had kept him hostage for his entire life. Knowing there was no time to delay, the boy had to make a split-second decision.

'Okay, let's go,' the boy agreed with great trepidation. Dylan and Remy each grabbed a hand of their still unnamed brother. They closed their eyes and their thoughts were instantly transmitted to their third brother as well. They could hear what was in his mind too and promised to answer all his questions as soon as they were safe. They silently communicated the need to create the most powerful transport portal that they had ever done before. Dylan's inner voice took control and concentrated on getting them home.

In a flash, the portal appeared, larger and stronger than any they had ever created as a pair. The churning, roiling air twisted and spun. Remy jumped in first. Followed by Thea. The third brother hesitated slightly, but Dylan coaxed him with words and when that didn't work fast enough, he gave him a small shove.

Just then, two figures stood in the entrance to the bedroom. One, Dylan recognized. The other he had never seen before in his life, and he knew that now was not the time for introductions. With a final glance behind him, Dylan jumped into the transport portal with Via firmly ensconced in his pocket.

Before the two figures at the door could reach them, there was nothing left. The portal was gone and the children were too.

Baltazar glared down at Reus, fury burning in his pale, translucent eyes. Words were not necessary. Reus knew exactly what his master was thinking. It did not bode well for Reus' survival. Reus bowed his head and waited for Baltazar's wrath to be unleashed.

EPILOGUE

Remy, Thea and the unknown brother gazed around at the unfamiliar surroundings, their eyes wide in a combination of astonishment, curiosity and fear. Via remained hidden inside Dylan's shirt.

The third brother had never before been outside the confines of his prison, where he had been kept by Baltazar his entire life. He didn't even realize that he had lived in a secluded wing of Baltazar's own underground castle. This young immortal had never seen the sky, had never felt the open air on his skin, and he certainly did not know what to make of the tall, brown things that stood on either side of him. He reached out a hand and tentatively touched the rough surface of the object that stood sturdy and barren.

Thea was transfixed by the sky. No longer the brilliant blue that she was used to – the only sky that she had ever known. This sky was dull and overcast. Big, dark puffy objects floated overhead, and she recalled from HCS class that these foreign bodies must be clouds. Tiny bits of what she thought were white dust drifted down and landed on her skin. They were cold and unlike anything she had ever witnessed before.

Remy was most fixated by the stuff under his feet. It was crunchy and hard and white. It even glittered a little bit in the hazy light that filtered from above. He reached down to touch it, and some of it stuck to his finger. He sucked on it and was surprised by the fact that it didn't taste like anything. He let the cold substance melt on his tongue.

Dylan stared across the street from where they stood. The surroundings familiar, comfortable and safe. His eyes knew where to look to find the dent he had made in the garage when he had thrown a wild baseball the previous summer. He could see the same rose-colored drapes fluttering softly in the windows on the main floor. He could even see the silhouette of one of his favorite people pass behind a closed curtain on the upper level.

Just then, Dylan felt something rubbing between his legs. He looked down and smiled when he saw two Siamese cats twisting between his ankles. He scooped them both up into his arms and gave them each a kiss on the top of their silky heads. Then he placed them back down on the snowy ground and sighed.

'Where are we?' Remy asked out loud.

'Home,' replied Dylan softly. 'Home.'

END OF BOOK ONE

Excerpt from the next book in the series

BOOK 2
DYLAN DOVER:
ORION'S QUEST

BY LYNNE HOWARD

CHAPTER ONE

Baltazar's eyes gleamed with malice as he glared down at his faithful but errant servant, Reus. All that remained of the three boys and their female companion was a wisp of smoke from the transport portal that had disappeared with the children. Reus looked up fearfully at his master who also happened to be one of the most powerful immortals in their world. Baltazar, a vampire, was double his size, and wielded great power. His life was literally in Baltazar's hands.

Reus could feel Baltazar's cold, penetrating stare and his worst suspicions were confirmed when he made eye contact with the vampire who towered before him. Baltazar's eyes were translucent which indicated that he had not consumed blood for many weeks, and Reus quivered slightly under his superior's unnerving and unblinking scrutiny. Reus waited anxiously for Baltazar to say something…anything at all, but Baltazar remained silent and just continued to scowl at him. Finally, Reus could not take the silence a moment longer and asked in a tentative voice,

'Baltazar, what are we going to do now?'

Baltazar took a step closer to Reus and placed his ice-cold hands on Reus' shoulders. A small smile played at the edge of his lips and a spark of amusement danced in his eyes.

'*We*, Reus? What are *we* going to do now?'

Reus nodded enthusiastically. 'Yes, master. How shall we proceed? Clearly, we must find the boys and the girl, I would think as well, although clearly she is dispensable.' Reus was playing a dangerous game, but he knew that he had to continue to deceive Baltazar. He could not let his true motivations be known if he was to have any chance of saving the children, and ultimately the entire realm from Baltazar's plans of total destruction.

'Oh Reus,' sighed Baltazar as he squeezed Reus' shoulder a little too hard to be comforting. '*We* shall not be doing anything to rectify this disaster that *you* have caused. I, however, will be taking appropriate measures to retrieve the children and bring them back where they belong, under my control.'

'So, my s-s-services to you will no longer be required?' stuttered Reus apprehensively. He already knew the answer to this question, but he hoped that his centuries of loyal service might persuade Baltazar to be lenient.

'Your services to the entire realm will no longer be required, Reus,' snapped Baltazar in anger. 'Time and again you have failed me, and in doing so you have placed our entire world in jeopardy. You are to blame for the children's escape and whatever consequences follow will be because of your ineptitude and stupidity. Your usefulness to me has run its course and now your incompetence makes you a liability. You know too much to be released on your own accord, and yet you know too little to be of any further assistance.' Baltazar's voice dropped as he delivered the final blow. 'You will be disposed of, Reus. I have no choice.'

'No, Baltazar. Please, I beg of you. Have mercy on me, your loyal servant who has always tried his best to carry out your instructions. Please, master…' Reus sank to the floor, his head bowed and waited.

Baltazar sighed again. 'Reus, the children's disappearance must be dealt with urgently. I don't have time for this. Every second that passes puts us in greater peril.'

'Baltazar, I know that I have made terrible mistakes – '

Baltazar brusquely interrupted Reus. 'You minimize the damage you have caused, Reus. You have not just made some mistakes; you have erred time and time again in such significant ways that the fate of our world is now in question. I must attend to this matter immediately. You, I will deal with later.'

From above, Reus heard a rattling noise and looked up. Coming down from the ceiling was a cage made of thick iron rods that Reus instinctively knew would not be penetrated by even his strongest magic. When the cage reached the ground, Baltazar opened the door and gave a formal nod to Reus in farewell. Reus, still on his knees, shuffled forwards into the enclosure. Baltazar slammed the door shut with a powerful kick and a moment later, Reus felt himself lifting off the ground.

The cage moved upwards at a steady pace and within moments, the ceiling was rapidly approaching. Yet the ascent did not stop even as the ceiling came closer and closer. Just when Reus was convinced that he would be killed by crashing into the immovable barrier above him, the ceiling split open and the cage was sucked up into a black abyss. An instant later, the opening slammed shut, leaving Reus trapped in an iron cage, in total darkness, somewhere in Baltazar's underground castle.

Is this how I am going to die, wondered Reus. *Trapped here forever?* Reus cradled his face in his hands and tried to think of a way out. Baltazar himself had no magical powers, since vampires are immortals with incredible strength and speed but do not actually possess magical abilities themselves, but his castle was created by Atticus. One of the two warlocks who were the leaders of the realm, Atticus' magical powers were unparalleled by any other immortal. The magic that permeated every aspect of Baltazar's castle was designed to protect the secrets therein, and Reus' magic was not strong enough to penetrate any of the spells that had been cast. Reus' magic was useless everywhere in Baltazar's castle, unless Baltazar arranged otherwise. Reus, in all his centuries of existence, did not know of any supernatural being who had powers stronger than Atticus and who could counteract the magic imposed by the mighty leader. Except...

Reus' head shot up with the realization that the children's magic must have worked to get into the locked area where they were before they disappeared, and they managed to create a transport portal. Creating a transport portal in and of itself was an incredible feat for any immortal, but to create one strong enough to transport multiple people was unheard of. Even more astonishing was the fact that they accomplished this inside Baltazar's castle. Except for Atticus and perhaps his co-ruler Callista, Reus didn't know of any immortals whose magic worked inside Baltazar's underground, palatial castle. The magic of these children must have been so powerful that it could overcome that of Atticus. Reus shook his head in disbelief and wondered what would become of the three boys and their female counterpart that disappeared so swiftly. What more would they be capable of once they learned how to fully harness their powers? Reus closed his eyes in defeat and waited for whatever Baltazar had in store for him.

Hours passed in darkness and silence. Just before he drifted off to sleep, too tired to try to stay awake anymore, a thought sprung into his mind that jerked him into full alertness. *There's a fourth sibling. If they find her, who knows what they will be able to do. Our world and everything in it will be in their hands.* Reus knew that his work was not done. He had to get out. He had to intervene. The entire immortal world depended on it.

But what if this time, Reus had met his end? He had many close calls with Baltazar over the years, but this time was different. Baltazar had never put Reus in a cage and left him alone for hours on end, seemingly to die. Reus desperately wished that his magic would work. Not just because he would be able to escape, but also because he could not use the IM system (immortal mail) without magical powers. Reus knew exactly who he would communicate with, if he could. He knew without doubt that she would help the children. Reus closed his eyes and fondly recalled his friend, Lilly, who he had known for centuries. The only one he had trusted with his most guarded secrets. He remembered his first letter to her twelve human years prior.

My dearest Lilly, I hope this letter finds you well. I know we haven't seen each other in some time, but I hope you know that is not for lack of desire on my part, but simply due to the circumstances that I find myself in which prevents me from leaving the immortal world to come visit you. I wish I was able to deliver this message to you in person, but for reasons that you will understand, I cannot. Please read this letter carefully as it will disintegrate five minutes after it is opened.

Lilly, the immortal world is in danger. Baltazar has plans to take it over and destroy everything but he cannot do so without first seizing the magic of four siblings, who have been prophesized by one with the power of foresight to be powerful beyond any immortal that has ever existed. These children will be delivered, I think later today and Baltazar has instructed me to hide one of them in the human world. I don't have time to fully explain his plan to you now, and I am not even sure if Baltazar has fully shared his intentions with me, but I do believe that for now at least, he trusts me, and that I will be placing the child within the mortal realm very soon. Please watch over this child and keep him safe from harm. I beg of you to let me know instantly if Baltazar ever comes around so that I can intervene. I will send you another message with the child's precise location as soon as I know it. We can communicate by IM for now, but I promise that I will make every attempt to come see you in person soon. You are the only one that I trust with this matter, my dear friend. And I have faith that together, you and I will be able to save this child, and the entire realm from Baltazar's evil objectives. Watch for my next note, it shall be arriving soon, I'm sure of it. With great fondness and deepest respect,

Reus

Reus knew exactly what he would write to Lilly now, if he only had the ability to do so. He could only hope that word of his death would quickly spread, and that the news would reach Lilly's ears very soon. He knew that she would instantly understand what fate had befallen him, and that she would be aware of the consequences that would follow. He could only hope that Lilly would know what to do when he was no longer alive. He no longer had the strength to keep his eyes open. He finally drifted to sleep with Lilly's smiling face firmly entrenched in his mind. His final conscious thought was how grateful he was to Lilly for her past assistance and for her future help. When he died, she would be his only hope.

ACKNOWLEDGEMENTS

Writing a novel is a daunting task, but the steps that follow are equally challenging. Dylan Dover would never have been read by anyone but me, if not for the contributions of so many people.

First, thank you to my agent, Eric Lincoln Miller at 3ibooks Literary Agency. You had faith in me from our first interaction, and your never-ending optimism, wise counsel, expertise, and hard work are what took Dylan Dover the dream to Dylan Dover the reality. Thank you to my publicist Roxy Runyan for all your creative ideas and your positive energy.

To all the amazing people at The Conrad Press who put such great efforts into the publication of this novel. I can't thank you all enough for your professionalism, dedication and hard work.

I am fortunate to know many people who were willing to preview *Dylan Dover: Into the Vortex* and so graciously wrote endorsements of the novel. And I am grateful for the support of my many friends/colleagues for their ongoing encouragement and enthusiasm. Thank you to Marvin Zuker, Danny Goodman, Beth Hurd, Andrew and Johanna Wise, Jordan Erdman, Stefanie Stockhamer, Stacey Shuster, Carmelo Nanfara, Sherene Sahib, Nadira Persaud, Lynda Watters, Michael Zuker, Ruth Kelly, Puja Chadha, Gail Kemper, Aiman Flahat, Marc Saltzman, Judi Morris, Sara Black, Nick Maes, Suzanne Gluchy, Sandra Miller, Leorah Marcu, Lyla Abells, Tobi Bongard, Emily Henderson, Michelle Silverberg, Stacia

Wolle, Suzanne Socken, Michelle Hyde, and Jenny Lewis who is no longer with us, but her memory is a constant inspiration.

I would also like to thank my family, starting with my parents Lawrence and Maxine Polon. You have always been my biggest fans, constant support system, and greatest advisors. Thank you for absolutely everything. You have been the greatest role models and I hope that I can live up to your example. Thank you to my brothers, brother-in-law and sisters-in law, Jon and Dina Polon, Geoff Polon, Rick and Ellen Howard, and to my nieces and nephews Josh Howard and Tiffany Tanz, Jennie and David Kelman, Rebecca Howard and Mitch Pichosky for their ongoing encouragement.

And finally, my deepest gratitude and love to my husband Andrew, for giving me the time to write and happily picking up the slack, for your ongoing love and support, and never faltering faith in me even when I had been on the verge of giving up. Thank you to my son Matthew and daughter Jessie, for your amazing ideas, for always finding a way to make me laugh and for putting up with my moments of insanity. And of course, thank you to my son Dylan for letting me borrow your name and for inspiring the character of Dylan Dover based on the incredible person that you are. Thank you, Dylan, for the hundreds of hours you spent talking to me about the book, offering insights and for your candid critiques which made me revise chapters that I thought were finished but made the book so much better in the end! I am forever grateful to have the love and support of such a wonderful family.

Lynne Howard, June 2022